SHELL
GAMES

ALSO BY BONNIE KISTLER

House on Fire
The Cage
Her, Too

SHELL GAMES

A Novel

BONNIE KISTLER

HARPER

NEW YORK • LONDON • TORONTO • SYDNEY

HARPER

This is a work of fiction. Names, characters, places, and incidents are products of the author's imagination or are used fictitiously and are not to be construed as real. Any resemblance to actual events, locales, organizations, or persons, living or dead, is entirely coincidental.

HarperCollins books may be purchased for educational, business, or sales promotional use. For information, please email the Special Markets Department at SPsales@harpercollins.com.

FIRST EDITION

Library of Congress Cataloging-in-Publication Data

Names: Kistler, Bonnie, author.
Title: Shell games: a novel / Bonnie Kistler.
Description: First U.S. edition. | New York: Harper Paperbacks, 2024.
Identifiers: LCCN 2023054990 | ISBN 9780063378964 (trade paperback) |
ISBN 9780063378933 (hardcover) | ISBN 9780063378957 (e-book)
Subjects: LCGFT: Thrillers (Fiction) | Novels.
Classification: LCC PS3563.A2917 S54 2024 | DDC 813/.54—dc23/
eng/20231204
LC record available at https://lccn.loc.gov/2023054990

ISBN 978-0-06-337896-4 (pbk.)

24 25 26 27 28 LBC 5 4 3 2 1

In memory of

Rosemae Richards MacDougal,

my mother

Between lovers a little confession is a dangerous thing.

—HELEN ROWLAND

CHAPTER 1

"I have a confession to make," Charlie Mull said as he rose to his feet.

His big booming voice cut through all the shouts and laughter in the courtyard, the ringing of crystal and the clinking of silver on china. The guests hushed at once and swiveled their heads his way and scraped their chairs around to listen.

This wedding was the premier social event of the 2023 season. Kate Sawyer was a somebody, after all, not only in Florida but up and down the East Coast. A hugely successful real estate developer and a glamorous woman of a certain age, she appeared regularly in both the business journals and the society pages. Gossip had it she was a billionaire, which was true only occasionally depending on where the market was, but close enough to true that Kate did nothing to dispel the rumors. And she'd been squired about by some prominent men during all the years of her widowhood, including, rumor had it, Ted Turner. She did nothing to dispel that rumor, either.

The wedding venue was Kate's own home, logically enough, since Sarasota had few rented halls or hotel ballrooms that could rival it. La Coquina was a Mediterranean-style palazzo built on a narrow spit of land between the gulf and the bay. Only a single bridge linked the barrier island to the mainland, and parking was at a premium, so Kate had chartered a party boat to ferry the guests over. They'd filed out to the beach for the sunset ceremony, then flowed back into the courtyard for dinner al fresco. A string quartet had played Mozart on the beach, and now a twelve-piece dance band was tuning up in the

center island of the circular drive outside. Young people in cummer-
bunds and bow ties glided through the array of tables, some clearing
plates, some refilling wineglasses, some still cradling magnums of
Dom Perignon in their arms for those guests who continued to drink
champagne long after the introductory toasts were over.

Charlie stood at a table for two, what the caterers called a sweetheart table. He and Kate had no use for a head table, not at their age.
Their parents were decades dead, of course, and Kate thought a lineup
of geriatric bridesmaids would have looked ridiculous. Charlie wore a
tuxedo—unusual for a beach wedding, but Kate was a staunch believer
in formal attire. Her gown was made of pale gold lace, and Charlie
wore a waistcoat and bow tie to match. He was a big man, barrel-
chested, with a broad back that was ramrod-straight even if tilted
forward a few degrees off vertical. He had a shock of white hair and
ruddy cheeks and watery blue eyes that still knew how to twinkle.

"I have a confession to make," he said again, and grinned.

Kate gazed up at him with a look of fond exasperation. This was
the expression she customarily bestowed upon him. The fondness
was real enough; the exasperation she put on to moderate it a bit, so
she wouldn't appear besotted to her assembled friends and colleagues.
There was only one way she aimed to appear tonight—amazing—and
in that she'd succeeded. Her form-fitting gown fitted a form that still
drew wolf whistles from construction crews, at least from the ones
high up on the girders. Her jawline was tight, her skin smooth, her
hair a soft shade of ash blond.

"As some of you folks know," Charlie was saying, "I've taken two
bullets in my life. Once in Da Nang and the second time in Beirut.
Barely winged me either time. But there was one time I took a direct
hit to the heart. It wasn't a bullet, though. It was an arrow. A Cupid's

arrow back in the eighth grade, when I first laid eyes on a little gal named Katie Weller."

Laughter came from the guests, amid an audible groan from Kate.

"So that's my confession," Charlie said. "I fell in love with Katie the minute I saw her. Not that I ever stood a chance. I mean, come on, she was honor roll, and I was auto shop. She was country club, and I was junior ROTC."

Kate shook her head in denial, but she was smiling.

"She was so far out of my league I didn't even have the guts to talk to her. She never would've known I existed if not for one Saturday in November." He looked down at Kate, and his face softened with the memory. "I was out on the football field, she was up in the stadium, and I kept her in my sights between every play. During every huddle. Then, I don't know what happened, but she fell headfirst down those concrete stairs."

"It was the heat," she said, with enough firmness that no one thought to wonder about the November temperatures in Massachusetts.

"I stopped dead in my tracks there on the twenty-yard line and watched her tumble. It was like in slow motion. A whole flight of stairs, and at the bottom she landed on her head with a crack I swear I heard out on the field."

An *ooh* rippled through the crowd.

"I was a running back, and that's what I did. I ran back to the side-lines and around the bench and vaulted over the rail into the stadium. I picked her up and ran like I'd never run in my life. The hospital was five miles away, and I was halfway there when the ambulance caught up with me. They peeled her out of my arms and loaded her in and left me standing there on the sidewalk in my shoulder pads and helmet, wondering what the hell just happened."

There was little suspense to the tale—Kate had quite obviously survived—but the guests were listening raptly. They were charmed.

"What happened?" Charlie went on. "Well, we lost the game, and I got kicked off the team, but I didn't care about that. All I could think about was Katie. They said it was only a mild concussion, but I was worried sick. The next morning I screwed up my courage and went to see her in the hospital, clutching a ragged bunch of daisies. And there she was, sitting up in bed, pretty as a picture even with that bandage around her head, and she reached out a hand when she saw me and she said—I swear to God—*My hero.*"

Kate rolled her eyes. *I did not,* she mouthed.

"*Come here and let me hug you, she said.*"

She gave a shrug to concede that much might be true.

"So you see, it was way worse than a mild concussion. She was knocked clean out of her senses!"

When the laughter died down, Charlie continued with his tale. Kate went home the next day, and the day after that she astonished Charlie by asking him to be her date for the homecoming dance. The next few months were the happiest of his whole life, he declared. They went steady from Thanksgiving all the way through the Fourth of July.

"But it couldn't last past then," he said as a mournful look fell over his face. "Not when I was headed for Vietnam, and she was headed for Harvard."

Radcliffe, Kate mouthed, trying to look sad even as she corrected the record.

They promised to write each other, and they did for a while, but those kinds of promises fade when life intrudes, and theirs did, each in its own way. She was caught up in her studies. He was caught up in the war. They lost touch. He never knew she'd married and moved to Florida; she never knew he'd made the marines his career. He never knew she'd lost her husband, and she never knew he'd been married and divorced. But the worst thing of all was that she never knew he'd settled in Florida after he left the corps.

"So there we were," he said, "me up in Tampa and Katie here in Sarasota. Both of us single, living our separate lives only an hour apart, for twenty years. We would have lived and died that way if it wasn't for the most incredible stroke of luck."

Charlie was working at a car dealership, he told the crowd, selling luxury sports cars, mostly to rich retirees trying to relive their youth by driving something that could do zero to sixty in 2.8 seconds. But one day a young fellow came in, and Charlie nabbed him before any of the other salesmen could. The young fellow wasn't sure what he wanted, a Maserati, a Lamborghini, or a Ferrari, so over the next few weeks, he and Charlie went on a bunch of test drives in and around the city, up and down I-75, sometimes into the swampy interior of the state. They'd stop for lunch and get to talking, and before long, they got to be pals.

"I didn't even care about my commission anymore," Charlie said, but when Kate guffawed, he amended: "Well, I didn't care as much."

Finally, the young fellow settled on a Lambo and bought the car of his dreams. He took Charlie home for dinner to celebrate, and Charlie finally got to meet his sweet young wife. When they sat down to the table, he noticed it was set for four. *Expecting somebody else?* he'd asked. *My late mother-in-law,* the young fellow griped. They were starting in on dessert when the mystery guest finally swept in.

An excited murmur rippled through the courtyard.

"No, now, don't get there ahead of me." Charlie laughed as he held up two halting hands. "Let me tell it like it happened."

"In swept the mystery guest," he said again, and he felt like his jaw hit the floor. She stopped and stared. He stopped and stared. He stood from the table. *Charlie?* she said. *Katie!* he said.

"Yep. It was my own Katie Weller, fifty years later and a thousand times more beautiful."

She rose from the sweetheart table—fluidly; she did squats every day to make sure of it—and went into his arms for a kiss that brought a hearty round of applause from the crowd. When they finally broke apart, Charlie picked up his glass. "So here's to that young fella with the late mother-in-law. I'll never be able to thank him enough. Dr. Eric Hoffman!"

He lifted his glass in a salute to Eric's table, then turned his toast toward his bride. "And here's to Katie Weller, Kate Sawyer, and now Katie Mull. My one true love."

As they kissed again, the guests surged to their feet, and their applause swelled through the courtyard. Charlie's story was an inspiration, especially for the majority of the guests, who were three times the age of majority. It meant that their lives weren't done. The past wasn't past. They were still the same people they'd been at seventeen, and here was the proof. High school sweethearts separated for over fifty years, reunited. They weren't at the end of their lives. Their story wasn't over. A new chapter had begun, and the guests cheered and clapped and whistled as if they'd been handed a new lease on life.

Also, the cake was being wheeled out. Dessert was about to be served.

CHAPTER 2

Kate stumbled as Charlie was handing her into the limo. She might have sprawled onto the seat had he not steadied her descent. She uttered a brief expletive at the trailing hem of her gown, though she knew it was more likely the champagne that made her wobble. She never indulged as much as she had tonight. After George's death, she'd barely touched the stuff. But tonight was the start of a new life. She could throw away those old worries and enjoy herself. Celebrate!

But tipsy was one thing and sloppy another. A magnum of champagne sat waiting in an ice bucket on the limo bar, and she resolved to have none of it.

She tucked the train of her gown into the footwell and sank back with a happy, tired sigh. It had been a long day—week, really—but it was worth it. The wedding had been a total triumph, worth every goddam exhausting moment.

Though it certainly had been exhausting. She couldn't trust a wedding planner with an event that meant this much to her, so she'd done it all herself. The music, the flowers, the food. And God! The seating plan. Florida was a political land mine in the run-up to next year's election, and she had to tread carefully. The handful of Democrats had been easy enough to manage—she'd seated them with her daughter Julie and the few other guests under forty. But then came the two camps of Republicans, those who supported the former president and those who supported the current governor. It was Mar-a-Lago versus Tallahassee, and eventually the twain would have to meet but not in time for her wedding. Kate was a Republican, too, of course, but she was the genteel kind who liked low taxes and lax regulations. Not the kind who fretted about drag shows and public bathrooms. It was all such nonsense, this so-called *culture* war. It was being waged by people who had none.

Charlie bent to kiss her before he closed her door, and as he straightened, she couldn't help noticing the stiffness in his back. It had been a long week for him, too, moving the last of his belongings from his apartment into her home. She'd wanted to send one of her crews, but he'd insisted on doing the job himself. It was one of the thousand things she loved about him—his self-reliance. He loved her, but he didn't need her. It was such a refreshing change from most of the men who made up the dating pool for women her age. Florida women had an expression born of bitter experience: the men were only after a nurse or a purse. Sometimes both. But Charlie was after neither. He was in robust health, and it was he who'd insisted on the prenup.

Kate had made certain to leak that fact to the biggest gossips in her set. No one could ever gloat that he'd married her for her money. This was a love match, pure and simple. He'd get nothing if they divorced—not that they ever would. And if she predeceased him? He insisted he wanted nothing then, either, but how would it look if she left him a homeless widower? So the prenup provided him this house and the boat at the dock but nothing more. Not the New York apartment or the Maine cottage or the Key West conch house. Not any part of her investment portfolio. And most importantly, not her company.

He started to circle the limo, but the guests surged around him, pecking his cheek and shaking his hand, extending congratulations and saying goodbyes. They'd known him only these past few months, but already they loved him, too. Everyone did. He beamed his thanks and politely inched away until he finally gave a big departing wave to the crowd and opened the car door. Kate reached out an eager hand as he started to duck inside.

"Charlie! Buddy, hold up!" came a shout from the courtyard.

She scowled. It was Eric, her son-in-loathe, and her friends parted for him like he was the messiah he thought he was. Unfortunately, they thought so, too. As Sarasota's top orthopedist, he'd rebuilt most of the knees and hips around him.

Charlie turned as Eric strode up, and the two men embraced and whispered a few words to each other. Charlie thought the world of Eric, and with a heavy sigh, Kate resolved yet again to make more of an effort to like her son-in-law. But it was such an effort, in the face of all that arrogance. And it was so undeserved! What was he, after all, but a glorified mechanic? He just happened to work on joints instead of engines. And he was such a bad match for Julie, who was quite meek enough without living in the shadow of an alpha dog like Eric. She'd had her tail between her legs ever since she met him. Even now she was shrinking behind him.

Such a mousy little thing, her daughter. Her face so colorless, her hair a drab shade of brown, and that dress! Silver might have worked, but this was a dull pewter gray and a size too big. Kate hardly knew where the girl came from. She'd been a late-in-life baby, a final triumph after a string of miscarriages, and Kate and George had called her their little miracle child. But as the years went by, Kate sometimes wondered if Julie was the last gasp of her aging ovaries, if the better eggs had already been used up by the babies who never were.

But no, that wasn't fair. Julie was a sweet girl. Hardworking and reliable. Kate had installed her as general counsel of the company a few years back, and she'd been doing a perfectly adequate job.

But she paled beside Greta, her best friend from law school, who was standing there beside her. Greta was Eric's sister, but Kate didn't hold that against her. She was extraordinarily accomplished. A judge already—at thirty-three! But there was nothing sober about this judge. She was an icy blonde—like her brother, but on her it worked—and she dazzled in a dress of shocking pink taffeta. Her husband cut a dashing figure, too. Alex Blanco was a neurologist who probably had the same god complex as Eric. But in Alex's defense, he treated the brain, which was in a whole different league.

Eric finally stepped aside to let Julie say her goodbyes, but Charlie's own daughter got there first. Becky was a big woman, broad-faced with shoulders almost as wide as her father's. Those shoulders wore angry blotches of red across fish-belly–white skin. Her husband was behind her, equally broad and equally sunburned. They'd flown in from New Hampshire for the weekend and had obviously spent the day at the beach.

Julie's turn came at last. Charlie wrapped her in his arms in a bear hug, and Julie clung to him with tears of joy on her face. He was the father she wished she'd had, and there were times Kate wished it, too. Oh, to turn back the clock, to take a mulligan on life's choices. For a moment she was almost teary herself.

But no, she had no real regrets. If she'd married Charlie all those years ago, she never could have built her billion-dollar business. Today KS Development owned or managed more than three hundred properties. Its portfolio included a hundred million square feet of office buildings, industrial parks, shopping centers, residential communities, and hotels.

It took an unfulfilling marriage to make that happen. Yes, George taught her about business, but largely through negative example. His companies manufactured industrial parts, and she'd watched as one product line after another failed, done in every time by cheaper foreign-made goods. It taught her that a business had to be import-proof to be safe. It had to be rooted in the good old U.S. of A., and what could be more rooted than real estate? What could be more irreplaceable than coastal Florida real estate? People thought that George left her a fortune when he died, but the truth was that his business had already gone bust by the time he died. He left her nothing but life insurance, and only enough of that to provide the seed money for her next project.

So—no regrets. Now she had her company and Charlie, too. The best of all worlds.

He climbed in beside her at last, and as the limo slowly rolled out of the circle drive and onto the road, Charlie leaned over. "Kiss me, Kate," he said—an old joke—and she obliged as the crowd cheered.

His bones creaked as he settled back in his seat. Kate patted his knee. "A long day at our age," she said.

"At my age," he insisted. "Not yours." They were both seventy, but she looked at least fifteen years younger, a fact in which they took equal pride. For Charlie, it was the pride of possession tempered by his disbelief that he was actually married to this beautiful creature; for Kate, it was the pride of accomplishment. She'd accomplished a great deal in her life, but tonight the accomplishment that most filled her heart—and admittedly, swelled her head—was that she'd kept her looks. Thanks to healthy eating and exercise, of course, but also thanks to her other hero, Dr. Russell Shein. She wished she could have invited Russ to the wedding, but plastic surgeons were like backstreet lovers—adored but necessarily hidden away. Which was silly, really. After all, this was Florida, land of perpetual self-renewal. Ponce de León would have succeeded in finding the fountain of youth if only he'd waited five hundred years and searched in doctors' offices.

Charlie popped the cork on the champagne and poured a glass for each of them. They clinked their flutes together.

"You're a big fat liar," Kate said, and took a swallow, her earlier resolve forgotten.

"What?" he protested, laughing.

"Your speech! There was hardly a word of truth in it. I had the hopeless crush on you, Mr. Popularity, with your string of cheerleader girlfriends."

He grinned. "I didn't think you noticed. You with your nose always in a book."

"I was sneaking peeks at you the whole time. You were the only reason I went to those Saturday football games. It was a chance to stare at you without anybody noticing."

"Which is why you took that fall. You were watching me instead of your feet."

They'd told each other this story many times before, back in high school and again over the last year. It never got old. The wonder of it all. That they were watching each other that whole time. The miracle that he loved her just as she loved him.

And oh, how she loved him. She didn't even wait until their third date to cast off her virginity. It was a good thing she already had her Radcliffe acceptance letter, because she barely cracked open a book the rest of their senior year. They spent it all in carnal delight. The backseat of his car, the locker room after hours, the motel room they'd saved up for on prom night. Fifty-two years later and she felt flushed just thinking about it.

Though, again, that could have been the champagne. They polished off the bottle before the lights of Tampa began to swirl through the smoky windows of the limo. They would spend tonight at a hotel near the airport, in readiness for their early-morning flight to L.A. Another night there, then on to Tahiti, where they'd board the yacht for their monthlong cruise of the South Pacific. Carnal delights at their age would mostly take the form of fine meals and deep-tissue massages, but those would be delightful, too.

No regrets, she reminded herself. She mustn't think of the fifty years lost, only of the utter joy they'd take in however many years remained.

THEIR LUGGAGE HAD been sent ahead and was waiting for them at the hotel in the premier suite they'd booked. Another bottle of Dom was waiting, too. Charlie headed for the bathroom in an exaggerated cartoon run that made Kate giggle. She stepped out of her gown in the living room and let it puddle where it fell. One of her employees would be along in the morning to collect it.

She went into the bedroom and changed into a dressing gown and sat down at the vanity table. She leaned close to the mirror and blinked a few times to clear her vision. Yes, despite all the champagne, despite all the clammy hugs and smooches, she still looked fine. Makeup flawless and not a hair out of place. Not a hint of gray, either, though that was nothing special. Florida women of her set never went gray. The first telltale silver strand would be offset with golden highlights. As the years marched on, the highlights turned increasingly ashen and increasingly abundant until the women were completely blond and no one remembered a time when they weren't. For any who happened to reach their eighties, the ash turned to platinum. The few who made it to ninety then sported a brilliant white—brilliant because they'd arrived there without ever having to endure a single gray hair. This was the trajectory Kate planned on.

She opened her cosmetic case. She had a nightly routine, and she followed it religiously, whether or not she was tipsy, even on her wedding night. First to carefully remove her makeup and peel off her lashes. Then to apply all the various serums and lotions, glycolic, hyaluronic, collagen, retinol—it was a chemistry lab set for women of a certain age. Finally, she picked up the syringe that she'd preloaded with her daily dose of Sermorelin peptides. This was the other miracle in her life, an anti-aging cocktail that she swore by, courtesy of Dr. Shein.

Charlie came up behind her wearing a white terry robe. He wrapped his arms around her and grinned at their reflection in the vanity mirror.

"Shoot me up, darling?" Her hands were trembling too much to line up the injection.

He took the syringe from her. "You know I love you just the way you are."

"Then it's important that I stay just the way I am," she said. For a moment there were two of him and two of her in the mirror, until she blinked and got her vision back.

"Seriously, you don't need this stuff," he said, but he dutifully plunged the needle into her thigh and did it so deftly she didn't feel a thing. Though that might be due to the champagne, and suddenly, he had another bottle in his hand and a pair of crystal flutes that he set down beside her chemistry set. *My chemical romance,* she thought, and laughed out loud as he popped the cork and filled their glasses.

She felt a sudden stab of pain behind her eyes, ten times sharper than any of her usual dull headaches. Too much alcohol, she knew. But there was no way she was going to plead a headache on her wedding night to her one true love. She fished a bottle of Tylenol out of her cosmetic case and squinted at the markings on the cap. The arrows swam in her vision. She lined them up, she thought she did, but the cap wouldn't dislodge. "Open this for me, darling?"

A cloud seemed to fall over his face as she handed him the bottle. He stared at it a long moment before he groped for a chair and sat down heavily beside her. "Katie," he said after a long moment. "You know how much I love you."

"No more than you, I," she said, but that didn't sound right. "I mean, no more you than—oh, what the hell!" Laughing, she gave up. "Me, too!"

"I want us to always be completely honest with each other."

"Of course."

"Do you remember the Tylenol murders?"

"What?" She blinked hard. She couldn't imagine why he was bringing this up now.

"In Chicago, back in the eighties, when somebody tampered with the bottles on the store shelves and put potassium cyanide capsules in with the pills? Seven people died?"

Oh, now she understood. "God, yes," she said with a groan. "That's why we all have to suffer now with these damn tamperproof caps."

He had no trouble, though. He flipped the cap and tapped a pill into her hand. She popped it in her mouth and took a big swallow of her champagne to chase it down her throat. *What fool ever said you couldn't have it all?* she thought. She had everything now, everything she'd ever dreamed of.

"Katie. Darling," he said sadly as the room tilted leftward. "I have a confession to make."

CHAPTER 3

J ulie was supervising the clean-up crew when she felt a shiver run up her spine.

Every hair rose on the back of her neck, and with a moan, she turned into Eric's arms. He ran his hands over the curve of her hips and up to her breasts, and his eyes bored into hers, posing the question, making the challenge. She threw a look over her shoulder at the men loading the banquet tables into the truck. The caterers still had to load their vans, and the cleaners still had to sweep and mop and put everything back as it was. Her mother had charged her with the responsibility of overseeing all of it. But Eric charged her in every other way.

She gave one quick nod, and he grabbed her hand and tugged her after him. They ran past his sports car, parked where no one was supposed to park and no one else would dare to. It was low-slung and flame-orange and smoldered like an ember in the dim glow of the houselights. Beyond it was darkness, and they plunged into it, across the road and onto the beach.

The sea was a void, black water against black sky, demarcated only by the shimmering white foam of the surf. Her shoulder bag banged against her hip as she struggled to keep up, and when they reached the beach, she kicked off her heels. The sand was warm against the soles of her feet, and it squished between her toes as she followed Eric over the dunes. He peeled off his dinner jacket and tossed it into the wind. Julie had dressed so carefully that afternoon, but she undressed now with wild abandon, and so did Eric, until they were both naked and gleaming like mother-of-pearl in the starlight. She dropped to her knees, but he was already hard, and he pushed her down onto her back.

He didn't need to check if she was ready. She was always ready for him. All it ever took was a glance across a room, a knee squeeze under the table, a fingertip traced along her spine. She'd been in thrall to him from the day they met, from the moment she twisted her ankle stumbling off the deck at Greta's backyard barbecue. She was dazed from the fall and blinded by the sun and barely registered the faceless hands reaching out to help her up. Until another pair of hands touched her and lit a fuse that burned like wildfire from her foot to her face. It was Eric, squatting at her feet, cradling her calf in one hand while he probed her ankle with the other. "Trust me. I'm a doctor," he'd said, and given her a smile that made solar flares radiate from his face, as if he were a sun god.

From that moment on, her fuse never stopped burning. Even on a moonless night like tonight, he dazzled her. Even in the dark. Especially in the dark. All those people who questioned the happiness of her marriage, the friends who pitied her, they didn't know about this. They could never imagine this.

He plunged into her, and she closed her eyes and watched pinwheels whirl across the sky. "So fucking hot," he moaned as he pounded her into the sand, then his mouth was on her breast, and depth charges detonated inside her, and the wind roared and the waves crashed, and she was in the sea and the sky and everywhere and nowhere.

Until another sound penetrated. A ringtone from her bag a yard away on the beach. "Mamma Mia."

Julie froze, but Eric didn't. "Leave it," he said through gritted teeth, still thrusting.

"But—it must be an emergency. She wouldn't call—I mean, it's her wedding night!"

"Exactly. She has Charlie now to step and fetch. You don't have to be at her beck and call anymore. Leave it!"

She couldn't. She was programmed to respond to her mother's voice and, by proxy, her ringtone. She twisted to reach for her bag under the pile of clothes. Eric slipped out of her, and he reared back on his knees with a growl of frustration.

"Mom?" she exclaimed into the phone as he jumped to his feet and ran to the water's edge.

"Is this Julie Hoffman?"

Her breath caught at the sound of a man's voice. "Who's this?"

"Sergeant Oster, Tampa PD. Your mother is Katherine Sawyer?"

"Oh my God! What's happened? Is she all right?"

"She's not hurt, but she's upset," the officer reported in a flat voice. "She wants you to come up."

Julie could hear Eric diving into the sea, breaking the surface with fast, furious strokes. "What is it? What's happened?"

"She called 911. She reported a murderer." The man's tone didn't change as he added the rest. "A mass murderer."

CHAPTER 4

No fucking way," Eric shouted, and slammed his palm against the steering wheel for emphasis. He was driving too fast. He always did in the Lambo, but more so now, at two in the morning, when the highway was nearly his alone. More so now, when he was so angry. "I can see her witnessing one murder, maybe, but there's no way to witness serial murders! Not unless she was following the guy around!"

"I know!" Julie had to shout, too. The top was down, and the wind was roaring in her ears and tearing through her hair. "I don't get it, either. But that's what he told me." Though suddenly, she wasn't so sure. "I think. Maybe he said mass murder? Like maybe she witnessed a mass shooting?"

Eric shot her a look. He got annoyed when she doubted herself that way. "She wouldn't need to call 911 for that. It would be all over the fucking news."

"Right," Julie said. None of it made sense. She'd been trying to reach her mother for an explanation, but every call went to voicemail. The cops must have held on to the phone, which made her worry even more.

"I tell you, she's losing it again! I bet she hallucinated the whole thing. That's why she's at the hotel and not at the police station. The cops know she's crazy."

Julie didn't respond to that. He'd never liked her mother, and over the years he'd come up with a host of reasons why. She was too controlling. Too vain. Too meddlesome. Lately, it was her supposed dementia. He claimed he could see it every time she misplaced her keys or ran late for an appointment. As if such things didn't regularly happen to him and everyone else in the world. And even if Kate had been a bit more forgetful of late, who wouldn't be? She'd been in a frenzy of activity these last few months, organizing the wedding and the honeymoon, not to mention her business affairs, to keep all her projects on track while she was away. And if she'd seemed a bit giddy at times, almost girlish—well, no wonder. She'd been reunited with her high school sweetheart; she'd fallen in love all over again.

Anyway, Julie knew exactly why her mother would be in her hotel suite and not at the police station. Because she was Kate Sawyer. No one would dare to inconvenience her, not even law enforcement.

"Hey," Eric said, more softly. He lifted his hand from the gearshift and squeezed Julie's knee. "I'm sorry. I know you don't like to hear that. It's just—I thought once she was with Charlie, we'd be done with all her drama. We could focus on us. But here we go again!" He returned his hand to the gearshift. "I mean, why the hell does she need you? She's got Charlie right there!"

Julie didn't respond to that, either, because that was her darkest fear. That whatever kind of murder her mother had witnessed, Charlie—dear, sweet Charlie—was the victim.

ERIC DIDN'T TRUST the valet parkers at the hotel, not with this car. He dropped Julie off at the entrance and roared off in search of his own parking space.

She expected to find the lobby swarming with police, but there was only the usual late-night crowd of partygoers returning to their rooms. She followed a giggling trio of girls in sparkly minidresses across the hotel lobby to the elevator bank. They side-eyed her as they waited for a car to arrive, and she was suddenly aware of her own post-party appearance. Her elaborate updo had come elaborately undone. She'd lost her bra on the beach, and her breasts felt loose and saggy inside the bodice of her dress. She could feel sand in her shoes, in the crack of her buttocks. "Fun night?" one of the girls snarked as the elevator doors opened.

Julie said nothing as she got in and pushed the button for the penthouse. The police officer on the phone had carefully recited the suite number, as if she didn't already know it. As if she hadn't booked and confirmed the reservation herself.

The party girls peeled off on a lower floor, and Julie rode alone to the top of the hotel. When the doors opened, a man brushed past her into the elevator. He was silver-haired and sun-bronzed and wearing a business suit in the wee hours of a Sunday morning. But it wasn't until she spotted the flag pin in his lapel that she realized. "Senator Richards?"

He put an arm out to hold the doors open. He squinted at her. "Ah. Judy, is it?"

She'd been introduced to him many times before at various fund-raising events, but there was no reason for him to get her name right. It was her mother who was his largest donor, not Julie.

"I'm sorry I can't stay any longer," he said. "I have an early flight back to D.C. But it's all in hand. I called Roger Engel." At her blank look, he clarified: "The U.S. Attorney. He owes me, so he's got the FBI pulling their archives and checking the military records. We'll get to the bottom of this. Don't you worry."

None of this made any sense. She wondered if he was confusing her with someone actually named Judy. "I'm here for my mother?" she said.

"Yes, I've just seen her," he said as the elevator beeped its impatience. "My doctor's with her now."

"Doctor?" she exclaimed. The officer on the phone had said her mother hadn't been hurt. "Is she all right?"

He withdrew his arm. "She's—well, she's pretty upset. What a thing to happen on her wedding day." He thought of something else as the doors slid shut. "She got my gift, I hope?"

She turned and ran down the corridor, but the room numbers were going the wrong way, and she had to turn and run the other way until she arrived breathless at the door. It was locked. She rattled the knob and was starting to knock when it swung open. Another man in a suit stood inside. This one was younger, with russet-colored hair and skin that was more sunburned than sun-bronzed. He wore an earpiece with a coiled wire disappearing into his shirt collar. "Mrs. Hoffman?"

"Yes?"

"Mrs. Eric Hoffman?"

"Yes," she said again, baffled.

He stepped back to let her through. "I'm Detective Brian Holley, Sarasota County Sheriff's Office."

Her eyes moved past him to sweep across the living room of the suite. There was no sign of a struggle, no disarray beyond her mother's wedding gown on the rug. Thanks to the stiff boning in the seams, the bodice stood upright while the skirt puddled into the floor. It reminded her of the melting witch in *The Wizard of Oz*.

"Your mother's in there with the doctor." The detective nodded at the closed door to the bedroom.

"Where's Charlie? Her husband?"

"He's been detained downstairs."

That meant Charlie was alive, but Julie's relief lasted only a second before her confusion swelled to crowd it out. Why would he be down in the lobby now? What could he be doing? Consulting the concierge? Browsing in the gift shop while his bride was up here in hysteria?

"Sarasota?" she said as she recalled how the detective had introduced himself. "I thought the murder happened in Tampa?"

He shook his head. "Chicago. And I guess the feds have jurisdiction. But your mother called the sheriff, and he sent me up to see if I could be of any assistance."

Now Julie was totally lost. How could Kate have witnessed a murder in Chicago? And called the Tampa police to report it? While she was also calling a U.S. senator and the sheriff of Sarasota County?

The door to the bedroom opened, and another man emerged. He was gray-haired and gray-bearded and wore an aloha shirt and sandals. He was carrying a doctor's satchel. He eyed Julie. "You the daughter?"

"What happened? How is she?"

"Hysterical when I arrived. I gave her a sedative. She'll drift off to sleep in ten or fifteen minutes. Go on in. She's been asking for you."

Julie hurried past him into the bedroom. Her mother was lying on a white linen duvet with her eyes closed and one arm trailing toward the floor. She looked so different, so powerless, that for a second Julie was afraid to come closer. "Mom?"

Kate's eyes fluttered open. "Oh, Julie. Finally!" She was wearing her favorite silk dressing gown, the one with the peacock fanning its tail on the back. Julie had just picked it up from the cleaner's on Thursday.

"Mom, are you all right? What happened?" Julie squatted by the bedside and took Kate's loose hand in hers.

"Oh!" A single sob escaped Kate's lips on a rush of air. "Why did he have to tell me? We could have lived out the rest of our lives without—If only he hadn't opened his damn mouth!"

"Charlie?"

Kate jerked her hand free and pressed it to her forehead. "He said he had to tell me. Oh, God, my head—it's splitting! What was I supposed to do with that information? Live with it?" Another sob tore out of her. "Did I do the right thing? God, I don't know!"

"What? What did he tell you?"

Her eyes sank shut. "I didn't know what to do. The love of my life . . ."

"Mom!" Julie jostled her. "What did Charlie tell you?"

"Those people. All those people." Her arm dropped off the side of the bed again.

"What people?"

"Tylenol," Kate mumbled.

"You need a Tylenol?" Julie looked around the room. "Where is it? In your cosmetic bag?" But she remembered the doctor had given her a sedative. "No, I don't think you should take anything else now."

"He killed them," Kate said in a whisper, barely more than a breath.

"What? Who?" Julie leaned in closer.

"Tylen—Tylen . . ."

Julie jostled her again. "Mom?"

A light snore was the only response.

Julie sat back on her heels. Charlie had told her he'd killed some people? In Chicago? And now he was blithely killing time down in the lobby? She didn't believe it for a minute. But the only other explanation was Eric's favorite theory—that Kate was losing her mind—and she couldn't believe that, either.

"Mom?" she said again, but Kate was out cold.

CHAPTER 5

"Julie!"

Eric's shout sounded from the hotel corridor. Julie hurried out to the living room of the suite. He stood in the doorway, and the Sarasota detective had one hand on the knob and the other on the jamb, blocking his entry.

"Out of my way," Eric snapped at him.

The man glanced at Julie over his shoulder. "You know him?"

"My—my husband."

The detective immediately lifted both arms in apology and backed away.

"Julie!" Eric charged at her. His dinner jacket was open, his cummerbund and tie lost to the beach. "What the hell's going on? Charlie's sitting in the backseat of a locked cop car in the parking lot."

"What?" she gasped. Then she realized. Charlie hadn't *been* detained. He was *being* detained.

"I knocked on the window, and all he could do was shrug and shake his head. Where's your mother? What's this all about?"

Julie threw a helpless look at the detective, but he was touching a finger to his earpiece and listening to another conversation. "I—I'm not sure," she said. "Mom's been sedated. She's out now, and she wasn't speaking clearly before that. But I think she said that Charlie confessed to killing some people?"

"Get out," Eric scoffed.

"I know. I mean, I don't know. Maybe she's got a migraine? She kept asking for Tylenol."

"If I might . . ." the detective said quietly.

Eric wheeled on him. "Who the hell are you?"

"Detective Brian Holley, Sarasota County Sheriff's Office. Ms. Sawyer reported that her husband—Charles Mull?—confessed to her tonight that he was responsible for the Tylenol murders."

Eric stared at him a long moment before letting out a hoot. "And you bought it? You actually took that seriously? For fuck's sake, the woman's got dementia!"

"No, Eric—" Julie began.

"The FBI's running it down," Holley said. "It shouldn't take long to check dates and alibis."

"Jesus Christ." Eric raked a hand through his hair. "I don't fucking believe this."

"I don't understand," Julie said. "What are the Tylenol murders?"

Eric shot her an astounded look. "Jeez, did you grow up in a cave? How do you not know that?"

Detective Holley ducked his head and sidled to the door. "I'll be right outside," he said as he slipped into the corridor. "If you need me."

Julie returned to the bedroom and closed the door before Eric could see her cry. It wasn't the harshness in his voice or the pitying look on the detective's face that made the tears burn in her eyes. Or it wasn't only those things. Because under it all was terror. Either dear sweet Charlie was a murderer or her mother had completely lost her mind, and she didn't know which possibility frightened her more.

Eric opened the bedroom door without knocking. "Julie?" He scowled at Kate on the bed, but his face softened when he saw Julie's tears. "I'm sorry, babe." He put his arms around her. "I didn't mean to snap at you."

She hid her face against his chest.

"It's just—seeing Charlie in the back of that cop car. In a bathrobe! I mean, jeez."

Eric turned to study Kate where she lay on the bed. Julie turned, too. Even in repose, Kate's skin was smooth and nearly unlined. Her sleep looked peaceful, and Julie felt a brief burn of resentment that she could rest undisturbed while everyone else was in turmoil.

"She needs a doctor," Eric said.

"He was just here—"

"Not that kind of doctor. A neurologist." He pulled his phone from his pocket. "I'm calling Alex."

"Eric, no. It's three in the morning!"

He continued scrolling through his contacts. "I think this qualifies as an emergency, don't you?"

He went back into the living room to make the call, and Julie pulled out her own phone to google *Tylenol murders*. The Wikipedia entry came up first in the search results. She heard Eric leaving a voicemail message for Alex as she scrolled through the article. Drug tampering, she read, in 1982, and she felt somewhat vindicated for not knowing about events that had happened forty years ago, before she was even born. She read on: *Chicago metro area. Tylenol capsules replaced with potassium cyanide. Seven deaths. Murders remain unsolved.*

This was ridiculous. It wasn't possible that Charlie had confessed to such a heinous crime. It wasn't possible that Charlie could have *done* such a heinous crime. He was the gentlest man Julie knew. So much so that she once felt compelled to ask him how he'd ever survived in the marines. *It was tough sometimes,* he'd admitted, *but I did what I had to do. I had my buddies to think of, and later I had my men. They counted on me.*

That was how he survived: by thinking of others first and putting their well-being ahead of his own. It was impossible that such a man had committed these murders. Any murders.

She gazed at her mother. It was equally impossible to believe that there was anything wrong with Kate's mind. Only two weeks before, she had closed on a three-hundred-acre tract near Naples and done so with the most creative financing vehicle their outside lawyers had ever seen. It had involved multiple shell corporations and cross-guaranties and buyback schemes too complicated for Julie to process without pages of flow charts.

I don't know how she comes up with these ideas, Jack Trotter had marveled when they celebrated the deal afterward. Jack was the company president and managed the mundane affairs of the business, leaving Kate free to imagine and scheme and create. Those things she sometimes forgot, the blunders Eric kept harping on—they were trivial matters she could depend on Jack and others to handle. That was her brain's way of prioritizing the details of her life and business. No one needed a flow chart to understand why that made sense.

Eric was leaving his message for Alex. His voice was too loud. Julie closed the bedroom door, then toed off her shoes and stretched out on the other side of the bed. The warmth of her mother's body radiated through her silken robe and brought back a wave of memories of all those long-ago times they lay together like this.

When she was a little girl, her mother lay beside her every night to read her bedtime stories. She worked a frenetic schedule then as always, but she seldom missed a bedtime. She didn't read the usual picture books or fairy tales that other mothers read to their children. No, Kate read the classics: Peter Pan and Narnia, then on to Dickens and Twain and Jules Verne. *She's not getting a damn thing out of those books,* Julie's father sometimes complained, and maybe he was right, but Julie loved lying there and listening anyway. She loved the sound of her mother's voice, the smell of her perfume, the warmth of their cuddles.

Eventually, she outgrew the bedtime stories—or Kate abandoned her attempt to raise a mini-me. But they came to share a bed again when Julie was thirteen, during those long months when the nightmares wouldn't stop. Her mother slept with her almost every night then, and when Julie woke up shivering and sobbing, Kate was there to hold her and calm her and whisper, *It's okay, it's all right, I'm here.*

It's just the two of us now, she often told Julie after her father died. *But that's two better than most people. You and me. We're the Dynamic Duo!*

All those people who questioned Julie's loyalty to her mother, all those friends who pitied her for the way Kate sometimes treated her, they didn't know about that time. They could never imagine it.

She closed her eyes now and listened to her mother breathe. This day had started out as the best in Kate's life and ended up as the worst, and Julie felt so awful for her. But the same thing was true of Charlie, and she didn't know what to feel, except, at this moment, exhausted.

CHAPTER 6

Julie jerked awake at the knock on the outer door of the suite. She dragged herself off the bed and went into the living room. Eric was asleep on the sofa, his shirt undone and his dinner jacket draped over a lamp. He looked like a dissolute rake passed out after some Gatsbyesque bacchanal. He was so handsome it made her heart hurt.

The knock came again, louder. Julie opened the door to Detective Holley. He looked contrite. "Excuse me, Mrs. Hoffman, but there are some people here—"

Behind him stood Greta in yoga pants, her face full of tragedy. "Oh, Jules," she cried, and reached around the detective to grab her into a hug.

"Greta?" Julie was too startled to return the hug. "What are you doing here? Alex?" she said next. He was behind his wife, wearing gym shorts and balancing a cup carrier loaded with four coffees.

"Okay, so you know them," the detective mumbled, and stepped aside.

Greta gave her a tight squeeze. "You poor thing!"

"Dude," Eric called from the sofa. "Thanks for coming." He swung his feet to the floor as Alex ducked through the doorway and put the carrier on the coffee table.

Julie looked to Eric. "You told them to come?"

Greta answered for him as the men gave each other a handshake and a one-armed hug. "We drove up as soon as Alex got the message."

Detective Holley remained in the corridor, on his feet, eyes averted. Julie averted her eyes, too, and quickly closed the door. Eric and Alex went into a huddle by the windows. The sky was black beyond them.

"What time is it?" Julie asked.

"Just after five." Greta seized both her hands. "Oh, God! What a terrible thing for you to have to deal with!"

"Right. I'll have a look," Alex said to Eric.

It wasn't until he started for the bedroom that Julie realized what he meant: he'd have a look at her mother. "No, don't." She pulled her hands free. "She's asleep."

He ignored her and leaned into the bedroom doorway. "Hey, Kate. It's Alex Blanco. Okay if I come in for a chat?"

"Alex, no—she's been sedated."

Kate's groggy voice drifted out. "Alex? That you? Yes, come."

He raised a single eyebrow at Julie and went in and closed the door.

She threw a hot look at Eric as he sank back on the sofa. He had no business calling in a neurologist at five in the morning, brother-in-law or not. He had no business calling in a neurologist at all. That wasn't his decision to make. But she couldn't say that, not with his sister standing there. "I wonder," she said instead, "if it would be better to wait for the FBI—"

Eric didn't look at her. He was busy peeling back the lid on his coffee cup. "We couldn't wait." He took a trial sip of the coffee, then, apparently satisfied with the temperature, a full gulp. "She could've had a stroke."

Julie blinked. "A stroke!" She sat down hard on the sofa beside him. She'd never considered that possibility, and it both terrified and elated her. It would be awful, of course, but it might also be the best possible answer. Charlie wouldn't be a murderer, and Kate wouldn't be losing her mind. She'd simply had a stroke, and with the right treatment, she'd soon be herself again. She and Charlie could have their happily-ever-after.

But doubt crowded in on the heels of that thought. Wouldn't the senator's doctor have checked for symptoms of a stroke as soon as he arrived? Shouldn't Eric himself have checked instead of taking a two-hour nap? Wasn't that first hour critical?

Greta tucked herself in on the other side of Julie. She took the lid off a coffee cup and handed it to her, then opened another for herself.

"Did you see Charlie down there?" Eric asked her.

She nodded. "The poor guy. Half asleep in the back of that squad car while the cop babysitting him played on his phone."

Eric made a noise of frustration in his throat.

"Jules, did you call his daughter?" Greta asked.

"No, I—" Julie was embarrassed to admit that it hadn't occurred to her, and even more embarrassed that she didn't know where Becky and her husband were staying. She'd planned to put them up in one of her mother's hotels, but Charlie had insisted their trip should be on his dime, and he'd already booked them a room. She never asked where. She was afraid they might be at some budget motel.

"No, Charlie wouldn't want that," Eric said, and the certainty in his tone was enough to close the subject. The three of them sat in silence, slurping their coffee and listening to the low rumble of Alex's voice from inside the bedroom, followed by the throaty sound of Kate's replies. The words were indistinct, but the tone was as familiar as a thousand doctors' exams anywhere.

Greta put her hand on Julie's knee and softly squeezed. After a moment Eric picked up her hand and held it loosely in his own.

When Alex finally emerged, he looked at Eric and shook his head, and Eric gave a nod of acknowledgment.

Their wordless exchange rankled Julie. It was like a secret code used by boys in a tree house posted with a NO GIRLS ALLOWED sign. "What?" she demanded. "What is it?"

Alex finally looked at her. "Your mother shows no facial weakness. No eye droop. Her smile is symmetrical. She can raise both arms above her head. Her speech is clear. So—no indication of a stroke."

"But—that's good news!"

"No," he said with exaggerated patience, as if speaking to a child. "She's incoherent—"

"Because she just woke up. After being sedated."

He took a seat in the armchair across from her. "She's imagining things. Seeing things. She thought she saw a meteor streak past the window."

Julie felt a jolt of fear at that. But she remembered something. "No, the sedative could have caused that. What's it—Ativan?—can cause hallucinations in the elderly?"

"Withdrawal from Ativan," Alex corrected her. "And we don't know that's what she took. It was more likely Valium." He looked back to Eric. "We'll need to schedule a full workup tomorrow. But my preliminary impression is that she's experiencing auditory and visual hallucinations consistent with dementia."

Eric sighed. "I knew it."

Julie pulled her hand from his and got to her feet. "We don't know anything. You're jumping to conclusions."

Eric stood, too. "Julie, babe, I know this is a lot for you to handle." He started to reach for her as another knock sounded.

She wheeled away to open the door. Detective Holley was there with another man. This one was older, also in a suit.

"Sorry to disturb you," Holley said. "This is Special Agent Martin Hertz."

Hertz was holding a folder in one hand and a small billfold in the other. He flipped the billfold open ten inches from Julie's face. His photo was on one side; a gold shield was on the other. "FBI," he said. "We've completed our investigation. I have a report."

"Already?"

"Come in. Come in," Eric said behind her. He pulled her aside to admit the two men to the suite. Greta and Alex were on their feet, too. The room had seemed so spacious when she first arrived, but now there were too many people in it, and the walls were closing in. The disembodied torso of Kate's wedding gown still stood in the middle of the room, and Julie hurried to move it to the corner. One less body in the way.

"Have a seat," Eric said.

"I'll stand," the FBI agent said. "This won't take long."

He seemed put out, Julie thought, and of course he would be—roused from his bed in the wee hours of a Sunday morning to obey the summons of a U.S. senator who was obeying the summons of a mega-donor. He had every right to be annoyed. Julie couldn't help cringing sometimes at the way her mother threw her weight—her money—around.

Detective Holley retreated to the far side of the room and leaned against the desk. The others shuffled awkwardly back into their seats. It made for a strange tableau. Two men in business suits, two people in disheveled evening clothes, and two more in athleisure wear.

Special Agent Hertz cleared his throat and opened the folder he was holding. "'Early this morning,'" he read, "'Tampa PD received a report that one Charles Mull had informed his wife that he was responsible for the deaths of seven people in the greater Chicago area back in 1982. When questioned, Mr. Mull denied that he said it and also denied that he could have done it. He was detained, with his consent, while further inquiries were made. The matter was referred to the FBI field office here in Tampa.'" He spoke in a drone without lifting his eyes from the page.

"'We accessed archives and reviewed the original investigatory reports and all updates and supplements. The deaths in question were caused by potassium cyanide poisoning. It was determined that capsules containing the poison were inserted into bottles of acetaminophen sold under the Tylenol label. The murders became known as the Tylenol murders. It was determined at the time that the bottles in question had come from two different manufacturing facilities, one in Pennsylvania and one in Texas, so the tampering must have occurred after the bottles were placed on the store shelves for sale. Dates of delivery to the stores in question narrowed the time window of tampering opportunity to September 26, 27, and 28, 1982. Therefore, the perpetrator must have been in the Chicago area at that time. Charles Mull states that he was stationed overseas during all of September 1982 and for at least six months before and after.'

"'We accessed the NPRC'"—Hertz did look up then to explain—"that's the National Personnel Records Center—'to review Mr. Mull's military service records. In August 1982, Sergeant Mull was serving with the Thirty-second Marine Amphibious Unit when it was deployed to Beirut to assist in the evacuation of PLO guerrilla fighters. It was meant as a peacekeeping mission, so the fighters were permitted to retain their weapons as they marched to the harbor to board the vessels. Some rioting took place, and a number of weapons were fired, mostly into the air, but one of the bullets struck and wounded Sergeant Mull.'"

"Yeah, that's right," Eric said. "He mentioned that just last night."

The FBI agent ignored the interruption and read on. "'Sergeant Mull was airlifted to the U.S. military hospital in Landstuhl, Germany, where he received medical treatment and therapy. Hospital records show that he was admitted on August 22, 1982, and he was discharged from their care on October 5, 1982. He returned to active duty with his unit in Rome the next day.'

"In other words"—Agent Hertz finally looked directly at his audience—"Charles Mull was in a different hemisphere at the time of the drug-tampering. He has a solid alibi for the Tylenol murders."

"I knew it," Eric declared on Julie's left.

"Thank God," Greta breathed on her right.

The agent snapped his folder shut and headed for the door. Halfway there, he paused. "Off the record?" he said, turning back. "We know who the actual perpetrator is. We've known almost from the start. The lawyers wouldn't charge him because we can't prove that he was in Chicago in September 1982. But we know for certain that Charles Mull wasn't."

CHAPTER 7

"That can't be right."

All heads swiveled to the bedroom doorway where Kate stood in her peacock dressing gown.

"You've made a mistake," she said. "He told me he did it. Why would he confess to something he didn't do?"

The room went very still. The FBI agent shifted his eyes to Detective Holley, who looked at the floor. Kate peered closely at the two officers, and when neither answered, she looked to the others, who all looked away.

"Oh," she said. Her voice was suddenly different—small and thin and nothing like the voice of Kate Sawyer. Her face was deathly pale against the vibrant blues and greens of her robe, and in the next moment, it seemed to collapse; her cheeks sagged into jowls, and her eyes sank deep into their sockets. "Oh," she said again.

She swayed on her feet and had to clutch both sides of the door-jamb to steady herself. For a moment she froze like that, an iron cross, before she spun away into the bedroom, the peacock's tail fanned wide across her back. She slammed the door.

A soft thud sounded from the corner of the room. The upright bodice of Kate's wedding gown had toppled over.

Julie got up and started after her mother, but Greta tugged her back. "You should give her a minute," she whispered.

"It's a lot to process," Alex agreed. "And it's hardest for those patients who still have enough self-awareness to understand what's happening to them. You'll find it's actually easier on her after the dementia's more advanced."

"Stop," Julie said. "It's too soon—"

Agent Hertz gave a parting nod to Detective Holley and left the room.

Eric got to his feet. "I'm gonna go down and spring Charlie."

"He's been sprung," Holley said. "He's on his way up now." He looked back at Julie. "If there's anything else I can do?"

She wasn't sure what he'd done so far. "No," she said. "Thank you."

"Good night, then," Holley said, and he left the room, too.

"Alex," Greta said quietly. "I guess you'll want to dictate your notes?"

"Oh, right." Alex took out his phone and stood by the window looking out over what remained of the night. Bands of pale gray light were striated across the sky. "Patient presented with auditory delusions," he began. He spoke softly into the recorder.

A few minutes later, the corridor door opened again, and there stood Charlie. His hair was disheveled, and he wore the hotel's terry-cloth robe. On his feet, incongruously, were the black patent-leather Venetian loafers he'd worn with his tuxedo.

"Charlie!" Eric flung his arms around him and thumped him on the back. "Are you okay?"

"Where's Kate?" Charlie's gaze moved blearily across the room.

Julie's heart pinched to see him like this. "She's in the bedroom," she said as she came up to hug him, too. "She's a bit groggy," she whispered. "Let's give her some time."

Alex was dictating into his phone. "Call the hospital. Schedule a full workup and order a rush on all the tests."

Charlie's attention snapped up. "What's that?" he said. "What tests?"

Alex turned from the window. "We need to do a full neurological workup," he said. "And see how far the dementia's progressed."

"What are you talking about? I don't have dementia."

Eric huffed a laugh. "Not you, buddy. Kate."

Charlie stared at him, then at Alex. "You're a damn fool," he said finally. "The both of you. There's nothing wrong with Katie's mind. She's as sharp as a tack! Lord, she can calculate compound interest in her head."

"Charlie." Eric put a hand on his shoulder. "She thinks you confessed to the Tylenol murders. She hallucinated it. There's no other explanation but dementia."

Charlie shook him off. "There damn sure is! She was drunk!"

Julie drew a sharp breath. It was one part shock—she'd never in her life known her mother to be drunk—but also one part hope: drunkenness seemed so ordinary, so reversible.

"All that wine with dinner," Charlie said. "All that champagne before and after. We overdid it. Both of us, but I was used to it. She wasn't."

"That doesn't explain how she came up with something as crazy as the Tylenol murders," Eric said.

"It sure does," Charlie insisted. "Remember my wedding speech? *I have a confession to make.* Those words must have been swimming around in her mind when I handed her a Tylenol. We got to talking about the tamperproof caps, then about the Tylenol murders, and she put the two things together and came up with me confessing to the Tylenol murders. There's nothing more to it than that!"

"Charlie—" Julie touched his arm. "You're sure?"

His face softened as he looked down at her. "Trust me, sweetie. I used to see it all the time when my boots came back drunk from weekend liberty. Those kids'd be telling the craziest stories you ever heard. Full of bits and pieces of things that really happened but all mixed together into the wildest concoctions. You woulda thought it was LSD, but all it took was tequila. That's the power of alcohol and the power of suggestion. And that's all that happened to your mom."

Alex shook his head at Julie, but he spoke to Charlie more tactfully. "Well, it wouldn't hurt to get her in for some tests this week, anyway."

"It damn sure would," Charlie said, stiffening. "Since we'll be in Tahiti. On our honeymoon. And now if you'll excuse me, I'd like to rejoin my bride for what's left of our wedding night!"

Julie laughed and gave him a hug. "Let me go in first. She'll probably want to fix her face."

"Bah. You girls and your faces," he griped, but he was smiling as he sat down and crossed one hairy leg over the other.

"You want some coffee?" Eric was saying as Julie slipped through the bedroom door. "Let me get room service."

Julie closed the door behind her. Kate was indeed at the makeup mirror, but she wasn't fixing her face. She was staring at her reflection while tears streamed down her cheeks.

"Oh, Mom." How devastating it must have been for a woman like her mother—one who took such pride in her own mental prowess—to be told she was losing her mind. Julie hurried across the room to put her arms around her. "There's nothing wrong with you. It was just the alcohol. Charlie explained everything."

"Charlie." With a moan, Kate dropped her head into her hands. "I was such a fool."

"To get so drunk? No, really, there's no harm done." Apart from wasting the time of three different law enforcement organizations, not to mention a U.S. senator, Julie thought. But people like her mother got passes for transgressions like that.

Kate moaned again, louder. "I was a fool to fall for him. A fool to believe a word he said."

Julie straightened, and a look of fear crossed her reflection in the mirror. Her mother wasn't making sense. "Mom," she said carefully. "You heard the FBI agent. Charlie didn't do it. He couldn't have. He has an absolute alibi."

Kate sniffed loudly. "Of course he does. That was the whole point, wasn't it?"

"The point? Of what?"

"Of the confession. It had to be something he couldn't have done. How else would it work?"

"Would what work?"

"The gaslighting."

Julie stared at her in utter astonishment. "What?"

"I have to give him credit. It's the smartest way around a prenup I've ever heard. Have me declared incompetent. Then appoint himself guardian. Of me and my money. All he needed was some expert testimony, and look at who he summoned up here." Kate let out a bitter laugh. "A neurologist!"

Julie wasn't following any of this, but she knew that much was wrong. "Mom, no. Charlie didn't ask Alex up. Eric did."

"Oh, yes. Eric." Kate spat out the name like a bad taste.

"What's that supposed to mean?"

"And his sister, the probate judge! It's brilliant, all of it!" She plucked a handful of tissues from her case and wiped off her face. "Now." She stood up. "Get Charlie out of here and take me home. Then you need to call Grady. Or Greggson. What's-her-name. Whoever does my family law. I want the divorce papers ready to file Monday morning. Or should it be an annulment? Yes, an annulment."

"Home?" Julie was stuck three sentences behind. "Mom, your flight's in a couple hours. Your honeymoon trip, remember?"

"My honeymoon," Kate repeated dully. She collapsed back into the chair. "Oh, God. Charlie!" she wailed. "He was the love of my life. He was everything to me. And I was nothing to him—nothing but a bank account!" A torrent of tears streamed down her face before she buried it in her hands.

CHAPTER 8

Julie did exactly as instructed. She called her mother's fleet manager to have a company car delivered to the hotel for the drive back to Sarasota. She called Luisa, her mother's housekeeper, to alert her to their unexpected return and to pack up Charlie's things. She reached her mother's lawyer to schedule a meeting first thing Monday. "No! Today!" Kate shouted from the hotel bathroom, and a time was set for that very afternoon. Julie packed her mother's bags and called a bellman to cart them down to the lobby.

Then she went out into the living room to explain what was happening. Charlie was devastated and Eric was furious, but there was nothing else she could do. Nothing else they could do, either, and along with Alex and Greta, they vacated the suite long enough for Kate to make her exit.

They drove in silence back to Sarasota. Normally, Kate had much to say about Julie's driving—usually something like *get around this jerk*—but today she sat silent. She was dry-eyed, but her mouth was quivering, and her hands clenched and unclenched in her lap. Now and then a buzzing sounded, like a fly trapped inside the car. It was coming from Kate's handbag at her feet. Her phone, on vibrate. Charlie, trying and failing to talk to her.

IT WAS STILL early morning when they crossed the drawbridge to Cascara Key, and the clouds reflected a rosy glow from the sun as it climbed through the sky behind them. Julie drove north along the narrow road, passing mansions to the right, the beach to the left, until she reached La Coquina.

It meant *The Shell*. Kate had chosen the name because it meant roughly the same thing as Cascara. Now it struck Julie as too accurate: the house would seem like an empty shell without Charlie in it. He'd been living here, albeit unofficially, for the past six months, and the place had never been jollier.

The circular drive looped past the big iron gates that led to the courtyard and continued around to the garages on the side of the house. Luisa was out the door and down the steps before Julie shut off the engine. She was a squat woman in her fifties with glossy black hair that she wore in a tight coil of braids on top of her head. She helped Kate out of the car and circled to the trunk to unload the bags. Even though she'd been exhaustively involved in the wedding preparations—not to mention the wedding cleanup, thanks to Julie's early departure the night before—she expressed no surprise and asked no questions about Kate's return without Charlie. She said not a word beyond *good morning*. But after Kate went ahead into the house, Luisa gave Julie's hand a quick squeeze.

"How's the packing going?" Julie asked in a low voice as they sorted out the bags.

"Done. Ferdy is driving to your house right now." Ferdy was Luisa's husband. They lived in an apartment over the garage and ran the entire household. Luisa did all the day-to-day cooking and cleaning while also supervising the twice-weekly cleaners and the private chef on weekends. Ferdy was the maintenance man and supervised the twice-weekly landscapers. They'd been part of the household since Julie was a little girl, and though they would never presume it themselves, she thought of them as family.

Julie went inside, through the back entry hall and the mudroom, past the pantry and the laundry room, into the kitchen and from there down another hallway into the foyer. Kate was already halfway up the curving staircase. "I'm taking a nap," she announced to the ceiling twenty-five feet overhead. "Wake me when the lawyer arrives."

Julie got her phone out at once and called the lawyer again, to change the meeting's venue from the law office to La Coquina.

THIS HOUSE WAS never Julie's home. Kate didn't have it built until after Julie was out of school and living on her own. She visited often in the daytime to swim in the pool or lie on the beach, but she'd never spent a night here before. She decided on the first-floor guest suite, with windows facing the Gulf.

She was in the shower when Eric called. Ferdy had arrived at their house with all the bags and boxes of Charlie's things, but Eric refused to send him back with any of Julie's things. Not even a toothbrush.

"This is stupid," he said. "Come home."

"I can't," she said as water streamed down her body and pooled on the marble floor. "I can't leave her alone when she's—" She searched for a word. Heartbroken? Yes. Deranged? She just didn't know.

"Then don't. I'll drive Charlie over and pick you up."

She shuddered at the thought of the scene that would follow. "No. Please, Eric. Give it a day. Let things—clear up."

His heavy sigh came over the line. "Things like this don't just clear up, babe. You need to face facts."

Facts she could face. Theories and arguments she could only consider. She caught a glimpse of herself in the mirror and turned away. She looked so drawn, haggard, even. She'd hate for Eric to see her like this. "Give it some time," she said.

"One day," he said finally, grudgingly.

FACE FACTS, HE'D said, and as she toweled off, she tried to. Fact one: Charlie couldn't have committed the Tylenol murders. Facts two and three: he said he didn't confess to them, and Kate said he did.

So what was the explanation? Charlie said she was drunk. Eric said she was demented. Kate said she was being gaslit.

That was such a strange word, Julie thought. She wasn't even sure exactly what it meant. She'd seen the old movie once, long ago. She remembered it was about a husband trying to drive his wife insane. Or to make her think she was insane, which was basically the same thing. These days *gaslighting* was a term people threw around a lot, whenever they thought someone was yanking their chain. It seemed to come up all the time in politics.

She picked up her phone and looked up the actual definition: *the psychological manipulation of a person, usually over an extended period of time, that causes the victim to question the validity of their own thoughts, perception of reality, or memories, typically leading to confusion, loss of confidence and self-esteem, uncertainty of one's emotional or mental stability, and a dependency on the perpetrator.* Gaslighting sowed self-doubt in the victim's mind, forcing them to question their own judgment and intuition.

Well, Julie thought, closing the website, *if that's really what Charlie is up to, lots of luck.* No one would ever succeed in getting Kate Sawyer to question her own judgment and intuition.

CHAPTER 9

Julie's role as general counsel of KS Development required her to keep rosters of all the company's law firms, and there were dozens—the national firms that handled the big-picture matters, along with the local firms in every city where a KS project was underway. Julie's role as Kate Sawyer's daughter required her to keep a roster of her mother's personal law firms, and there were several of those as well.

Foster & Greggson was the name of this one. Franklin Foster did Kate's estate planning, advising her on how to give away her money, while his partner, Lenore Greggson, advised her on how to keep it. Lenore was the author of the prenuptial agreement that Kate and Charlie had signed the week before.

Lenore arrived punctually, driving up to the iron gates in a black German sedan that managed to convey both wealth and gravity. Even though it was a Sunday afternoon, she was dressed in business clothes, a smart trouser suit and heels that obliged her to mince her way through the tiled courtyard to the heavy double doors of the house.

Julie asked Luisa to show the lawyer to the living room while she headed up the stairs to wake her mother. But Kate was already coming down, fully dressed in her customary business attire: a silk blouse and tailored trousers. Julie wore a tropical-print muumuu and flip-flops. Swimsuits and cover-ups were the only clothes she kept at this house.

"No, bring her to my office," Kate said, and swept past Julie to the back of the house. Her office had the same clean modern decor as the rest of La Coquina. The upholstery was crisp and white, the case goods dark and gleaming, the art abstract, and the desktop a clear beveled expanse of glass. The French doors opened onto a terrace that overlooked the bay and the dock where her cabin cruiser, the *Half-shell,* bobbed gently on its moorings. Kate circled the desk and stood waiting for Lenore to come through.

"Ms. Sawyer, a pleasure," the lawyer said as she entered the room and gave an admiring glance about. She was a woman of indeterminate middle age, younger than Kate, older than Julie, with auburn hair and tasteful jewelry. She carried not a briefcase but a slim document case in oxblood leather.

"Lenore, thank you for coming." It was one of Kate's surprising gifts, to remember names in a pinch. She pointed the lawyer to a chair and took her own seat behind the desk. It was an inversion of the usual lawyer-client positioning, and Julie suspected that this was the reason for today's meeting venue. Another guest chair sat at an angle next to Lenore's, but Julie took a less obtrusive seat in the corner of the room.

"How may I be of service?" Lenore asked, and Julie had to admire her diplomacy. She certainly must have known that yesterday was the wedding day, so she certainly must have guessed that something was already amiss. But she didn't express shock or demand explanations. She was letting Kate set the tone. She had the kind of demeanor that Julie had tried and failed to adopt during her brief unhappy stint in private practice.

"I want an annulment," Kate said.

"I see." Lenore opened her document case, revealing a clean lined legal pad. "Under Florida law, a marriage can be annulled if it is either void or voidable. Void covers marriages that were invalid from the outset, such as in cases of incest or bigamy."

"What else?" Kate said, and waggled her fingers in a *give me more* gesture.

"A marriage is voidable if it was procured through fraud or duress."

"Yes. Yes, that works. Fraud."

Lenore nodded and made a note. "If you could give me the specifics of how Mr. Mull defrauded you?"

Kate drew a deep breath and leaned forward, her elbows on the desk. "He entered the prenup pretending to disclaim any interest in my assets while he was secretly scheming for a way to get around it and get control of everything."

"How?" Lenore said with a sharply arched eyebrow. Julie imagined this was the closest she would come to showing an emotional reaction. The prenup was her work, after all; she'd drafted it to be ironclad.

Kate hesitated before answering. "By having me declared incompetent."

"How?" Lenore said again. This time she sounded puzzled.

"It's a long story." Kate did a quarter-swivel in the desk chair so she was facing the windows, the bay, the dock, the boat. She seldom went out on the *Half-shell* anymore, and she'd been on the verge of selling it when Charlie came back into her life. He was an avid fisherman and an excellent helmsman, and now it was more his boat than hers.

"Last night, after the wedding," Kate said, "Charlie confessed to me that he committed some murders back in the eighties. I called the police, naturally. Then, when they questioned him, he denied that he'd told me any such thing. Further investigation revealed that, in fact, he didn't commit those murders. So why did he tell me otherwise? Why did he make his grand confession? To make me look like I'm losing my mind!"

Lenore didn't say anything for a long moment. "Has he said as much?" she asked.

Julie spoke up. "No, he chalked it up to confusion brought on by alcohol consumption. Actually, he argued against the idea that—that she was losing her mind."

"Argued with whom?"

"Ha! That's it exactly," Kate said. "He had a neurologist and a judge there—in our honeymoon suite!—so he could have witnesses and build a record."

"Mom, I told you," Julie put in quietly, "it was Eric's idea—"

"Oh, I don't doubt that for a minute!"

Julie pulled her mouth tight.

"Regardless," Lenore said, "a finding of fraud requires clear and convincing evidence of intent. We'd need to prove, one, that he made this false confession. Two, that he did it with the goal of having himself appointed your guardian. And three, that he did all of the above with the specific intent of avoiding the prenup." She spread her hands. "I'm afraid that would be a difficult burden." Her tone made it clear that by *difficult,* she meant *impossible.*

Kate bit her lip. "Divorce, then. I want to file for divorce."

Lenore nodded. "Of course. On grounds that the marriage is irretrievably broken. This we can certainly establish."

Kate exhaled. "Good. Then—proceed."

"Certainly. We can prepare the papers immediately. But let me caution you on one point."

Kate squinted at her. "Yes?"

"If you're correct about Mr. Mull's endgame, then I expect that your filing for divorce would cause him to accelerate his petition for guardianship. And unfortunately, that would bolster his case."

"How so?"

"Seeking a divorce the day after the wedding—a lavish, long-planned wedding—might very well convince the court that—well, that you were in fact mentally incapacitated. And your only rebuttal would be Mr. Mull's confession to you, which he denies, and which might further convince the court—"

"That I've lost my mind."

"I'm afraid so."

"I see." Kate stood and went to the windows and stared out at the *Half-shell*. Two gulls had landed on the flybridge, and their wings flapped furiously as they squabbled over some morsel. "So I'm damned if I do and damned if I don't." She laughed, short and bitter, and added in a whisper, "I'm damned."

Julie rose from her chair. "Mom?"

Kate didn't answer. She turned and left the room without another word. A moment later, her steps sounded on the stairs, heavy and slow.

Lenore zipped up her document case and stood. "I don't believe I have my instructions."

Julie gave a weak shrug. "I guess she needs to think?"

Lenore lifted an eyebrow and turned to go. Julie trailed after her across the fifty-foot expanse of the foyer and out the front door. Something occurred to her in the courtyard, and she hurried to catch up with Lenore before she reached her car. "If only the prenup included some language, you know, prohibiting Charlie from ever serving as guardian—"

Lenore wheeled on her. "In the event of her mental incompetence?" She scowled. "As if she would have allowed me to include a provision like that."

Julie flushed. She hadn't meant to criticize, but Lenore obviously prided herself on how unassailable her prenups were. Any suggestion of a loophole would have to rankle. "No, of course. You're right," Julie murmured. She tried to recover before Lenore drove away. "About your instructions—how about this? Draft the divorce petition, but don't file it until further notice."

"That works." Lenore nodded and slid behind the wheel.

A nondescript gray sedan pulled into one side of the circle drive just as Lenore was pulling out of the other. The sun glinted off its windshield, obscuring the driver's face. Julie visored her hand over her eyes but couldn't make him out. She didn't recognize him until he climbed out of the car. It was the detective who'd stood sentinel in the hotel all night.

"Detective—Holley?" She hadn't expected to see him again, and she felt ridiculous in her muumuu.

"Mrs. Hoffman. I have something for you." He pointed to the rear of his car.

She couldn't imagine what. He circled around to the trunk, and she met him there as he opened it. Inside was a long package that took up the whole of the trunk, cased in black plastic with a zipper that ran its full length.

She froze. It was a body bag. It was Charlie, she knew it. She knew it at once.

He'd killed himself.

She backed away and squeezed her eyes shut, but that was where the nightmare lived, behind her eyes, and it was playing already, flickering against her retinas like a black-and-white film. A handheld camera shuddered as it tracked a slow-motion walk down a hallway. A glance inside a doorway. A pair of black wingtips on the floor, toes pointed to the ceiling, and beyond them, a pair of trousered legs, then fast-forward, hyperlapse speed, police and paramedics, a sound like a fusillade of gunfire as the body bag was zipped up. It was happening again. She couldn't believe it was happening again.

No. Stop. Stop the movie. Block the memory.

She forced her eyes open, forced herself to watch as Holley lifted the body bag out of the trunk. He did it effortlessly. It looked almost weightless in his arms. Julie blinked. She didn't understand. How could Charlie be so light? Until she saw the logo stenciled on the bag. The designer's logo. "Oh! My mother's gown." It was a garment bag, not a body bag, but still her voice quaked as she spoke.

"You forgot it when you left the hotel," the detective said.

It wasn't forgotten. It was abandoned. *Leave it,* Kate had snapped as they'd left the suite that morning. *I never want to see the damn thing again.*

"Oh, don't worry," Holley said when he turned to her and saw the look on her face. "I didn't touch it. The hotel staff bagged it up."

He thought she was trembling with anger. "No! No, I didn't—I mean, you didn't need to go to such—" She couldn't finish the sentence. It was twenty years since that other body bag, and yet she reacted like this. She was so embarrassed.

"It was no trouble. I was headed back this way anyway."

She held out her arms awkwardly, and he shifted the bag to her. She swayed a bit to keep it from dragging on the ground. "Well—thank you."

He peered at her. "Rough day, I guess."

She shrugged. Up close, she saw that his eyes were rimmed with red. "It was a long shift for you, I guess."

"My job," he said, shrugging, too.

She nodded. "Well."

"Well," he said. Their conversation was as awkward as the handover of the gown bag. "If there's anything I can do—well, here, take my card." He pulled it from the breast pocket of his suit coat.

She swayed again as she freed a hand to take it from him. "Thanks." She turned and started for the house.

"I know how hard this must be."

She looked back. He was gazing at her with such kindness on his face. She could hear the sympathy in his voice. Maybe it was even empathy. Maybe he had a parent with Alzheimer's. Obviously, he thought she did.

Sometimes it seemed she'd spent her whole life defending her mother against the slings and arrows that were so often directed at a woman of her stature. And now here she was, doing it again.

"Thank you," she said. "But we don't even know what this is."

SHE HUNG THE gown bag in the hall closet. Later she'd worry about what to do with it. She'd barely closed the closet door before Kate came down the stairs. She'd changed out of her business clothes. Now she was wearing a long linen tunic and loose linen pants, all in pure ethereal white. On her head was a broad-brimmed hat with a neck flap trailing like a veil behind her. She looked like a bride trekking the Sahara.

"I'm taking a walk," Kate said.

"Oh! Wait, I'll come with you."

Kate shook her head in a quick, firm *no*.

"Okay," Julie said. Nonetheless, she followed her mother out the door and all the way through the courtyard. She stopped in the driveway and watched Kate cross the road to the beach and turn left. The island was almost five miles long. *Don't go far*, Julie started to call before she heard echoes of those same words in her mind, shouted after her a thousand times by her mother. It was what parents always said to children, not children to parents. She knew this sometimes happened, that a child became the parent of an aging mother or father, but she couldn't imagine it ever happening between her and Kate. She couldn't imagine herself doing it, and she definitely couldn't imagine Kate tolerating it.

Julie went out as far as the road. Kate wasn't moving with her usual purposeful stride. She drifted along in an aimless amble along the water's edge. The wind was blowing off the surf and rippling her clothes, and when her tunic billowed out, Julie realized that it wasn't a bride she looked like. It was a ghost.

A gust of wind blew in off the water and lifted Kate's hat off her head, and she didn't reach for it. She didn't seem to notice it was gone even as it went floating up into the sky. The neck flap streamed out like a woman's hair in the wind. Julie had a morbid thought: the hat looked like a severed head as it sailed off to sea.

Her mother was disappearing in pieces.

CHAPTER 10

Kate had made detailed out-of-the-office plans and contingencies for her honeymoon month, but Julie hadn't, and she was expected at work Monday morning. At seven, she crept out of the first-floor guest suite, had a brief consult with Luisa about meal plans, and headed out to the company car. A minute later, she returned for the gown bag in the hall closet. She'd stash it in her own house until—until whenever.

Eric had surgeries Monday mornings, so it was safe to go home and change. Not that it was ever unsafe. She just didn't want to start the week off with a quarrel.

She drove across the bridge to the mainland and north to Sarasota in a sluggish stream of traffic. Even resort cities in the land of vacations and retirements couldn't escape rush hours. Viewed from outer space, Florida was a strange little peninsula, with ten-mile strips of packed-tight development along either coast and a wide swath of nothing much in between. Kate owned thousands of acres of that marshy wasteland, anticipating the inevitable sprawl inward, but for now most of it was leased to ranchers who grazed their cattle on the swamp grass.

Julie's drive took her past a school where a well-dressed group of picketers had assembled. MOMS FOR LITERACY, their signs proclaimed. They were protesting the latest round of book bans pushed through by their counterparts, the Moms for Liberty. Julie had skimmed the list of books deemed obscene by those particular moms, and she wasn't too surprised to see *Moby-Dick* among them. It confirmed what she'd suspected—that the book banners never read past the titles of the books they wanted banned. Kate had made a generous contribution to Moms for Literacy, claiming to be appalled by all the far-right politicians and their anti-education fervor, while conveniently forgetting that it was her other contributions that had put those same politicians in power.

A woman of too many contradictions, her mother, Julie thought with a heavy sigh.

Ten miles and thirty-five minutes later, she pulled into the driveway of her home. It was a two-story sepia-colored house in a settled part of town close to the hospital. It was modest by neighborhood standards, a shack by Kate's, but nonetheless pricey. Near-coast real estate came at a premium.

It wasn't Julie's dream house. That one was a little cottage a few blocks west that reminded her of her childhood house, before the money started to multiply and they had to move up. Her dream house was a cheery yellow with a wide front porch and fun nooks and crannies inside and a sweet little gazebo in the garden out back. It was nothing palatial. It was actually smaller than their current house. But because of its bayfront location, it carried a big price tag.

Eric had liked it, too, but they'd needed a mortgage to buy it, and he was dead set against incurring debt of any kind. Understandably, after having watched his father gamble away every penny he had and quite a few that he didn't. His parents were in a senior community now, all expenses paid by Eric. It was a sickness, his father's gambling addiction, but one that couldn't be fixed by medication or surgery, so this was Eric's way of dealing with it: ensuring that not another penny ever passed through his father's fingers again, and remaining steadfastly debt-free himself.

If she really wanted the cottage, Eric had told her then, she'd have to find another quarter million in cash. He knew what he was asking;

there was only one place she could find that kind of money. She'd never asked her mother for money before, not since she'd finished school, but this was her dream house, so she'd finally worked up the nerve to ask. *Oh, darling,* Kate had said, *I'd give you a million dollars if I could. But I can't.*

Julie was confused, then alarmed. *Mom, is the business—are you in trouble?*

God, no! We're flourishing. But Julie, darling, how can I give you any money when you don't have a prenup?

Julie could hardly tell Eric that was the reason for Kate's refusal, not given how he already felt toward his mother-in-law. All Julie had told him was that Kate turned her down.

Figures, he'd snorted, and they'd settled on this mud-colored house instead.

Julie let herself in the front door and went upstairs. The guest room door was closed—Charlie must be asleep or trying to be. She tiptoed into her own bedroom and past the unmade bed where Eric had slept alone last night. She showered and dressed and packed a bag and, thirty minutes later, tiptoed past the closed door again. She wondered if Charlie had been able to get any sleep at all.

She parked her suitcase at the bottom of the stairs and headed to the mudroom at the back of the house to get her briefcase. She stopped short in the kitchen. On the floor, sticking out from behind the island, was a pair of legs. They ended in Charlie's favorite tennis shoes.

She squeezed her eyes shut. He wasn't asleep upstairs. He was here, passed out on the floor, maybe already dead. Of course he couldn't sleep last night, he couldn't even live, and the nightmare reel started to play.

"Oh, hey there, honey."

Her eyes flashed open. Charlie was lying on the floor, twisting his head out from under the kitchen sink.

"I noticed you had a leak under here." He held a wrench in one hand, a rag in the other.

"Oh." She took a deep breath to steady herself. It was okay, he was fine, nothing was happening again. "Right. I—I've been meaning to call the plumber. We've just been so—"

"No need." His head disappeared under the sink again. "Thought I might as well make myself useful for however long I'm abusing your hospitality."

"Charlie." She took another breath, slow and calming. "You know you're always welcome here."

"Thanks, sweetie." His chuckle sounded hollow from inside the cabinet. "I guess the big question is when I'll be welcome *there*." He made one final turn of the wrench and hauled himself to his feet. "Meanwhile, I'm glad you're there with her. I know Eric's giving you a hard time about it, but you stick to your guns. You're doing the right thing." He turned on the tap, ducked his head to check the trap, and gave a satisfied nod.

"I'm so sorry about—all this."

He shrugged, but with a smile. "Here's two things I know about your mom. Two things I know and love. She's proud and she's stubborn. Her pride's wounded just now by that little fantasy she imagined, and she's too stubborn to admit that's all it was. But she'll come around in time." He sighed, but then his eyes twinkled. "Not too much time, I hope. Not like we have an endless supply of it."

"Oh, Charlie."

"Never you mind." He picked up the toolbox and turned toward the mudroom. "I notice you got a squeaky hinge on that door back there."

She collected her briefcase as he eyeballed the hinges on the door. "Charlie—" She hesitated. "If Mom ever did—lose her faculties? What would you do? Would you have her committed?"

"Julie." There was a *tsk* in his tone, like he was disappointed she could even ask. "I'm the one who's committed. Committed to her. In sickness and in health, right? I mean to take care of her for the rest of my life. You don't need to give that a second thought. Now—" He gave her a kiss on the cheek and a pat on the shoulder. "You get off to work and let me do the same."

CHAPTER 11

KS Development's headquarters were in a downtown high-rise near the banks and law firms and insurance companies it necessarily had to deal with. Kate's office suite was on the top floor and included a terrace with a putting green. Julie's office was smaller and a floor below.

She'd occupied it for four years now. Her first job out of law school had been with a small firm that had no ties to either her mother or KS. But it soon became obvious that the firm had hired her not for her abilities but for her connections—or what they hoped would be her connections. They were counting on her to tap into her mother's Rolodex and bring home the bacon. Even if she'd been comfortable with that kind of cronyistic schmoozing, she was no good at it. After two years with no rain made, they let her go.

She moved then to a government job where there would be no need to generate business. The work would be clean—pure, she thought. She was soon disillusioned. Everything was about connections there, too—what they called *clout*—who you knew, who would write you a letter of support or recommendation, who would boost you up one more rung on the civil service career ladder. Even positions that weren't political were oh so political.

The only way to escape the expectations that came with her name would have been to leave town, leave Florida altogether. But by then Eric was already setting up his practice in Sarasota, and although he hadn't mentioned marriage yet, she had hopes. Anyway, she couldn't have left him if she'd tried. She knew because she had tried once. It hadn't taken, and she'd felt like a fool, and she'd never tried it again.

So she'd buckled to nepotism and accepted her mother's offer of the GC position at KS Development. If her sole value as a lawyer was her connection to her mother, it seemed only fair that her mother should be the one to profit from it.

SHE HAD A meeting that morning with a lawyer named Thaddeus Ainsworth IV, a name that suggested he was representing the Boston Bank of Abundance, if there were such a thing. But no, he was representing a notorious environmental activist named John "Figgy" Newton who claimed he'd been injured by security guards while picketing a KS construction site.

There were cell phone videos of the incident—there were always videos—and the evidence was clear enough. Figgy and a dozen other protestors were marching along the chain-link fence surrounding the site where KS was breaking ground on a new project. It would eventually include four high-rise towers housing luxury condominiums along with high-end retail and gourmet restaurants, all set around a central plaza so vast that jokesters were calling it Tiananmen Square. The protestors carried signs, some reading SOS, some STOP KS NOW, and a crowd favorite—KS IS FULL OF BS.

One of the protestors—presumably Figgy—spotted a break in the fence that made him stutter to a stop and throw himself to the ground and start to wriggle his way through. Then two burly men in black loomed into view. They each grabbed a leg and hauled Figgy out, scraping his back against the jagged prongs of the cut chain links. He screamed, the other protestors shouted, and the screen went black.

A photo was in the file along with the demand letter from Attorney Ainsworth. It showed Figgy's bare back, cervical to lumbar, raked with a half-dozen long bleeding stripes. Unless a suitable accommodation could be reached, he threatened to file suit for his physical injuries as well as mental distress and psychological suffering.

KS had insurance to cover such liabilities, of course, and Julie easily could have referred the matter to insurance defense counsel to handle. But all the insurer would care about was money, not the reputation of its insured. KS didn't need any more bad publicity. More than a quick settlement, Julie wanted a non-disparagement agreement from Figgy. So she'd opted to be self-insured for this claim and to meet with his lawyer directly.

Thaddeus Ainsworth IV didn't have a listing in the Martindale directory, where almost all lawyers in private practice could be found. That gave Julie a good guess that he was an old white-shoe lawyer from the North, now retired to the golf courses and marinas of Florida like hordes of other Northerners. There was a reason the Sunshine State was also called God's waiting room. Lately, the governor had been flexing his favorite sound bite on the campaign trail—*Florida's where woke comes to die*—but the truth was it was where *people* came to die.

A lot of old lawyers liked to keep a hand in while they were waiting, so many that the homegrown lawyers were threatened by the competition and had successfully lobbied for a rule denying reciprocal bar admission to those retired-from-out-of-state lawyers. It was a comical sight twice a year to see the nodding gray heads sitting for the bar exam amid all the bright-eyed twentysomethings. Julie's guess was that Mr. Ainsworth wasn't actually practicing anymore but that he'd agreed to dust off his credentials just long enough to snag a quick settlement for Figgy, who was likely a nephew or grandson of an old friend. She didn't plan to use that against him, though. She had enough other material.

AMY IN RECEPTION buzzed her at two-thirty to announce that Mr. Ainsworth had arrived and was waiting in the main conference room. He was half an hour early, a habit he'd probably acquired after a few years of early-bird dining. Most Florida restaurants were SRO at five o'clock.

Julie gathered up her file and went down the hall to the conference room. A man stood up as she entered, but he wasn't the silver-haired patrician she'd expected. Amy must have made a mistake in conference rooms. Julie turned to go.

"Ms. Hoffman," the man called after her.

She turned back. "Mr. Ainsworth?" she said doubtfully.

"Call me Tad," he said.

He looked more like a surfer dude than a Boston Brahmin. He had a head of shaggy, sun-streaked hair and a day-old beard stubble that made his suntanned face look like a fuzzy peach. He wore a suit, but instead of a button-down, a T-shirt peeked out from under his jacket. Some sort of graphic design showed between the lapels.

She shook his outreached hand, briefly, before sitting down at the head of the table. He returned to his seat. In front of him was a water bottle with a cork top and a legend that boasted it was plant-based. On the chair beside him was a bicycle helmet.

If his game was to throw her off hers, he'd nearly succeeded. She decided on a quick pivot from her planned strategy. She'd show her cards right up front.

"We've taken a look at the video files you sent over." She pressed a button to lower the TV screen from the ceiling at the far end of the conference table. "Let's take a look at one you didn't send over."

"Sure." He leaned back in his chair to watch. His suit jacket parted enough to give her a glimpse of his T-shirt. The graphic was a cartoon image of Planet Earth.

She pressed another button, and the screen lit up as the clip played soundlessly. This one was taken from a slightly different angle than the others. It showed Figgy crawling under the fence, then looking back over his shoulder with a grin before he planted both hands on the ground and arched his back like an upward-facing dog in yoga class. He held that pose while the guards pulled him out, with the result that the jagged ends of the fence scraped his back.

"As you can see," Julie said, "Mr. Newton's injuries were entirely self-inflicted. If he'd lain flat, he would have come out as easily and painlessly as he went in."

Ainsworth seemed unimpressed. "Who can say how any reasonable man would react to a sudden assault like this one? It was an ordinary defensive reflex."

"Sudden?" Julie said. "I notice none of your videos had audio tracks. But this one does. Let's watch it again."

She turned on the volume and replayed the clip. This time the crowd could be heard egging Figgy on. There was also singing in the background: *All we are saying is give Earth a chance.* Then, from off-screen, a sharp shout: *Hey, stop! You're trespassing!* Figgy looked back and laughed. *Back it up!* Figgy went into his yoga pose. *I'm warning you! Count of three. One. Two.* On three, Figgy was yanked out.

"It wasn't sudden," Julie said as the screen went dark. "It wasn't unexpected. Mr. Newton was trespassing. He was warned repeatedly. And rather than heed the warning and retreat, he deliberately put himself in a position that would result in injuries. Which, by the way, were superficial only."

Ainsworth took a sip of his eco water and waited.

"Nonetheless," she said, "in return for a full confidential release and a non-disparagement agreement, the company is prepared to make Mr. Newton a very generous payment of twenty thousand dollars."

He nodded, so quickly that Julie was afraid she'd overbid. Ten thousand might have done the job.

"You've got a deal," he said. "If you add two zeroes to that."

She stared at him in astonishment. "Two million dollars? For scratches?"

"Two million dollars for SOS."

"What?"

"Save Our Shores. Our nonprofit."

She was lost. "What are you talking about?"

"Your company, your mother, has basically paved over all of coastal Florida. You know what the consequences of that are?"

Your mother. Julie deliberately used her married name at work so that outsiders wouldn't make the connection. But this surfer dude had obviously done more opposition research than she had.

"SOS—that's some kind of environmental activism entity?"

"It's a 503(c)(3) charitable organization. Which means your two million will be tax-deductible." He grinned.

"What's your connection to this—SOS?"

"Founder. President. General counsel. Take your pick. I almost called it Save Our Bay, SOB, but you know, that's who we're fighting against." His grin went wider.

An environmentalist with a sense of humor. This was something new. "You don't actually represent Mr. Newton, do you?"

"He's not looking for a settlement, if that's what you mean. He doesn't care about personal compensation." Ainsworth straightened his shoulders, and the full graphic on his shirt was revealed: Planet Earth had two eyes, one in Puget Sound and the other in Lake Erie. A single teardrop ran from Erie to the Gulf of Mexico. "He cares about the bay and what your mother has done to it."

Her mother cared about the bay, too, and all the other waterfront property in the state. It was irreplaceable real estate, and sea-level rise threatened to erode it, so every project she built was engineered to preserve as much shoreline as possible. But that was as far as her environmental protectionism went. Whenever Julie tried to bring up climate change, Kate shut her down at once. *These things are all cyclical,* she'd say. *The planet's a billion years old. It's survived meteorites and the Ice Age and God knows what else. It'll survive this.*

The planet, maybe, Julie had once dared to venture. *But what about the human race?* Kate's only response had been an airy wave of her hand.

Ainsworth was watching her with a sly smile, as if he could tell where her own sympathies lay. She needed to shut that down at once. "Well, lots of luck proving causation," she said. Her eyes narrowed. "If you're even really a lawyer?"

His grin went wide again. "You don't remember me, do you?"

"What?" she said, startled, but a second later, it came to her. "Oh! The Kaplan Foundation." They'd both clerked there one summer during law school. He was at Yale, she remembered next, and nobody liked him. "But you quit after like two weeks."

"I was there to practice Good Law. I quit when I found out I wasn't."

"Working to feed and shelter the homeless wasn't good enough law for you?"

"Come on," he scoffed. "Like that was the real mission of that foundation. Their only goal was to keep them invisible."

She couldn't argue with that. Wealthy retirees and seasonal tourists didn't want to step over sleeping-bag lumps on the beach. They didn't want to skirt panhandlers outside restaurants. The Kaplan

Foundation did lots of good work, funding shelters and soup kitchens along with laundries and clinics, but only in far-flung parts of the city that weren't serviced by public transit. Keep them fed and sheltered and out of sight.

"*Karenia brevis*," Ainsworth was saying. "You know it as red tide. That's the neurotoxin that kills fish, dolphins, manatees, sea turtles, and seabirds. And makes people sick besides. I bet even your mother finds her eyes watering and her throat closing up during red tide."

Julie knew it too well. Walking on the beach through a litter of decaying fish. Wheezing so hard she had to flee inside for breath. "Red tide is caused by agricultural products," she parried. "Fertilizers. Pesticides. Animal manure." She gave him a haughty look. "KS doesn't do farming."

"*Karenia brevis* explosions are caused by the runoff of all those pollutants into the bay. Which is caused by the lack of ground absorption. Because your mother has paved over the coast."

"You can hardly turn back the clock on decades of coastal development."

He shrugged. "Maybe not. But you can tear up the parking lots and put in greenways along the coast. Install groundwater filtration systems."

Julie knew that would never work. "It's interior agriculture you should go after," she said.

"We have a program for that, too," he said. "And two million will help us kick-start it."

This had gone on long enough. "Well, I wish you luck raising it." She closed her file and stood.

He stood, too, and buckled his bike helmet on his head.

"May we validate your parking ticket?" She allowed the smallest smirk to show.

He laughed and shook his head. "Till next time," he said, and left the room before she could.

THAT AFTERNOON SHE researched Save Our Shores. She checked its incorporation status, got the names of the directors, downloaded its Form 990 from the IRS website, then went to GuideStar.com and garnered all the other details: its business address, which doubled as Ainsworth's residential address; its employees, which were none; its mission, which was pie-in-the-sky. SOS was obviously Ainsworth's pipe dream, kept alive, barely, by a few good-hearted donors and a small army of volunteers.

They wouldn't be much of a threat to KS, she decided. Figgy's personal injury claim was nothing but a gambit to get a meeting and make a pitch for a donation. She doubted that Ainsworth would ever follow through with a lawsuit, but if he did, she'd pass it along to the insurance company like all the rest.

LATE IN THE day, company president Jack Trotter poked his head in her office doorway. He wore a suit and tie but held a hard hat at his side: an affectation, she'd always thought, to convey that he was more construction foreman than accountant—though he actually was a CPA.

"Morning, Julie," he called out cheerily. "You recovered yet?"

She gave him a puzzled squint.

He beamed at her. "I mean, that was some shindig Saturday night. Everybody seemed to have a blast."

It hit her then—he didn't know. Nobody did. As far as the rest of the world was concerned, Kate and Charlie were off on their South Seas honeymoon. Julie didn't know what to say. If Charlie was right, the whole thing would blow over, and Kate would be appalled—

furious—if anyone knew what had happened. Even if Charlie was wrong and it didn't blow over, she'd be furious. Julie didn't know how to answer, so she didn't. "I met with that protestor's lawyer today," she said instead.

"Oh. Right. Funky Winterbeam?"

"Figgy Newton."

"Settle it, did you?"

She shook her head. "Turned out to be a shakedown for some environmental activist group. Two million."

He hooted. "I can hear your mom all the way from Tahiti. Hell, no!"

"I showed them the door."

"Good. And hey, give my regards to the lovebirds next time you talk to them."

SHE HAD EMAILS to answer, and phone calls to return, and contracts to review. But it was no use. All she could think about was the lovebirds. Her mother had been transformed these last many months, glowing with optimism and happier than Julie had ever known her to be. Then, in a single night, it was over. Julie and Eric had suffered some rough patches in their marriage, but they'd never done that kind of one-eighty. They'd never gone from love to hate in an instant. How could any person—any sane person—turn on a loved one so suddenly and completely? Until the FBI confirmed Charlie's alibi, her mother had actually believed that Charlie did it. It was unthinkable that he could have committed such a monstrous crime. So what did it say about Kate that she'd thought it?

Julie closed out her email and opened a browser and did a Google search for symptoms of Alzheimer's. She ticked off each item on the list. *Memory loss that disrupts daily life?* No. *Challenges in planning or solving problems?* No. *Difficulty completing familiar tasks?* No. *Confusion* with time or place? No. *Trouble understanding visual images or spatial relationships, trouble speaking or writing, misplacing things?* No, no, and no.

But then she reached the last three symptoms on the list. *Withdrawal from work or social activities?* Check. *Change in mood or personality?* Check. *Decreased or poor judgment?* Well, that put the rabbit in the hat, didn't it? It wasn't poor judgment if Kate was right about Charlie's intent.

Delusions and hallucinations, Julie read, didn't appear until late-stage Alzheimer's. But the most common delusion experienced by such patients was that someone was stealing from them.

A MESSENGER WAS in reception with a package for Julie as she was leaving for the day. It was from Lenore Greggson, and she knew what was inside without opening it. The petition for divorce.

CHAPTER 12

The only difference between a sandbar and a barrier island, so went the old joke, was that developers hadn't built any houses yet on the sandbar. Cascara Key was five miles long and in some places no more than a hundred feet wide—barely enough room to squeeze in a Gulf-front mansion, though plenty of mega-millionaires had managed to do just that. The island was winter home to three hundred people, year-round home to far fewer. A single narrow twisty road ran from one end of the key to the other. Speed limit 15. No traffic lights. At times the only difference between the beach and the road was that the sand was deeper on the beach.

La Coquina occupied a triple-size lot on the north end of the island. Julie was driving there, the beach to her left, the mansions to her right, when she spotted a lone figure walking along the edge of the surf. Dressed all in white with pale blond hair, she blended into the white-sand beach almost to the point of invisibility.

There was no place to pull over. Julie put on her flashers and left the car in the road. "Mom!" she called, but her voice was swallowed up by the roar of the wind and the water. She walked out to the edge of the wild sea oats and called again, louder. Her heels sank into the sand, and she was starting to toe them off when Kate finally heard her and turned her way. "Want a ride?" Julie hollered. It was at least another mile to La Coquina.

Kate waved her off with an exaggerated swoop of one arm, like an impatient crossing guard. Then she turned back to the surf and kept on walking.

"I DO NOT understand," Luisa said when Julie came in from the garage. English was her second language, but she spoke it with grammatical perfection, so much so that she refused to use contractions. "All she does is walk on the beach. That is all she does all day. She does not eat. She only walks and plays her sad music. It is like she is in mourning."

It was like she was in mourning, Julie thought. She'd lost the love of her life. That was natural enough until Julie questioned why. Because she'd also lost her mind?

Luisa folded her hands at her waist and waited—for her marching orders, perhaps, or for some kind of explanation.

"She thinks Charlie isn't who she thought he was," Julie said. "She thinks their marriage is over."

"Why would she think so?" Luisa's chin came up. This was as bold an inquiry as she ever made. "Mr. Mull is the best man I know."

"I know." Julie sighed. Kate was generous with her help but never particularly friendly. Certainly she never confided in them. But Julie had a different relationship with Luisa. She told her about the impossible confession and what Kate thought it had to mean.

Luisa looked dumbfounded. "I cannot believe it."

"I know." Julie hesitated. "Luisa, have you ever seen signs that maybe my mother was, you know, losing it?"

"Losing what?" Luisa looked puzzled then, abruptly, outraged. "Her mind? Never!" Her eyes narrowed a bit. "This is what Dr. Hoffman thinks?"

Julie gave a weak shrug. "I guess I'll go unpack." She wheeled her suitcase out of the kitchen. A large round table stood in the center of the foyer, and on it was a vase of flowers. It was a strange-looking bouquet—daisies drooping on their stems, their leaves curled and browning, at least three days past their prime.

"From Mr. Mull," Luisa explained, coming up behind her. "Shall I remove it?"

A smile spread across Julie's face as the meaning dawned on her. It was such a romantic gesture. "No. No! It's fine!"

She took her bag into the ground-floor guest suite and changed out of her business suit and into shorts and sandals so she could join her mother on the beach ramble. But by the time she was heading out the door, Kate was coming in.

"Mom?" Julie stopped and tried to smile. "How are you?"

Kate rolled her eyes and strode past her. "How do you think?" She stopped short at the sight of the desiccated daisies. "What the hell is this?"

"It's a callback!" Julie exclaimed. "You remember? In high school, those pitiful daisies he brought you in the hospital? Isn't that sweet?"

Kate brushed past the table. "Luisa!" she shouted. "Get those weeds out of here!"

Julie's face fell as Luisa scurried in and whisked the vase away. Kate started up the stairs, and Julie trailed after her. "I saw him today," she ventured.

Kate didn't even glance back. "Ha. Still working his charms? Spinning his lies?"

"He was fixing our kitchen sink."

"Which endeared him to you even more, I imagine."

Kate went into her bedroom suite and pushed a button on the control panel by the door. Music swelled through the room, some operatic aria pitched at full melodramatic volume.

Julie stopped at the threshold. The room had been redecorated since she was last here. It used to be done up in soft tones of peach and aqua, but now the headboard and duvet were covered in camel-colored suede. So were the two wing chairs that stood side by side at the French doors opening onto the balcony. The curtains were in a geometric pattern in the same shade of camel. Or not camel, Julie realized. Khaki. It was a military look, decidedly masculine, and obviously undertaken for Charlie's benefit.

She recognized the aria then. It was the farewell song from *La Traviata*.

Julie lowered the volume on the control panel. "Mom"—she took a few steps into the room—"you don't really think he's gaslighting you?"

Kate shot an exasperated look over her shoulder. "Not me! For God's sake, Julie, he knows he could never manipulate me. It's you he's gaslighting."

Julie blinked. "Me? What possible reason—"

"Think about it. It's your testimony that would push this whole thing over the edge. Anyone might be skeptical when a brand-new husband tries to get his wife committed. A brand-new, dirt-poor husband, I might add. Even Greta might have a hard time ruling against me on his evidence alone. But if my loving daughter backs him up? If she says, *Yes, Mom's losing it. I've seen a thousand signs?*"

"No, that's crazy—"

"What do you think all his fatherly affection is about? He knows that's the way to get you. Eric told him, I'm sure, how starved little Julie is for a daddy in her life."

Julie drew a sharp breath. That was something they never spoke of, a hard and fast line in the sand of their mother-daughter relationship. Never speak of her father. Never speak of how he left her. The remark stung so hard that she couldn't keep the sarcasm out of her voice. "Oh, so Eric's part of this big plot, too?"

"Of course he is. Who brought Charlie back into my life? And who's related to a probate judge and a neurologist? Alex provides his medical opinion and Greta sits in judgment. She's the one who decides guardianship petitions, you know. It couldn't be a more perfect combination. Cabal. Whatever."

Julie stared at her mother in horror. She couldn't imagine where all this paranoia was coming from. Her mother had real enemies out in the world—cutthroat business rivals, jealous socialites, rabid environmentalists—and faced them all with a rational, measured response. She'd never cooked up crazy conspiracy theories like this.

Kate exhaled with the impatience of one speaking to a slow child. "Listen to me," she said. "I've spent my whole life remembering things Charlie said to me back in high school. I've memorized almost every word he's spoken to me since he came back into my life. I know exactly what he said to me Saturday night. *Darling Katie, remember the Tylenol murders? I have a confession to make. It was me.* Clear as day. I didn't imagine it. I didn't hallucinate it. So okay, now we all know it couldn't be true. But ask yourself: What possible reason would he have had to lie about something like that?"

Julie could only shake her head.

Kate threw up her hands. "To make me look crazy!" she said. "Crazy enough that he'd have to take control of my money. Who would even question his good faith? Not the lawyer who drew up the prenup. She'd testify about how he insisted he didn't want a penny from me, and how I had to force him even to accept the house if I die. And not my darling daughter, either, if he succeeds in gaslighting her."

Kate flopped across her bed, fully clothed. She still had her sandals on. Sand was caked in the tread on the rubber soles.

"Well," Julie said finally, "if that's the case, then I guess you'll want to proceed with the divorce petition? Lenore sent over a draft today."

Kate heaved a sigh. "No. No. She was right about that. He'd only use it to bolster his own petition for guardianship. And then he gets everything. Like I said, I'm damned if I do and damned if I don't. Unless I die. Then he only gets the house and the boat. And maybe not even that."

"Let's not talk about dying," Julie said. But her lawyerly curiosity got the better of her. "Why wouldn't he get the house and the boat?" The prenup clearly gave him that much in the event of Kate's death.

"The Slayer's Act," Kate said. "Look it up."

Julie rolled her eyes. She didn't need to look it up. She already knew what it said: a murderer couldn't inherit from his victim. "Mom," she chided, "Charlie hasn't killed you."

"Hasn't he?" Kate closed her eyes. "He broke my heart."

That was what this was all about, just as Luisa had diagnosed. Kate was in mourning for her lost love. *È tardi,* the soprano sang. It is too late. *Or tutto* finì. Now it is all over. This aria was a seventy-year-old woman's version of a break-up song. Maria Callas subbed in for Taylor Swift.

"Okay," Julie said finally. "If that's the case, you have nothing to worry about. If Charlie's scheme depends on my testifying against you, it's doomed to fail. Because I never will. If Alex is his expert witness, we'll hire our own expert witnesses. As many as you want. The most prominent doctors in the field. And if Greta is the judge, we'll get her disqualified. There's no way they can beat us."

Her mother lay very still, with her eyes closed. Julie couldn't even tell if she'd heard her over the music. "Well, I'll see you at dinner," she said. She went to the door and started to close it behind her.

"No, Duo, don't leave." Kate opened her eyes with a smile and patted a spot on the bed beside her. "Come and tell me about your day. You had that meeting today, didn't you? With the protestor's lawyer? Tell me about it."

Just like that, Kate was back, remembering a date on Julie's calendar that was set weeks ago. Her mother's mind was a marvel.

Julie perched on the side of the bed and told her about Thaddeus Ainsworth IV and his real agenda. Kate hooted when she heard his demand. "Two million dollars! He must be smoking some organic cannabis."

"I know."

"We're not responsible for the contaminants flowing into the bay."

"I know. I told him that. Not that he could hear me way up there on his high horse."

Kate eyed her. "Sounds like you didn't much like him."

"Not at all," Julie said with a shudder. "He's such a self-righteous—" She hesitated.

Kate's mouth twitched. "Prick?"

"Exactly!" Julie laughed.

Kate laughed, too. "Anyway, we already give to all those eco charities. Nature Conservancy, Greenpeace, whatever."

"Right," Julie said, though she knew that those contributions never exceeded the low five figures. Nothing like the seven figures Ainsworth was angling for.

Her phone rang, and when she fished it out of her pocket, she saw Alex's name on the screen.

Kate saw it, too. "Go ahead," she said, frowning. "See what he wants." She propped up on an elbow to listen in.

Julie winced a little as she answered. "Hi, Alex."

"Julie, listen, I booked all those appointments. We had to bump other patients who've been waiting weeks, but we got everything all set for tomorrow."

"What appointments?"

"A full workup. A cognitive assessment. A neurological exam. An MRI—that's to rule out stroke or tumors. Then a lumbar puncture to check her CSF for the markers associated with Alzheimer's. First appointment, nine a.m. at my office, then across the street to the hospital for the rest."

Kate snorted and shook her head.

"Thanks, Alex, but Mom says no."

"They always say no. You have to force her."

Julie's temples began to throb. "Like I could do that."

"Hey, I worked all day to get these tests booked."

"We never asked you to."

"Yes, you did. Eric told me to put a rush on it."

"See?" Kate hissed in her ear.

"He must have misunderstood," Julie said.

"Julie," Alex said in a different, softer tone, "I know this is hard. Greta is so worried about you. After all that you've been through."

"Thanks anyway, Alex." She hurried to disconnect.

Kate flopped back on the pillow. "See?" she said again. "They're all in on it. And they're all working on you. Charlie with his charms, Alex with the guilt trip, Greta with the sympathy act. And Eric with—" She rolled her eyes. "I guess we know what kind of hold he has on you."

Julie's head was pounding as she got to her feet. "I'll go see how dinner's coming along."

Kate threw an arm across her eyes. "I don't want anything."

"Mom, you have to eat."

"Send up a tray," she said, and drew her knees to her chest. A trail of sand marked the path of her feet across the duvet.

Julie sighed and went to the door.

"Wait. Before you go." Kate sat up straight. "Shoot me up with my peptides, would you, dear?" She waved a hand toward her cosmetic case. "My hands are too shaky."

Julie trudged back across the room. Her mother's vanity, she thought bitterly, would be the last thing to go.

CHAPTER 13

The dining room table at La Coquina seated twelve. Julie felt dwarfed by it as she sat alone in a side chair and picked at her dinner. She had the draft of a construction contract propped up against her water glass—a multimillion-dollar project that Kate had awarded to DeMarco Construction after a fierce-fought bidding war. Now the battle of competing contract drafts was being waged. But the words on the page went in and out of focus. She kept thinking about that dinner when she first met Charlie.

It had seemed strange when Eric told her he wanted to throw a dinner party for his car salesman. It had seemed even stranger when he insisted that Kate round out their group. It was the first time he'd ever initiated an invitation to his mother-in-law. When Julie couldn't hide her surprise, he'd simply said that his new friend Charlie would be more comfortable with someone his own age there. But it was plain to her after only a few minutes' acquaintance that Charlie was comfortable around people of every age.

She gave up on the DeMarco contract and carried her plate to the kitchen. Luisa and Ferdy were lingering over their dessert there. Ferdy was a sweet-natured man, no taller than his wife, with skin the color of wheat bread. He'd been in this country even longer than Luisa, but he spoke no English at all. He understood it well enough, but embarrassment about his accent or some other insecurity made him choose never to speak it. He spoke in Spanish, and Luisa provided simultaneous interpretation whenever it was required.

It wasn't required tonight. He wished Julie *Buenas noches,* and she wished them both the same and went down the hall to the home theater.

It was a windowless room equipped with a giant projection TV. Like the dining room, it seated twelve, in three rows of leather recliners in stadium-level tiers. Julie sat in the second row and scrolled aimlessly through all the subscription streaming platforms in search of something to distract her. A mystery, a thriller, fantasy, sci-fi—every genre was represented, and none of them appealed to her tonight. She switched to the weather. The National Hurricane Center had issued a tropical storm watch for the Florida peninsula, but this was hardly cause for alarm, or even much notice, since it was still early May and hurricane season didn't start until June.

She scrolled again and landed on the final scene of a rom-com, a bride and groom emerging from the chapel under a shower of rose petals. That made her think about Charlie's wedding speech, the bit where he talked about the serendipity of meeting Kate again, how he might have lived his whole life never knowing that she was only an hour away.

Was he living under a rock? Julie wondered now. Her mother's name was everywhere throughout the state, on hotels and shopping centers and office buildings, and okay, so he didn't know her as Kate Sawyer, but her photo was everywhere, too. He'd recognized her the moment he saw her in Julie's dining room, so why didn't he recognize her photo?

But no, that wasn't fair, she decided. Charlie wasn't in the real estate business. He didn't read the society pages. There was no reason to think he'd ever seen those photos.

Her mother was making her question things that were perfectly reasonable. Which made her wonder: Who was gaslighting whom?

She gave up on TV. When she opened the theater door, a colossal swell of music nearly knocked her over. Kate was now blasting her music through the entire house. She'd moved on from *La Traviata* to *Madama Butterfly*. One tragic opera after another.

Julie's head was pounding. She retreated to her bedroom and closed the door to muffle the noise. A bottle of Tylenol was in the bathroom cabinet. She frowned at it a moment, trying to imagine what kind of person could take something so innocuous, something meant to relieve pain, and use it to kill. Which begged the second question—what kind of person could believe, even for a moment, that the love of her life could have done such a thing?

She swallowed a pill and got into bed. But she couldn't sleep. Her head was aching, and her thoughts were swirling: the Tylenol murders, the movie *Gaslight*, Charlie in her dining room, Charlie on his back on the floor of her kitchen, and when that image morphed to her father on his back on the floor, she gasped out loud and heaved herself out of bed.

The windows of La Coquina weren't supposed to be opened. It would disrupt the carefully calibrated climate controls to admit any outside air. Nonetheless, Julie got up and opened the window overlooking the courtyard. She couldn't see the Gulf from there, but she could smell the salt air and feel the sea breeze stir her hair and hear the faint rhythmic laps of the surf against the sand. The night was moonless, but a hundred stars glittered in the clear black sky.

Her mother was a lot, as Greta often said, but Julie had come to terms with that long ago. Kate was the only mother she'd ever have and, after age thirteen, the only parent. They were a team—a badly mismatched team, maybe, but a team. The *Dynamic Duo*. Kate had started calling Julie by the nickname *Duo*. She meant it as an endearment, but as Julie grew older, she couldn't help feeling that she'd been tacitly stripped of the word *dynamic,* because she wasn't. Kate was the dynamic one, while Julie was merely what made them a duo. Her mother was the sun that would always eclipse Julie's moon. Of course, Julie resented her sometimes, and there had been times she'd wanted to rail and rebel and even cut her mother off. But to what end? Kate would never change, and spite was a meager reward.

But that was when it was simply Kate versus Julie. It was easy enough then to cede the battle to her mother. When it was Kate on one side versus Eric and Charlie and her dearest friends on the other—Julie didn't know where to plant her flag.

She left the window open and went back to bed.

CHAPTER 14

Julie woke with a scream in her throat and a hot hand clamped hard over her mouth. A heavy weight pinned her to the mattress, from her shoulders all the way down to her shins. She felt the hard bone of a knee between her legs, pushing them apart. She heaved up and tried to buck him off. She tried again to scream.

"One day," he grunted in her ear. "You promised it would only be one day."

Relief washed over her at the sound of Eric's voice. She sagged into the mattress.

"You have to come home. I can't live without you. You know that."

He took his hand from her mouth and kissed her hard. Her heart was racing, but she twined her arms around his neck and raised her hips as he entered her. "Come home," he chanted with each thrust. "Come home. Come home." After a time—a long time—his chant changed. "Come on," he muttered. "Come on. Come on!"

She never faked it—she never had to—but he'd never been this impatient before. She managed a short cry and a long shudder, and he was satisfied even if she wasn't.

"What's going on, babe?" he said afterward, when he could breathe again. "You never take that long."

"Eric, you broke into the house! You scared me!"

"What are you talking about? You left the window open for me."

"I left it open for the breeze."

"Oh." He reached for her and pulled her head against his chest. "I thought we were having—you know, a tryst. I'm sorry if you were scared."

A tryst? She supposed it was kind of romantic of him, like a teenager climbing up a trellis to be with his girlfriend. "It's okay," she said, and snuggled closer. They lay together, their legs entwined, in silence but for the soft sound of the surf through the window. Their breathing slowed and deepened. Julie was drifting off to sleep when Eric spoke again.

"She is in your head, though. I know it."

"Eric." She pulled free and rolled onto her back.

"I thought once she was married, Charlie would take over all the emotional heavy lifting. I thought you'd be mine for real."

"I am yours."

"I even thought we could start talking about that baby again."

Her head spun on the pillow. She was too astonished to speak. All she could do was stare at him. She'd stopped talking about a baby a year ago, and he never talked about it at all beyond saying she was too fragile, it would be too hard for her to raise a child with her PTSD, they should just lavish that love on each other. "Really?" she said. Her voice was thick.

"But not now, obviously, with all this going on. We need to get Charlie back here. And we need to get you back home." He kissed the top of her head with a loud smack. "Gotta take a leak," he said.

He heaved himself out of bed and padded into the bathroom. She watched how the starlight filtered through the window and played across the breadth of his shoulders and the firm round flesh of his buttocks. He disappeared behind the door, and after a moment, a different light entered the room. She looked to the nightstand. Eric's phone was on silent, but the screen was lighting up with an incoming call.

She couldn't remember if this was an on-duty night for him, but she knew he wouldn't want to miss a call from his service. "Eric?" she said, but he couldn't hear her over the ringing stream of his urine. She reached for the phone and froze at the name on the display. *Paula.* She hurried to put it back face down on the nightstand.

Paula was once his fiancée. She'd been by his side at that backyard barbecue where Julie first met him. She was a California blonde, tall and athletic, a fellow doctor, and perfect in every way. Yet he'd broken off their engagement two weeks later to be with Julie. A triumph, she'd thought, a clear sign that their attraction to each other was something truly special, a once-in-a-lifetime romance. It was their relationship that was perfect in every way.

Until a year later, when Julie happened to glance at his phone and was shocked to see Paula's name on the screen. She was still in his contacts, and when Julie looked at his call history, she saw that they'd been talking to each other regularly. They'd never stopped.

That was the one and only time Julie had tried to leave him. He found her packing her things, sobbing as she threw armfuls of clothes on the bed where they'd just made love. He erupted when she told him why. *Paula's a colleague,* he'd roared at her. She and her husband ran a pain management clinic. They referred patients to him all the time and vice versa. It was an important business relationship—and by the way, he'd sneered, a very lucrative one— and that was all. He'd dragged Julie to the computer in his study and opened up folder after folder of file notes and referral letters. *What kind of insecure, jealous, prying shrew are you?* he'd shouted at her. *And now look what you made me do—violate HIPAA a dozen times just to prove I love you.*

She'd apologized to him over and over, she'd begged his forgiveness, and when he'd only set his jaw and folded his arms, she'd dropped to her knees to show exactly how abject she was. Afterward he'd helped her to her feet. "I forgive you," he'd said. "Let's never speak of it again."

The whole experience was so humiliating that Julie had vowed never even to think of Paula again.

"What?" Eric said now, coming out of the bathroom.

"Mmm, nothing. Just missing you."

"Then you know how I feel with you living here." He picked up his phone and glanced at it. If he noticed Paula's name, he didn't show it. "Look at the time," he said. "We better get going." He reached for his clothes on the floor. "Come on. Get dressed."

"Dressed for what?"

He stepped into his pants. "We need to beat the morning traffic over the bridge. Come on. Pack your things."

She sat up. "Eric, I—I can't leave."

He turned on her. "For fuck's sake, Julie! Didn't you hear a word I said? You belong at home. With me."

With him and Charlie, too, she thought. She'd obviously be planting her flag then. "I can't leave Mom alone," she said.

"Then don't! Let Charlie come back here."

"That's not up to me."

"Who, then? Her?" He shook his head like it pained him. "Julie, you have to face facts. She's not capable of making decisions on her own anymore. But maybe, if you'd stop indulging her in this fantasy, maybe she'd wake up and Charlie could come back and we could get on with our lives. Can't you see that you're making the situation worse by staying here?"

She didn't answer, but she didn't move, either. He stared hard at her a long moment, then he bent over and kissed her just as hard.

But slowly, his lips softened. The kissed deepened. It was the kiss that made her melt every time. She almost did now. She could feel her body softening in his arms. She could feel herself submitting. Until he shifted his weight and she felt the hard rectangle of his phone in his pocket and remembered Paula and that other time she'd humbled herself before him. Literally at his feet. The memory of it shamed her.

She pulled back. "I'm not coming," she said. "Not yet."

He made a disgusted noise in his throat as he straightened away from her. He finished dressing without looking at her again, and climbed out the window the way he came.

CHAPTER 15

Julie felt more foolish with each passing day. Her only justification for staying at La Coquina was so her mother wouldn't be alone, but Kate chose to be alone anyway: she walked the beach all day and shut herself up in her room all night. The only companions she seemed to want were her sister-divas—Callas and Sills and Sutherland. She plugged their voices into her ears on her daytime rambles and blasted them through the house every night.

By default, this meant Julie was alone, too. Luisa and Ferdy had their own routine, and they were entitled to their privacy, so Julie ate alone in the dining room and watched TV alone in the theater room and slept alone in the guest room. She left the window open every night, but every night she slept alone.

Charlie called every day, multiple times a day, to both house lines as well as Kate's cell. He talked at length to Luisa and Ferdy, but Kate never picked up or came to the phone. He continued to send his symbolic daisies every day, too, and Julie wondered where he could be getting them; surely no florist would keep such ragged things in stock. In any event, it was to no avail, since Luisa was now under strict orders to refuse delivery at the door. Nevertheless, he persisted. Persistence, Julie supposed, was the point.

Eric didn't call, and he didn't pick up when Julie called him. But he texted once or twice every day. The same two words and nothing else: *Come home.*

WAS CHARLIE A con man or was her mother insane? Those were the questions Julie kept wrestling with. Her mother wasn't herself—

that much was obvious. But her behavior made perfect sense if she'd just discovered her brand-new husband was scamming her.

He wouldn't be the first man to romance an elderly widow to con her out of her fortune. But Kate Sawyer hardly fit the profile of one of those lonely, trusting old women, and Charlie Mull didn't fit the profile of a swindling lothario. Although—Julie considered—if he really was a con man, he wouldn't have waited until age seventy to launch his career. Maybe he'd done this or something similar before. Maybe it had landed him in court.

At the office on Tuesday, Julie logged into the court records database and searched for Charles Francis Mull and every permutation she could think of. But he didn't appear as a party in any federal court case, at least not since 2004, which was as far back as she could go. Nor did his name come up in any of the state court dockets she could access online.

She gave up on court records and did a plain-vanilla Google search for his name. This time she got pages of hits: Charlie being sworn in as an officer of the Rotary Club, sitting on a committee of the Tampa Chamber of Commerce, heading the local drive for Toys for Tots, teaching boating safety for the Coast Guard Auxiliary, wielding a hammer and saw for Habitat for Humanity. It was the profile of a good all-around citizen. A good man.

LATER THAT DAY Jack Trotter stuck his head in Julie's office. "Heard anything from the honeymooners?" he asked. There was an anxious crease behind his smile.

"Not a word," Julie said, which was not a lie, exactly.

"You think you could get a message through to your mother?"

"I don't know. What's up?"

"This storm over the Caribbean."

"It's just a watch, isn't it?" Like any native-born Floridian, Julie knew all the stages: storm watch, storm warning, hurricane watch, hurricane warning, and only after that, a hurricane. Half the tropical storms never graduated to hurricanes.

"Yeah," Jack said. "But still, I'm wondering. Do we batten the hatches or what?"

It was a tricky decision and one Kate always made herself—whether to ignore the forecast and risk damage to her properties, or go to the expense of elaborate precautions against a storm that might never materialize.

"Your call, Jack," Julie said.

He scrunched up his face. "Kinda seems like I'm damned if I do and damned if I don't."

He was right—Kate would haul him on the carpet if he guessed wrong and cost the company money—but Julie was thinking about Kate using those same words: damned if she filed for divorce, damned if she didn't.

GRETA CALLED JULIE that night. She seldom did now that she was so busy with her professional and social obligations. Before she went on the bench, they used to spend hours on the phone, talking about love and law and everything in between. They were the same age, but Greta assumed a sort of big-sister role in Julie's life. She was the one who egged Julie on to try new things and who calmed her through every case of jitters. She liked to play the role of dating coach, too, dispensing advice, warning Julie away from toxic boyfriends, trying to build up her self-confidence. No one was ever good enough for Julie, Greta seemed to think, at least until her brother came along. Julie used to relish those calls, tucking herself into an easy chair and settling in for a long chat.

But being sisters-in-law was a trickier business than being best friends. Julie couldn't go to Greta with romantic problems anymore, not when it was Greta's own brother who was the cause of them.

Tonight she had to be especially on guard. She knew Greta was calling as Eric's proxy, albeit ten times more tactful. "You're such a good daughter, Jules," Greta said after barely a minute's small talk. "You always have been. Even though your mother can be a lot sometimes. But do you really think you're helping her by inserting yourself into the situation?"

"I'm not—"

"You're living in her house."

"Well, she asked me—"

"But ask yourself why. What if it's just to drive a wedge between you and Eric? You know she's never liked him."

And he never liked her, Julie thought. The wedges were coming from both sides. "I think she's more concerned with her own marriage right now," she said.

Greta sighed. "Here's the thing. What if she has a brain tumor or something? Something that could be treated." So she was calling as Alex's proxy, too, Julie realized. Greta went on, "You'd want to find out as soon as possible, wouldn't you? You'd kick yourself if you missed something like that."

Julie knew she was right. She'd regret that for the rest of her life. But she also knew that the only way she'd ever get her mother to submit to a neurological workup would be to drug her and wheel her in on a gurney.

"Yes," she said finally. "And that's why I have to stay here. I'm working on persuading her to go in for Alex's tests."

"Oh," Greta said, clearly surprised. "Well, good for you."

There, Julie thought as they ended the call. Greta would report that detail back to Eric and Alex, and it would placate them both. At least for a while.

SHE'D PLANNED TO spend the next day working on the DeMarco contract. Instead, she spent the morning researching brain tumors and their symptoms.

Headaches. Vision loss. Weakness in one side. None of the above, at least nothing Kate had complained of. Cognitive decline. Emphatically no. Balance and coordination difficulties. Maybe? Her mother's meanderings on the beach came to mind. Personality changes. Yes, the paranoia was new, but that could easily be attributed to recent events. Hearing loss. Possibly? She kept playing her music at full volume. Seizures. Muscle twitches. Speech difficulties. No. No. No. Depression. Oh, God, yes. But wasn't that due to the collapse of her fairy-tale marriage? Lethargy. No, not when she was logging ten or fifteen miles of beach walking every day.

The research session was interrupted by a call from Amy in reception. "Tad Ainsworth's here to see you?"

Tad had to be Thaddeus Ainsworth IV. Julie frowned. He didn't have an appointment, and they had no further business. He needed to be sent on his way. "Tell him—" she began. But it was hard for Julie to be rude even when rudeness was warranted. "Tell him I'll be out." At least she didn't say *right out.*

She waited a full minute before she got up and made her way to reception. She could hear Amy's giggles all the way down the corridor. When she rounded the corner, she found Ainsworth perched on the edge of Amy's desk, his head bent close to hers. He was grinning as he showed her something on his phone.

"Hey," he said, turning that grin on Julie as he stood. He hadn't bothered with a suit today. He wore a T-shirt with a manatee graphic over a baggy pair of cargo shorts.

"May I help you?" Julie stopped ten feet away, her arms stiff at her sides, as Amy pretended to busy herself with a stack of mail.

"Just a courtesy call." He pulled a manila envelope out of a battered backpack. "We filed suit on behalf of Figgy this morning and made service on your company's registered agent. Here's a copy." He held the envelope out to her.

She didn't reach for it. "How very kind," she said. "But no need. Our insurance company will be handling this. You should deal with them from now on."

"Oh." His hand dropped, and his smirk faded. "I'm sorry to hear that. I was looking forward to us working together."

"We were never going to be working together."

He ignored that. "I even brought lunch," he said. "I thought we could sit and chat while we ate."

She eyed his backpack. "Let me guess. Bean sprouts and chickpeas."

He laughed. "Maybe next time. This time I brought burgers and fries."

She caught the aroma then. It did smell good. But he was crazy if he thought a ten-dollar burger was going to win him a two-million-dollar donation. "No, thank you," she said. "As it happens, I'm vegan."

She wasn't, and her cheeks burned as she walked away. She couldn't imagine why she'd lied to him.

"Then bean sprouts for sure next time," he called after her.

CHAPTER 16

Late in the afternoon, she heard an unusual volume of voices coming from the other end of the floor. Excited-sounding voices that made her wonder if Figgy-type protestors might have stormed the office. She went down the hall to find out. The voices came from Jack's office, but he was in there alone, bouncing on his toes in front of the giant TV on the wall. On-screen was a stack of squares with a face inside each one. It was a Zoom call mirrored from Jack's desktop to the TV. Half of the participants seemed to be talking at once, and she could pick up only a few phrases—lower the cranes, truckload of sandbags, secure the tarps.

"What's up?" she asked from the doorway.

Jack lurched around, and the clamor of voices died down. "Oh. Julie. We're—well, we're pulling the trigger."

She recognized some of the faces then. A couple of property managers, a few project engineers. They waved and shouted out, "Hey, Julie," while the rest just shouted, "Hey!" They knew her only as the boss's daughter.

"Trigger on what?"

Jack looked sheepish. "The hurricane."

"Oh! Have they upgraded it? I hadn't heard."

"No. Well, no. It's only a storm watch."

"But get this," one of the on-screen faces said, "Bart Clemmons and Stacy Wilbur were both spotted at Tampa International."

"On-air meteorologists," Jack explained at her blank look. "If they're gearing up, I thought we should, too."

Julie doubted his logic. It cost the networks only a few plane tickets to gear up. It would cost KS Development tens of thousands of dollars to do the same. Then there was the question of whether the reporters had actually been spotted and, if so, whether they were here on assignment. Maybe they were just vacationing. She should call her mother, she thought, and get Kate to make the decision. But that would mean giving up the pretense that Kate was off on her honeymoon and couldn't be disturbed. It would mean, she thought, giving up.

"Well, good luck," she told Jack, and waved goodbye to all the little faces on-screen.

THE BAY WAS a glittering turquoise as she drove to the island that night, the sky a brilliant blue and hung with clouds that puffed like giant cotton balls. Only the softest breezes stirred the tops of the palms along the way. According to the weather station on the radio, the watch remained a watch and not a warning. The likely track of the storm, something the meteorologists called the *cone of uncertainty,* was elusive.

Julie was struck by that term. It seemed like that was where they were all living now. Inside that cone.

There was a backup at the bridge—a tall-masted sloop was sailing south, and the bridgetender had to stop traffic and operate the hydraulic winch to lift the leaves to vertical and allow the boat to pass through, then activate the system again and lower the decking back to horizontal.

When Julie could finally cross, she was surprised to see that the traffic backup on the other side was even worse. Twenty or thirty eastbound cars were lined up to cross the bridge. She guessed they were all people heading downtown for dinner until she noticed the luggage piled into the backs of the cars. Some even had luggage strapped to their roof racks. This was the time of year for the annual migration of the snowbirds to their other homes up north. That could explain it. But she wondered: *Could they be evacuating?*

She stopped wondering once she crossed the bridge and the beach came into view. At regular intervals along the way, she spotted a young couple sunbathing, kids tossing a Frisbee, an older couple having drinks in their gazebo, and a man holding an empty leash while a yellow Lab romped in the surf. All normal seaside activities among the rich and private denizens of the island. All against a backdrop of the shimmering topaz waters of the Gulf.

There was nothing normal about the next person she spotted. Her mother, walking along the water's edge. By now Julie knew better than to stop and offer a ride, but something struck her—something was different—and she slowed to a crawl to look more closely. Kate's stride was long today, her carriage erect. She was talking on the phone. She looked animated. Herself again. Julie couldn't help hoping that she was talking to Charlie. That somehow they'd realized all this was nothing but a giant misunderstanding. Kate wasn't crazy and Charlie wasn't evil, and everything was fine again.

Julie drove on to La Coquina. A gray sedan was in the circle drive, and as she looped around it into the garage, a man in a suit swung out from behind the wheel. "Mrs. Hoffman!" he called.

She came out of the garage. It was the Sarasota County detective. "Hello—" she faltered, embarrassed that she couldn't remember his name, and after he'd been so kind.

"Brian," he said. "I was in the neighborhood and thought I'd stop by."

She threw a nervous glance down the road. There were no flashing lights or crackling flames that she could see. "Has something happened on the island?"

"Oh, no," he said with a quick shake of his head. "I was just, you know, making the rounds."

The police didn't make rounds on Cascara Key. They didn't need to. Every mansion had better security than any police force could provide. And the only resident criminals were market manipulators and Medicare fraudsters.

"I just thought I'd drop by and check in. You know, see if everything's okay."

Julie flinched a little at that. Kate had no use for her neighbors under the best of circumstances; she'd be appalled to think they were reporting her to the police. Speculating about her mental state. Probably dubbing her the Madwoman of Cascara Key.

"Everything's fine," Julie said. Instantly, she regretted the chill in her voice. She knew he meant well. He'd obviously been through something with a loved one of his own. He only wanted to help, however he could.

Suddenly, it occurred to her how he might. She walked a few steps closer to him. "But I wonder—if there's something you could do for me?"

He showed an eager smile. "Be happy to. What d'you need?"

"I was wondering about Charlie—Mr. Mull—if there was anything in his past. Any charges filed or anything like that?"

Holley didn't answer. He looked away and worked a hand over his jaw.

She realized she'd overstepped. "I'm sorry," she said quickly. "I shouldn't have asked. That's probably outside your jurisdiction."

"No, hold on," he said. "Let me think this through." He gazed off into the distance before he spoke again. "You're afraid he's scamming your mother."

She felt foolish. "No, sorry—"

"He tells her he's the Tylenol murderer, then he denies it. He's trying to drive her crazy. Or make the rest of you think she's crazy." Holley's eyes ran over the imposing facade of La Coquina. "And then he gets all this. Is that what you're thinking?"

She shrugged. "I wanted to rule it out."

"Huh." He thrust his hands in his pockets and rocked back on his heels. "If some con man's trying to defraud a resident of my county? That's absolutely within my jurisdiction."

"Oh," she said with a surprised smile. "Oh, but"—her smile faded—"I guess there's no point. The FBI already looked into that. He must be clean."

"Nah. They only had one assignment: check out his alibi for the Tylenol murders. Believe me, that's all they did. So let me do this for you. I'll run a search, see if he's ever been charged with anything."

Her smile returned. "That would be a big relief. Thank you, Detective."

"Brian," he said again.

"Thanks so much," she said, and she headed back into the garage.

"Oh, hey. About this storm?" he called after her. "I mean, you're watching the weather, right? You have someplace to go? If it turns into anything?"

"Yes, of course. But thanks for checking." She added, "Brian."

He smiled. "No problem, Julie."

LUISA AND FERDY were in the kitchen. They were old hands at hurricane preparedness, and Julie put the question to them. Was there anything they should be doing? They were discussing it when Kate came in from her ramble.

"Don't be ridiculous," she said. "It's only May."

Luisa and Ferdy looked at each other and shrugged.

"Good walk?" Julie asked her mother.

"Mmm." Kate opened the refrigerator and studied the contents.

Julie hesitated before she asked the next question. "I saw you were on your phone."

"So?"

Luisa looked at Julie and prompted her with raised eyebrows to press on. "Were you talking to Charlie?" Julie ventured.

"God, no." Kate slammed the refrigerator shut. "I'll never talk to him again." She looked around the kitchen. "What's there to eat? I'm starving."

Luisa leaped into action and assembled a cheese and fruit plate in record time. "I could make your favorite risotto for dinner," she said.

Kate popped a cheese cube into her mouth. "You know what I'd like instead? A steak. On the grill."

Ferdy raced outside to fire up the grill while Luisa bustled about the kitchen and Kate grabbed a banana and peeled it in three quick zips. Julie watched all the scurrying with a resigned sigh. All hope that her mother had reconciled with Charlie was gone. But so was at least one symptom of a brain tumor. Kate didn't seem to be depressed. She definitely had her appetite back.

On the spot, Julie made her decision. She wasn't needed here. She wasn't serving any purpose at all. And she wasn't willing to let her mother's marriage destroy her own.

"Hey, Mom, I was thinking I might go home."

Kate took a bite of banana. "Have you been away?"

"Mom," Julie said, pained. "I've been staying here."

"Here? For God's sake—why?"

JULIE WENT STRAIGHT to her room and packed her suitcase, prepared to leave immediately. But by then Ferdy had decided it

wouldn't hurt to bring in all the outdoor furniture and garden statu-
ary, just in case, and she went outside to help him. By the time it was
all stowed away, Luisa had dinner ready, so she stayed for that. Then
her mother summoned her upstairs for the nightly miracle potion injection, and by that time it was too late to leave. Eric had early rounds
on Friday mornings; he'd already be asleep.

For a second she thought about going home anyway and slipping
into bed and surprising him the same way he'd done to her Monday
night. But only for a second. He'd been on guard lately against possible intruders—inexplicably, Julie felt, since there hadn't been any
incidents in their neighborhood. He rationalized that the Lamborghini made them a target. Her solution was to get rid of it. His solution,
like every other homeowner in the state, was to buy a gun. So, no,
sneaking in was a bad idea. She could imagine the headline: *Florida
Man Fears Intruder, Kills Wife*. It was easy to imagine, since headlines
like that appeared regularly here in the Gunshine State.

She decided to go home early the next morning and catch him
before he left for work. They'd have a quick breakfast together and
make plans for a nice quiet dinner after work. As she got into bed, she
imagined how it would unfold. After dinner, they'd go upstairs and
make love, tenderly; then they'd lie in bed and talk out this whole
situation. They'd make a pact: she'd stop enabling her mother, and
he'd stop advocating for any kind of medical or legal intervention.
They'd agree to let Kate and Charlie sort out their own problems, live
their own lives. She and Eric would live theirs.

CHAPTER 17

Julie's phone woke her. It wasn't the ping of a text landing, it was an actual ringtone, a few bars of "I've Got You Under My Skin," and sure enough, it was Eric's name on the screen. A thrill rippled down the length of her body. It was as if he'd read her mind. He was calling to say, *Come home,* and she'd say, *I'm on my way.*

"Eric," she answered on a sigh of relief.

"Don't come home," he said.

She must have been half asleep. She must have heard wrong. "Wh-what?" she said as a terrible dread seized her. She'd delayed her decision too long. She'd already damaged her marriage beyond repair. He didn't want her anymore.

"The keys are gonna get the brunt of it," he was saying.

Keys? she wondered wildly. *To the house?* Had he changed the locks?

"But we might see some damage, too," he went on. "Charlie's boarding the place up now, and I volunteered for triple duty here at the hospital. So don't come home. Get in the car and head inland. Try Orlando. You'll be safe there."

She was more and more confused. "Safe from what?"

"The hurricane. Jeez, Julie, wake up."

"What?" She sat up straight. "No, it's only a storm watch."

"Not anymore. It's moving really fast now. Landfall's probably up north, but it's gonna swipe the coast all along the way. They're saying the surge could reach ten feet. You need to get out of there. Now. Before they close the bridge."

"Yes. Okay."

"C'mon, babe. Get up. Get moving. This is no joke."

"Okay, I'm up." She swung her feet to the floor.

"Listen, I gotta go. Call me when you reach Orlando."

"Okay. Love you," she said, but he was already gone.

She looked over at the open window. The curtains weren't even stirring. There wasn't the slightest breeze.

When she'd gone to bed, there had been only a tropical storm watch. No storm warning, no hurricane watch, and certainly no hurricane warning. Somehow this storm had leapfrogged over all the intermediate steps.

A finger of fear crawled over her. Not of the storm. Of Eric and what he was trying to do to her. He was making it all up, the hurricane, the emergency evacuation. It was nothing but a ploy to get her to leave her mother. He didn't say, *"You and your mother need to leave."* He didn't say, *"Take your mother and go to Orlando."* She'd been ready to go home, more than ready, but not like this. Not as a dupe who fell for his lies.

She reached for the TV remote and flipped through the channels until she landed on the local news. A giant map of Florida was on the screen, with a chyron scrolling across the bottom and an animated green blob rushing north through the Gulf.

She jumped out of bed and looked out her window. A steady rain was falling, and the sky was dark, too dark for six-thirty in May. A dim figure was moving on the other side of the courtyard. She squinted until she made out Ferdy. He was stacking sandbags against the threshold of the front door. Nearby a ladder leaned against the wall, and she craned her neck to look up at the balcony, where the French doors were already lined with sandbags. Then an electric whine sounded, and she ducked her head out of the way as the motorized hurricane shutter rolled down in front of her window and sealed shut with a snap.

For Julie, this was a surer sign than anything the meteorologist was saying on TV. Luisa and Ferdy knew what they were doing. If they were laying sandbags and closing the shutters, that meant it was real, it was a hurricane, and she was stricken with shame that she'd suspected anything different.

She pulled the window shut and latched it and threw on her clothes while the excited voices on the TV raved on about pressure systems and wind speeds and evacuations. Emergency shelters were being set up throughout the city, and the telecast cut to an on-air reporter at one of them. He talked about evacuations and food and water supplies.

Julie was in the bathroom grabbing her toothbrush when she heard a familiar voice from the TV. She ducked around the doorway, and the caption on the screen confirmed it: *Tad Ainsworth, Volunteer Coordinator.* He was wearing a windbreaker and a headset. The reporter asked him about the number of evacuees he was bracing for, but instead of answering the question, he faced the camera directly and delivered a speech. "There's never been a major hurricane in May before," he said. "The water's never been warm enough. But now it is, and guess why? Human-driven climate change. The lesson couldn't be clearer. If we don't stop destroying our plant, our planet's gonna destroy us."

Julie switched off the TV and called the manager of her mother's hotel in Orlando and told him to set aside two rooms plus the presidential suite for her mother. The hotel was already fully booked, but of course he would make it happen. "Whatever she needs," he assured Julie. "Anything at all."

Julie hurried out into the hallway with her suitcase. Luisa was in the foyer. "The shutters are all shut," she reported breathlessly. Strands of wet hair were plastered against her face, and her clothes were soaked through. "Ferdy laid sandbags at all the doors. The generator tank is full. The bathtubs are full. The flashlights and the emergency radio have new batteries."

"Thank you, Luisa. Any sign of my mother?"

Luisa started for the stairs. "I will go wake her now."

"Pack a bag for her, too," Julie said. "And you and Ferdy do the same. We're all driving to Orlando."

She was rolling her suitcase into the garage when something else occurred to her. She parked the suitcase and went outside through the open bay, the only door not already locked and sandbagged. The rain lashed at her as she raced around to the back of the house, and a sudden gust made her stagger and nearly lose her footing on the slick surface of the dock.

The *Half-shell* was rocking up and down on its moorings. If the storm surge pushed enough water inland, it would swamp the island and pour into the bay. The dock would be submerged, and the force of the current could break the decking apart. Underwater debris could slam into the boat's hull and bash it against the pilings. She remembered other boats in the bay that had been completely destroyed by storm surges in the past. She remembered how scornful her mother had been at the carelessness of those boats' owners.

Another gust slammed a sheet of water over her. She hollered for Ferdy, but there was no way he could hear her over the roar of the wind. She scrambled up the ladder to board the *Half-shell*. There were boxes and cushions on the deck, and she gathered them up and stowed them inside the cabin, then closed and locked all the windows. She went back out into the rain and cut the dinghy loose. Ferdy was there by then, and together they installed the fenders and gathered up the long lines. She climbed aboard again and wrapped her ends around the dock cleats while he tied his ends high up on the pilings. They left twenty feet of slack in the lines: enough, she hoped, for the boat to rise and fall with the surge and not tear up the pilings.

When it was done, they ran for the garage and found Luisa locking down the cover over the cargo bed of the pickup truck. "All the bags are in there?" Julie asked.

Luisa nodded, but there was a shadow in her eyes.

"What's wrong?"

Helplessly, Luisa said, "She went for a walk."

"Now?" Julie stared, first at Luisa, then at Ferdy, where he stood dripping on the concrete floor. "In a hurricane?"

"I tried to tell her."

A growl of exasperation sawed through Julie's throat. "All right," she said finally. She headed for the passenger side of the truck. "We'll pick her up on the way."

Ferdy said something to Luisa, who translated: "The radio says the bridge will close at eight o'clock."

Julie lurched to a stop. That was only twenty minutes away. She didn't know how far Kate might have gotten. She didn't know how long it would take to coax her to leave the island. "Okay." She took a deep breath while she recalculated. "Okay," she said again. "You two leave now. Take the truck and go to my house. I'll take my car and pick up Mom and meet you there, and we'll all drive to Orlando together."

Luisa's face was pinched with worry. "What if you do not make it over the bridge?"

"We'll make it," Julie said, and she got into her own car and backed out of the garage with a roar.

There was already standing water on either side of the narrow beachfront lane. Before long the road would be a river. The wind was whipping the surf into a roiling white frenzy, and flecks of foam floated in swirls through the air. The wipers squeaked in a heartbeat rhythm as Julie peered through the windshield, searching for a lone figure walking the beach. In a hurricane. Kate really was the Madwoman of Cascara Key now.

Cars were lined up at the bridge, waiting to cross to the mainland. Julie drove past them and continued south. There was no sign of her mother. Julie wondered if she could have taken shelter anywhere along the way. But Kate never had much use for her neighbors, even if they would have been willing to open the door to a crazy lady. In any event, most of the houses were closed up and dark. Some were probably snowbirds gone for the season. The rest were people gone for the duration of the storm. Rational people.

Eric would be so furious if she missed the crossing.

Julie drove on and tried to keep her eyes away from the digital clock counting down the minutes on the dashboard display. She wanted to go faster, but it was impossible on this narrow, twisty road, with the rain so hard and the wind so strong. The rain was blowing in almost sideways from the sea, and at times it hit the car with the force of a fire hose. From moment to moment, she was all but blind. She wondered if she'd even be able to see her mother out here.

If she was even out here. This could all be some sick prank. Kate could have circled the house and been hiding out in the cabana all this time. The ultimate power play. *I'll show you. I'm not afraid of some piddly little rainstorm.*

But suddenly, there she was. On the beach, walking into the wind, leaning into it with her shoulders braced, like a football player. A scarf was tied around her head, babushka-style, but it looked soaked through, and so did the rest of her clothes. They clung to her bones, so sodden and heavy that even gale-force winds couldn't stir them.

Julie jerked the wheel and pulled over with cascades of water spewing out from the tires. She put on her flashers and beeped the horn. Kate didn't turn; she didn't even react. Julie leaned on the horn, and still Kate kept on muscling her way through the rain. It was coming down harder now, and the surf was roiling.

The dashboard digits glowed: 7:55.

Julie jumped out of the car and ran out onto the beach, screaming, "Mom! Mom!" The rain slapped against her, shockingly cold, and instantly, she was drenched. She broke into a run across the soggy sand, calling, "Mom! Mom!"

She must have gone fifty yards before Kate finally turned. She stopped and laughed. "Julie! What are you doing out here? You're getting soaked!"

Julie gaped at her. "What are you doing out here? It's a hurricane! We have to evacuate, and the bridge is about to close!"

"Oh, don't be silly." Kate turned and started walking again. "I built the house to withstand winds up to a hundred and forty miles per hour. I put in a state-of-the-art storm drainage system. We'll be perfectly fine."

Julie ran to catch up and grabbed her by the arm. Kate's eyes widened in astonishment. "Mom," Julie said, her voice strung tight. "We're leaving. Now."

Kate heaved a put-upon sigh. "Oh, all right," she said, and allowed herself to be tugged across the dunes and up the road to the car. "All this panic," she grumbled as Julie pushed her into the passenger seat. "You'd think you'd never seen a rainstorm before."

Julie gritted her teeth as she ran around to the driver's side. She jerked the car into drive and cut a U-turn across the road and headed north again.

The trunks of the palm trees were doing backbends while their fronds flew off in a wild flurry. A gust of wind hit the car broadside and rocked it on its axles. She kept her hands tight on the wheel, her eyes fixed on the road. She ignored the dashboard clock, as though time would stop if only she didn't watch the digits change.

There was no lineup of cars as they neared the turnoff to the bridge, and Julie felt a little surge of hope. There was no traffic backup. She could zip across. She made the turn and screeched to a stop. Metal gridwork like a livestock gate blocked both lanes, and as if that weren't enough, there were also orange traffic cones and signs that read STOP and BRIDGE CLOSED.

Julie stared at the barriers and through them to the long string of cars on the other side of the bridge. All of them inching their way to safety. She let out a moan of despair. Beside her, Kate snorted a laugh.

Julie turned her stare on her mother. "Do you have some kind of death wish?" she shouted.

Kate's laugh faded. She turned her face to the window. "Wishing never gets you anywhere," she whispered.

CHAPTER 18

The house was dark as night inside, with all the windows shuttered. Julie turned on every light as she headed for her shower. Her mother did the same as she headed for her own shower upstairs. If—when—the power went off, the emergency generator would keep the refrigerators and freezers running, along with the wine cellar and a few auxiliary lights, but it wasn't connected to the plumbing, and there was no telling how long the hot water would last. Julie felt chilled to the bone and lingered under the hot stream of the shower until she heard her phone ring.

Eric, she thought with dread, and was relieved when it was Charlie instead.

"Hey there, Julie," he said. "Luisa and Ferdy just got here. They told me—did you find your mom? Is she okay?"

"She's fine, but we didn't make it off the island. The bridges are closed."

She heard him inhale sharply, but his voice was calm when he spoke again. "Okay. So you're with Kate at the house?"

"Yeah. She thinks it can withstand a nuclear holocaust."

"Well, she's probably right. But just in case, here's what you wanna do."

She knew the protocol, just like any native-born Floridian, but it was comforting to hear it from Charlie as he rattled off the instructions. Shelter in a windowless room. Take lots of food and water. Blankets and pillows. Flashlights and the emergency radio. A first-aid kit, just in case. Keep the cell phone charged as long as the power stayed on. The landlines would probably go down, but with luck, the cell towers would stand.

"Got it," Julie said. "Thanks, Charlie."

"Stay in touch," he said. "As long as you can." His voice cracked as he added, "Keep her safe for me, will you, hon?"

Julie dressed and hurried through the house, gathering all the supplies. She took them to the theater. It was a windowless interior room with an adjacent powder room, also windowless, and as long as the power stayed on, they could watch the weather on TV. It was as perfect a place to shelter as she could find on this side of the bridge.

Next she went looking for Kate and found her not in her bedroom, nor in the bath, but out on the balcony facing the sea. She'd actually rolled up the hurricane shutters and pushed aside the sandbags to get out there. The curtains were blowing into the room with so much force that they were nearly horizontal. Her mother was outside, leaning over the railing, arms outstretched, like she was Kate Winslet on the bow of the *Titanic*. Her hair and clothes were streaming water all over the tile floor of the balcony.

"Mom!" Julie screamed above the roar of the wind. "What are you doing? Get in here!"

Kate gave her barely a glance. She had a strange, exultant look on her face.

"Mom!" Julie grabbed her arm. "Come inside! We have to keep the house closed up!"

Kate said something, but her words were lost to the wind.

"What?" Julie leaned closer.

"I said it's magnificent! Isn't it? The power of nature!"

"Mom, you have to get inside." Julie tugged on her arm, gently at first, then harder, and when Kate didn't budge, she grabbed her with both hands. "Mom! You can't do this to me! Not again!"

Kate turned then. She cocked her head and studied Julie with an expression that slowly softened. "Perhaps not," she said finally. "But you're stronger than you think you are." Nonetheless, she stepped inside and dripped across the floor to the bathroom.

Julie rolled the hurricane shutters back into place and locked them, then closed the French doors and locked them as well. There was nothing she could do about the sandbags, not from inside the house. Instead, she went to the linen closet and came back with an armful of Triplo Bourdon bath towels and laid them along the threshold of the French doors. *There,* Julie thought. *A thousand-dollar leak stopper.* It would serve Kate right if her precious towels got ruined.

She waited on the edge of the bed until her mother emerged from the bathroom in her peacock dressing gown. The suitcase Luisa had packed for Kate was on its way to Orlando by now, but Julie grabbed some other clothes and toiletries and stuffed them in a carryall. Then she led Kate downstairs to the theater and closed the door.

"Find me a comedy," Kate said, yawning as she settled into a first-row seat. But Julie had possession of the remote, and the only thing she wanted to watch was the news.

The weather map was still there on the giant TV screen, and the green blob was still swirling sickly over the blue waters of the Gulf. Yesterday the cone of uncertainty had been hundreds of miles across at its wider end. Today it was barely twenty. It wasn't uncertain anymore. It was coming right at them.

Kate leaned way back in the recliner and closed her eyes. The storm that had so mesmerized her on the balcony moments before now seemed to bore her.

"Check in with your loved ones," one of the TV anchors exhorted, and Julie knew that she should. Eric would explode when he learned where she was and why, but he'd worry if he didn't hear from her at all. She took out her phone. It was fully charged, but it had zero bars of service. She panicked for a second—had the cell towers been destroyed already?—until she remembered that the room was soundproofed with dense acoustic baffles that must be blocking the signal.

Her mother was asleep now, her recliner tilted back as far as it would go. Julie opened the door to the hallway, and a blast of noise hit her from all sides. The wind roared so loudly it was like being sucked into a jet engine. She pulled the door shut behind her and checked her phone. She had service now, but even if the call went through, she'd never be able to hear. And she'd hate for Eric to hear how furiously the storm was raging; he'd worry even more.

She ran down the hall to the powder room, another windowless room where it might be quiet enough to have a phone conversation. But when she tapped on Eric's cell number, all she got was a robotic message that all circuits were busy and to please try again later. She tried Charlie's cell next, then Greta's, but got the same message each time. Too many people were calling at once. Everyone wanted to check in with their loved ones.

She ran back to the theater and closed the door as fast as she could to seal out the howl of the wind. Her mother slept on, undisturbed, and Julie returned to her second-row seat to watch the news. She rotated through the local news station to the Weather Channel to the cable news networks. The hurricane was the lead story across the dial.

She was watching one of the national networks when Tad Ainsworth appeared on the giant screen. It was the same clip she'd seen that morning—the network must have picked it up from the local affiliate—and Ainsworth was delivering the same diatribe.

"Not you again," she groaned. This hurricane must have been his dream come true; it gave him a national platform. She flipped the channel.

"Wait, go back." Kate lurched upright in the recliner. She'd been awake and watching after all.

Julie scrolled back to the network channel. Ainsworth was looking straight at the camera. "Climate change is real, people. It's happening, and this hurricane is proof."

"That's the boy you were telling me about? Oh, he's cute!"

"He's a jerk."

Kate twisted in her seat and gave Julie a curious look. "You took a real dislike to him."

"Anyone would. He's so self-righteous and sanctimonious and thinks he's so charming—"

"So I guess you wouldn't want to give him any money?"

"No, I told you—"

"Julie." Kate suddenly seemed deadly serious. "Promise me you'd never give him any money."

Julie rolled her eyes. How could she? She didn't have any money to give him. It was Kate's money he was after.

"You have to promise me," Kate insisted.

"Yeah, I promise," Julie said, and picked up the remote to change the channel again.

The screen went black.

For a second she thought she'd hit the wrong button—until all the lights in the theater flickered out, too. The room plunged into darkness. It was completely, utterly black. Never in her life had Julie seen or felt such darkness. She couldn't remember where she'd left the flashlights. On the seat beside her? On the floor? She was too frozen with fear to grope for them. With the TV volume off, the theater wasn't as soundproof as she'd believed. She could hear the storm outside, the winds pounding the walls and rattling the windows, and above it all, a high-pitched shriek like a woman screaming.

It was so dark she didn't even have to close her eyes for the nightmare reel to begin to play. The long walk down the hallway, the glance in the doorway, the toes pointing up. Her heart started to pound, and every terror seized her. The hurricane would kill them. Her mother was losing her mind. Julie was losing her mind. Charlie was gaslighting her. Eric was helping him. Everything was flying apart, and there was nothing she could do to hold it together. She was as insubstantial as a bit of wind-tossed flotsam. She was buffeted about, she grew dizzy, she was going to faint—

Then a beam of light penetrated the void. Kate must have found a flashlight, and Julie's breath left her body in trembling ripples of air.

"I've been wondering about the DeMarco contract," her mother said. "What kind of pushback are you getting on the penalty clauses?" Her voice was as calm and rational as if she were in a boardroom.

"What?" Julie managed to whisper.

"We'll probably be stuck here a while. We might as well get some work done. So tell me, what did their lawyer say about the daily penalty provisions?"

Julie's pulse started to slow. She knew what her mother was doing—trying to distract her—but the thing was, it was working. Her fears didn't leave her, but they drifted back to the corners of her mind as the mundane details of work pushed to the front.

HOURS PASSED, AT least according to the display on her phone. She had no sense of time beyond that. No sense of day or night. They ate cheese and fruit and granola bars, and it could have been breakfast, lunch, or dinner. They dozed, and it could have been afternoon naps or nighttime sleep. They talked about construction contracts and zoning appeals and tax avoidance, and every time a topic was exhausted and they lapsed into silence, Kate would bring up another matter.

The phone said it was five a.m. when Kate broke another long silence. "Listen," she said sharply.

"What? I don't hear anything."

"Exactly!"

"Oh!" Julie grabbed a flashlight and made her way to the door. She cracked it open an inch, then a foot. There was no jet-engine roar this time, no wailing-woman shriek, not even the rustling of a breeze. All she could hear was the distant hum of the generator.

The storm was over.

CHAPTER 19

An hour later, the emergency radio confirmed it. The storm was nothing more than that now. Rain was falling in Ocala, but the clouds were clearing away along the Gulf Coast. Now began the ordeal of assessing the damage the hurricane had wrought.

Julie ventured out into the foyer and swept the flashlight beam over the floor. There was no water, no breakage, no debris as far as she could see. She did a more systematic inspection after that, going from room to room, training the light on every windowsill and door threshold. All dry. She went upstairs and did the same to every room there. The towels weren't even damp at the French doors in her mother's room.

It was six-thirty by then, and there was enough daylight to do an inspection of the outside of the house. She found a pair of Ferdy's boots in the mudroom and started for the garage.

Her phone pinged. It suddenly had service again, and alerts were tumbling in. She had six missed calls from Eric and one voicemail. She bit her lip as she pushed play. She knew he'd be ranting about how stupid she was to stay behind to look for her mother. She only hoped no one at the hospital overheard him while he was leaving the message. She'd be so humiliated if anyone heard him speak to her that way.

"*Julie, baby,*" he said. He was whispering, so at least he'd been careful about that. But then he went on in the same soft voice. "*Charlie told me what happened. I'm so worried about you. Please let me know you're safe. Please. I don't know what I'd do—Call me. Please. As soon as you can. I love you."*

She thought her heart might burst with relief. She hurried to push the callback button and waited with a smile for the call to connect. She'd tell him she was safe, she'd tell him she loved him, too.

A robotic voice told her: "All circuits are busy. Please try your call again later."

She sighed. Everyone must have been checking in with their loved ones again now that the storm had passed.

She pocketed her phone and went to the garage. There was some water penetration here, a few puddles in the bay where Julie's car was parked. She raised the garage door and walked out into the morning light.

And into a vast sea. The Gulf and the bay were now one continuous body of water, with La Coquina rising like an atoll in the midst of it. There was no wind, and everything was silent. Eerily silent, she thought, and then she realized. The cries and calls and caws of the seabirds formed a constant background soundtrack here on the beach, but now there were no cries, because there were no birds. They'd gone for shelter when the storm struck, and they weren't back yet.

She scanned the immediate perimeter of the house. The flower beds and hardscape along the foundation were wet, but there was no standing water that she could see, at least nowhere immediately adjacent to the house. It seemed that Kate's state-of-the-art storm drainage system had worked.

The driveway was flooded, though. The palm tree that was the focal point of the garden circle still stood, but it looked like the mast on a sunken sloop. Other palms had been stripped of their fronds, and the trunks stood bald and naked against the morning sky. A giant palm tree had been uprooted, and it lay across the driveway entrance. It would have to be cut up and hauled away before she could hope to get her car out.

Not that there would even be a road to drive on until the tide went out. The road and the beach had disappeared into one continuous sea. Coconuts bobbed up and down like the heads of bathers in the water. The storm surge should have receded now that the hurricane had abated, except that the end of the storm coincided with high tide. The water level would remain high until the tide went out.

Splashing sounded behind her, and she whirled to find her mother making her way toward her. She'd changed from her dressing gown and now wore a linen shift and a pair of olive-green hip-high waders. She passed Julie and kept going, out toward the road. Or where the road should be.

"Mom, wait," Julie called. "Where are you going?"

"For a walk."

"Through the flood?"

Kate rolled her eyes at the obviousness of the question.

"It's not safe," Julie said. "There could be debris underwater. Nails or glass or"—she had a worse thought—"power lines!"

Kate waved a shushing arm at her and walked on. Julie grimaced as she watched her go. For the past eight hours, longer, her mother had been cool and collected. Sane. Now she was the Madwoman of Cascara Key again. Change in mood or personality? Check and check.

Julie turned back and resumed her inspection, clearing away debris as she went, until she made her way to the back of the house. The current was running fast in the bay. She squinted into the rising sun as a distant flash of bright yellow caught her eye. It was a small boat, a kayak, she thought, making its way across the bay. She thought how foolish its owner was to attempt a crossing when the water was this high and the current this fast. A storm chaser, probably, delighting in the thrill of the danger.

She continued her inspection. The poolside cabanas were flooded, cushions were soaked through and probably soon to mildew, and a foot of water lay over the pool cover.

She looked again out over the bay. It was a tandem kayak, she saw now, with two paddles swinging rhythmically from side to side. It was skimming fast and straight, cutting smoothly through the current. There were two men, she saw, both blond and athletic, expert kayakers, from all appearances. She wondered if they were part of a search-and-rescue team. Then she saw that the man in front, his hair wasn't blond. It was white. And the one in back was—

"Eric!" she cried.

She ran to the edge of the water, flapping her arms high above her head, jumping for joy in Ferdy's sodden boots. Eric spotted her and raised his paddle high. So did Charlie, then they both dipped their paddles hard and fast into the water, stroking even more rapidly as the kayak raced to shore.

Eric jumped out before the boat reached land, leaving Charlie alone to beach it while he splashed through the water to Julie. They caught each other in a fierce hug and held on tight, Eric breathing hard, Julie laughing and crying at the same time. "You're all right, you're okay?" he kept asking.

"I'm fine, everything's fine. You made it!" she cried.

"God, I was so worried," he moaned. He kissed her hair and her cheek and finally her lips.

Charlie stood next to the kayak, grinning at the pair of them, and she grinned back while Eric ran his hands over her shoulders and down her back as if conducting his own inspection for damage.

Then Charlie's gaze shifted away. His grin faded. A look came over his face, a sudden crease of worry, and Julie worried, too, about what he saw that so concerned him. She twisted out of Eric's arms to see what Charlie could be looking at.

Twenty feet away stood her mother. She was staring at Charlie.

Julie sucked in a breath as Eric's hand tightened on her waist.

Charlie stood silent, waiting. He was a combat veteran, a man who had faced the worst kind of danger, but there was no mistaking the look in his eyes now. It was fear.

Julie turned back to her mother. There was a look on her face she'd seen a thousand times before, in meetings, at construction sites. It was the look she wore when she was running numbers in her head, or weighing options, or calculating odds. When the wheels were turning.

A sudden cry broke the silence. *Ha ha ha.* The rasping call of a laughing gull, swooping over the water, returning after the storm.

When it came again, *ha ha ha,* Kate rushed at Charlie, so fast her waders spewed out a cascade of water like sheets of sparks.

Eric made a noise like *Hey!*

"Mom, don't—" Julie started to say, but her voice was drowned out by Kate's as she flung her arms around Charlie's neck.

"My hero!" she cried.

CHAPTER 20

The kiss lasted so long that Eric whispered they'd soon need oxygen tanks, the both of them. Julie frowned. "I don't get it," she whispered back. But Eric was grinning.

"It's over," he said, leading her away. "That's all we need to know." And he kissed her long enough to steal her own breath away.

"I DON'T GET it," Julie said again, this time to her mother when they were finally alone. The men were outside by then, dragging away the sandbags and opening the hurricane shutters manually, since the power was still out. Kate was at her vanity. *Need to make myself pretty,* she'd said with a coquettish smile.

"Hmm?" Kate said now as she outlined her lips.

"What brought on this change?"

Kate perused her assortment of lipsticks before settling on a soft peach.

"Mom," Julie said with an edge of impatience. "What does it mean? That you were wrong about all that—stuff?"

Kate smacked her lips together and leaned close to the mirror to inspect her work. "Oh, I don't know," she said vaguely. She rose and walked into her closet and started riffling through the hangers. "Things look different after you've spent a night staring death in the face. Priorities change."

Julie followed her. "I guess," she said doubtfully. "But does this mean he's not trying to gaslight me? And he's not after your money?"

Kate buried herself deeper in her closet. "Let's not talk about this now. Run and find your husband. I need to make myself look beautiful for mine."

THE BRIDGE WAS closed, the power was out, the road was impassable. The island was cut off from the world. "Perfect for a honeymoon," Charlie declared, beaming wide. "We'll be more isolated here than we would have been on any of those South Sea islands."

They'd decided then and there to spend the rest of the month at La Coquina. They didn't care about being cut off. There was plenty of food in the pantry, they could cook on the grill, they had candles enough for weeks of romance. Eric and Julie should take the kayak and go home. They weren't needed here. In fact, Charlie said with an exaggerated vaudevillian wink, they were kind of in the way.

"SHE'LL NEVER ADMIT it," Eric said as they paddled the kayak back to the mainland. He was in the stern, propelling them across the water with smooth, powerful strokes. "She'd rather pretend the whole thing never happened than admit she dreamed it up."

The tide was running out now, the waters were receding, and Julie was struggling hard against the current. She gritted her teeth and said, "It doesn't make any sense."

"She doesn't," Eric said from the stern.

"It doesn't make any sense that she'd hallucinate one solitary conversation and otherwise be perfectly lucid."

"Okay, then maybe it's what Charlie said. Alcohol haze."

Julie wondered if that was what was nagging at her, the fact that Charlie could be so undisturbed by his bride's insistence that he'd confessed to murder. That he'd brush it off so easily. Shouldn't he have been shocked and appalled? Unless he wasn't surprised at all—because he really had said it.

"Let it go, Julie," Eric said. "Your mother has."

But Kate's abrupt about-face was the biggest part of what troubled Julie. It wasn't like she'd actually had a near-death experience. She'd been totally undaunted all through the hurricane. Julie remembered how Kate had leaned over the edge of her bedroom balcony, thrilled by the power of the storm. Death hadn't stared her in the face; she'd laughed in its.

Julie was remembering something else, too. The way Kate and Charlie had looked at each other in that frozen moment before the gull cried. The calculating look in Kate's eyes was nothing new; Julie had seen it a thousand times before. But the look of utter fear on Charlie's face was startling. What was it? Fear of being rejected again? Or fear of being exposed?

She didn't understand any of it, including why she'd suddenly become suspicious of Charlie. At the exact moment her mother no longer was.

Maybe that was the answer right there.

"I just don't know what to think," she said.

"Leave it alone," Eric said. "She's Charlie's problem now."

"She's still my mother!"

"Yeah, but he's the one who has to live with her. And he's the only one who can get her to do those medical tests. So let him deal with it."

Charlie's car was waiting on the other shore. They beached the kayak and strapped it to the roof rack, and Eric got behind the wheel. But before he started the engine, he grabbed Julie and held her in a tight embrace. "Let them have their honeymoon," he said. His voice was soft and husky in her ear as he whispered, "And let's go home and have one of our own."

He meant to distract her, and it worked.

BUT THEIR HONEYMOON would have to wait. They had their own hurricane damage to contend with. Shingles had been torn from the roof, and the yard was a litter of downed branches and leaves. Eric ran first to the garage to check on the Lamborghini while Julie circled the house. The plywood sheets Charlie had nailed over the windows were intact, and the deck was in one piece. But when she stepped through the back door, her shoes made a squishing noise, and her heart sank. The water had penetrated.

They had power, though. Eric got out the wet vac, Julie got out the fans, and they spent the day trying to dry the place out before mold and mildew could take hold. She also spent the day trying to get through to the insurance company, but that was a lost cause. There were much bigger problems than theirs today.

Late in the afternoon Eric got a call from his service. People were breaking bones and pulling muscles all over the county. He showered and headed for the hospital.

After he was gone, Julie tried calling her mother's phone, but there was no answer. She sat at the kitchen table and watched the fan blades spin as all the likely scenarios ran through her mind. At the top of the list: Kate was ignoring the phone. Next up: the battery was drained, and there was no electricity to recharge it. At the bottom of the list, where Julie tried her best not to see it: something had happened. Something bad.

These were ridiculous thoughts. She knew Charlie. She loved him. How could she imagine for even a second that he was capable of—

whatever she was imagining. This was all her mother's fault. She'd succeeded in gaslighting Julie.

Or it was simply fatigue. She'd been awake for most of the last thirty-six hours. She deserved to be a little bit delirious. But somehow she knew she'd never be able to sleep, at least not until Eric got home.

She shouldn't sit and brood. She should try to do something useful. Alerts on her phone were broadcasting the community's urgent need for provisions and the addresses of emergency donation centers, so she loaded up the trunk of Charlie's car with canned goods and bottled water and paper products and drove to the nearest donation center.

It was downtown, near the bay, in a vast parking lot surrounding a performing arts venue. An open-sided vendor's tent was pitched in one corner near the street, and under it were a few folding tables and stacks of milk crates. A hand-lettered banner hung from one side of the tent: EMERGENCY DONATIONS HERE. An old pickup truck was parked behind the tent, and a couple traffic cones marked the lanes for cars to follow in and out as they dropped off their donations.

Julie pulled into the entry lane and got out to unload the trunk. A girl with a waist-long braid as thick as her wrist came out to help. Someone else came up behind her. "I got this, Angie," a man's voice sounded. Then: "Hey, we meet again."

Julie turned around with a case of water in her arms, and sure enough, it was Tad Ainsworth. No longer in the windbreaker and headset he'd worn on TV, he was wearing board shorts and flip-flops today. His stubble now looked to be several days old, less like peach fuzz and more like a beard.

"Well, no wonder," Julie said. "You're everywhere these days." At his questioning look, she explained, "I saw you on TV."

"Ah. Heard me, too, I hope."

He was as sanctimonious as ever. "Maybe a word or two before I found the mute button," she said.

He allowed a laugh. "You make it through okay?"

"Fine," she snapped.

He reached for the case of water, and they did an awkward little two-step as she shifted it into his arms. Close up, she could see the dark shadows under his eyes, and she felt a pinch of regret at her rudeness. He must have been working since early the day before. He probably hadn't slept for two days.

"Is there anything I can do to help?" she asked. Instantly, she regretted that, too. She hadn't slept much, either.

His weary eyes blinked in surprise. "You mean it?"

She couldn't back out now. "Put me to work," she said.

SHE SPENT THE next three hours accepting donations and hauling them into the tent, then repacking them into boxes she hoped would make sense to the families they were meant for: toilet paper and paper towels, bars of soap, an assortment of canned soup and beans, bottles of water. Other volunteers drove up from time to time, and she helped load the boxes into their cars and trucks, then off they went to distribute them to whatever neighborhood Tad had next on his list.

Dusk was falling by the time they hefted the last of the boxes into the bed of the old pickup truck. Julie had assumed it was somebody's abandoned junker, but no, she should have guessed it was Tad's, and he confirmed it when he got behind the wheel. The girl with the braid was long since gone, and Julie assumed her own shift was over, too.

She was heading for Charlie's car when Tad called after her from the pickup window. "Don't you wanna see the folks you've been doing this for?"

She only wanted to go home, but it seemed elitist to say so. As if she were Lady Bountiful, happy to give alms to the poor as long as she didn't get her shoes dirty. That was a feeling she always had around Tad, and she knew he was probably exploiting it. "Sure," she said.

She climbed into the passenger seat of his truck, and her door let out a long protesting groan when she pulled it shut. When he started the engine, it gave a cranky growl. The truck was vocalizing all of her feelings.

Instead of pulling out onto the street, Tad yanked the wheel and drove a big loop through the parking lot to the edge of the bay. She shot him a look. "I want you to see this," he said.

"I've seen it. I paddled across it this morning."

He looked surprised by that, but not enough to distract him from whatever point he wanted to make. "Take a look now."

She huffed a little but turned to look through the windshield. She knew this vantage point well. It was a favorite spot for sunset watchers, and the lucky ones sometimes got to see schools of dolphins leaping and plunging through the glassy slate-blue surface of the bay.

But the waters weren't smooth tonight, and they weren't blue or gray, either. They were the color of mud and churning with backwash. The surface was swirling with fallen leaves and branches. Human debris was everywhere, too, plastics bobbing on the waves, clumps of rags and cardboard. Sewage, too, she feared.

"The runoff's going to be devastating," he said. "The fish kill. The mangrove destruction. The shoreline erosion."

"All because of my mother?" she said. "Believe it or not, she doesn't actually control the weather."

"All because of development," he said. "Which she does control. The water can't sink into the ground, so it flows into the bay. Which is bad enough when the water's clean. But after something like this—" He shook his head with a sigh.

"Okay, look. Point taken," she said. "But what's the alternative? Living in huts with a population no greater than it was when the Seminoles had it?" Her voice grew louder as her argument built steam. "We've had a huge influx of people wanting to live here and mostly wanting to retire here. So we need an influx of young people to counterbalance that. And they need someplace to live and work."

"Oh, sure," he said. "Show me where KS builds affordable housing for young people."

As it happened, she could. "We built a thousand units last year," she said. "Come to the office and I'll show you exactly where." She didn't add that the affordable housing was a condition imposed by local zoning boards in exchange for luxury building permits.

He shrugged. He wasn't going to fight her on that point. "I'm not arguing for no development. I'm arguing for responsible development. Sustainable. With some serious planning for stormwater management. SOS wants to fund research into the science and engineering we need to do to prevent disasters like this." He nodded out toward the bay, and as if on cue, something that looked like a laundry tub floated by.

"That's what you wanted our two million dollars for."

He shook his head. "Two million would only be a drop in the bucket. Twenty would be a good start."

She rolled her eyes. "You ever feel like you're pushing a rock up a mountain?"

He shifted the truck into gear. "You ever feel like you're the rock?"

CHAPTER 21

Tad drove a route that skirted around downtown and turned east.

Julie seldom ventured far from the coast, and she didn't know this part of the city. He drove through working-class neighborhoods where the houses were small and squat. Cottages and ranch houses and tired-looking bungalows. But except for some downed trees and torn awnings, lots of overflowing gutters and swollen streams, the neighborhoods along the route looked largely unscathed.

Neither spoke for a few blocks. Then Tad said, "By the way, thought you'd like to know: Figgy's lawsuit is over."

She wasn't surprised. It had always been a small-change kind of case. "Insurance company settled?"

"No. He decided to drop it."

She wasn't surprised by that, either. "Because it was never about personal injury damages."

"No. But mostly because he's moved to Louisiana. There's an oil rig offshore that's exceeding the allowable leakage. He's organizing the protests now."

To Julie, that sounded like a far more serious threat to the environment than a few parking lots. "You don't want to join him there?" she taunted. "Get your face on international news?"

He didn't rise to the bait. He only shook his head. "This is my home," he said. "I'm committed to cleaning this up first."

He drove on. The houses grew farther apart, the neighborhoods sparser, as he continued east. The streetlights disappeared, and his headlights bored into swampy terrain dotted with pockets of oak hammocks and tangles of scrub brush. They were so far east, she wondered if he was too tired to realize where he was going. It was the coast that the hurricane had battered; it couldn't have done much damage this far inland. She sneaked a nervous glance at him. He was gripping the wheel with both fists. He squinted blearily through the fading light.

She cleared her throat. "Um, Tad?"

"Here we are," he said, and turned onto a muddy lane.

It was a mobile home park or, rather, the ruins of one, and instantly, she realized her error. The hurricane had hit here, disastrously. Giant sheets of corrugated metal lay in twisted heaps on the ground or leaned haphazardly against the structures they were once part of. One trailer looked like it had been pried open with a can opener, another with a corkscrew. Doors were ajar, some of them hanging by a single hinge. One trailer was sitting cockeyed on its foundation, as if the wind had picked it up and dropped it back down. Another trailer was missing its entire front wall, and the interior was on display like a schoolchild's diorama. Trash and debris were strewn everywhere.

People were everywhere, too, some of them standing by their former homes, gazing blankly at the devastation. Others were collapsed on the ground, hugging their knees and looking at nothing. Some were poking through the debris with sticks, flicking bits of trash out of the way, searching for anything worth saving. One young woman in a yellow dress was zigzagging through the property, screaming hoarsely, "Mariana! *Bebé!*"

A few people gathered around the truck as Tad rolled to a stop. He looked at Julie and grimaced. "Here comes the hard part." He swung out of the cab and leaped up into the cargo bed with more spring in his step than Julie would have thought possible. "Line up!"

he shouted, then added something in Spanish that she guessed meant the same.

The people were too desperate to be orderly. When they realized that supplies were on offer, they shouted to one another and swarmed the truck. Some of them vaulted over the tailgate and began chucking items to their friends and families on the ground. Tad didn't attempt to stop them, but he tried to work ahead of them, hurrying to pass supplies down to the women and children who were hanging back.

Julie hung back, too, and watched through the rear window, afraid to get out of the cab and ashamed of herself for being afraid. She thought how petty she'd been to worry about a little water on the floor of her house. How ridiculous to fret about the safety of a half-million-dollar pleasure boat. These people had lost everything.

In minutes the truck was empty. Tad called out something to the crowd—a promise to return with more, Julie thought—but the people were already hurrying away, clutching rolls of toilet paper and cans of beans as if they were treasure. At least some of the people were. Some, she saw now, had never left their huddles on the ground.

Tad climbed back in the cab. He leaned his forehead against the steering wheel and let out a long breath. A moment passed before he straightened and turned the ignition key. She didn't know what to say, and he didn't look like he wanted to talk anyway.

He backed out of the narrow lane and pulled out onto the road. Night was almost upon them. He turned on the headlights, and they lit up the green-black pines and palmettos in the distance. Scrubby evergreens grew thick in the roadside ditches, and Julie nearly missed the flash of white low on the ground among them.

"Tad, stop!" she screamed.

He stomped on the brake as she shoved her door open and flew out of the cab. She ran back the way they'd come, her gaze moving wildly through the weeds for that patch of white she thought she'd seen. But before she saw it, she heard it—a bawling wail that came from either an injured animal or a toddler.

It was a toddler, naked but for a drooping diaper.

"Mariana?" she said.

The child looked up at her, startled into silence.

"Want to go find Mama?"

The toddler reached both arms up, and Julie picked her up and ran back to the remains of the mobile home park. The crowd had dispersed by then, and little campfires were sending up flares of light. She scanned the area in search of the baby's mother, hoping her yellow dress would send out its own flare of light, but nothing appeared.

The toddler started to wail again, suddenly afraid of this stranger holding her.

Julie turned a full circle. She didn't know where else to look. Instead, she shouted, "*Hola! Bebé!* Mariana!"

"Mariana?" a faint voice echoed.

"Mamá!" the baby cried, her head twisting.

The yellow dress emerged from the shadows. "Mariana!" the woman shrieked. She ran to Julie and snatched the child from her arms. "*Gracias, gracias!*" she sobbed.

"*De nada,*" Julie said, though both mother and child were crying, and no one heard her.

The night was black now, and the truck was some distance down the road. She was picking her way through a minefield of rubble when a pair of headlights cut through the darkness. The pickup creaked to a stop beside her, and Tad leaned over to open her door. "Nice save, counselor," he said with a weary smile.

"Just lucky," she said. She climbed in and pulled her door shut.

"Yeah, but that's half the battle." He put the truck in gear.

"What is?"

"Realizing when you are."

She looked at him as he pulled back on the road. "You don't mean luck. You mean privilege."

He shrugged. "It's the same thing. My dad had this expression—*the lucky sperm club*."

"Sperm?" Her nose wrinkled.

"I mean, look at you and me. Both of us white, healthy, smart, good-looking." He ticked off these points matter-of-factly, neither boast nor compliment. "All thanks to our genes. Nothing we earned or deserved. That much alone gave us such a leg up in this world. Opened doors that would be closed to anyone else. Throw in family money, and we won the race before other people could even start. All because we belonged to the lucky sperm club."

Lucky egg, in Julie's case, but she understood what he was saying. She also understood now why he did all these good works. He was trying to atone for all his advantages. Still. "Easy to play altruist when you've got family money shoring you up."

He shook his head. "I don't take any of it."

"You're kidding."

"My grandfather devoted his whole life to making money. My father devoted his whole life to spending it. Both of them were miserable. So I decided I'd have nothing to do with it."

She hadn't expected that, and it chastened her a bit. "Well, whatever," she said finally, the lamest comeback in history. She tried a different tack. "Anyway, it didn't take privilege or wealth to spot that baby in the weeds. All it took was luck."

He blinked, and after a second, he laughed. "You're right. I'm too tired to make any sense. I probably shouldn't even be driving."

That gave her a little jolt of alarm. Here in the interior, the roads were dark and the ditches deep. "Want me to drive?"

"Would you mind?"

He slowed, and the truck rocked to a stop on the narrow shoulder of the road, so close to a thicket that she couldn't open her door. When he shifted over on the seat, she realized she was meant to swap places with him here in the cab. She unbuckled her seat belt and tried to pass over him without brushing against his lap. She failed, but it didn't matter. He was too exhausted to react. He slumped against the passenger door and seemed to be asleep before she even managed to get the truck back in gear.

It had been years since she'd last driven a stick, and the first mile was riddled with lurches, but muscle memory returned, and she gave herself a little smile of satisfaction as she managed to navigate the route back to the more familiar streets of the city. Tad slept on beside her, and he didn't even stir when she hit a bump and the truck bounced in the air on its ancient shocks. It was the deep sleep of a do-gooder, she supposed. Untroubled.

Charlie's car was where she'd left it, beside the donation tent in the parking lot. She pulled up beside it, and Tad sat up with a yawn.

"You okay to drive from here?" she asked him.

He sent a bleary look around the parking lot. "I think I'll just sleep here. I need to be here if we get any early donations in the morning."

She glanced skeptically at the cracked vinyl seat. It had at least one broken spring. He was making yet another sanctimonious sacrifice, and she couldn't help taunting him. "It must be exhausting," she said, "being such a do-gooder."

He snickered. "Yeah, but when I'm done, I sleep like a baby."

There it was. His insufferable moral superiority. She shook her head and climbed out.

"Hey, thanks for driving," he called after her. "And, you know, for all your help today."

"It was the least I could do," she said, because she knew that was what he was thinking. That she'd done the least.

She replayed their conversation as she drove Charlie's car home. She didn't disagree with anything he'd said, yet it irritated her. Yes, she had countless advantages that were denied to those poor souls in the trailer park, and yes, she knew she'd done nothing to deserve any of it.

But if half the battle was recognizing your luck, then she was halfway to a win, because she knew exactly how lucky she was, and she counted all the ways as she neared her neighborhood. She was lucky to have a home to go to. A home with a roof and walls and electrical power. Lucky to have a husband she loved who was on his way home now, too. A husband who was a real do-gooder, she thought with a flare of defiance, who'd spent the day alleviating the pain of others. And she was lucky to have a dry bed where she planned to sleep with him for at least the next twelve hours.

There was one more piece of luck she considered as she pulled into the garage. From the moment she'd arrived at the donation center that afternoon, she hadn't wasted a single thought on her mother and Charlie.

CHAPTER 22

A week passed. Power was restored to the islands, the roads were cleared, the bridges reopened. On Saturday, Eric drove Charlie's car over to La Coquina and drove home in Julie's. He reported that Luisa and Ferdy were back in residence, and the place looked pristine again. He'd spotted the newlyweds looking cozy in the hot tub and waved hello as they waved goodbye.

"See," he said to Julie, "I told you it would all work out if we just stayed the fuck out of it."

"You were right," she said, which was the quickest way to end a conversation she didn't want to have.

As soon as she was alone again, she tried calling her mother. Kate didn't answer her cell—maybe she hadn't recharged it yet. Julie tried the landline instead. Luisa answered that call.

"Fine, fine. Everything is fine," she said. "She is eating like a horse now. Breakfast, lunch, and dinner. Snacks all day and ice cream every night!"

Julie frowned. That didn't sound right. Her mother was always so vain about her figure and so careful about her diet. But it had to be a good thing that she had her appetite back. It showed she was happy. Besides, she probably thought she could stop worrying about her figure now that she was married. They were both seventy, after all. They could grow old and fat together.

Julie resolved not to worry about things, not to think about her mother and Charlie at all, and certainly not to brood about the strange looks on their faces when they'd first seen each other again.

She would let them live their lives and go back to hers. Her normal, lucky life.

LUCK WAS HOLDING at work. The KS Development properties had sustained almost no hurricane damage, and she was able to get prompt insurance payouts for the damage that was done.

They were a little less lucky at home. Insurance companies weren't nearly as responsive to ordinary homeowners as they were to their big corporate clients, and Julie hadn't been able to get anyone out to inspect the flooring and roofing issues. She hadn't been able to get any contractors out, either. The flooring in the living room and dining room had warped badly and still felt spongy in spots. They were trying to get an estimate to replace the hardwood with tile that would better withstand the next bout of water penetration. But every contractor in the city was triple-booked, and after a week they ended up removing the floorboards themselves. They'd been walking on concrete slab ever since. Roofers were booked even further out, and Eric finally gave up trying and decided to replace the shingles himself.

He was up on the roof that Saturday afternoon, and Julie was in the front yard raking up the last of the storm debris, when Detective Brian Holley pulled into the driveway. She had a moment of cognitive dissonance. He was driving a red Jeep, not a gray sedan, and he wore shorts and a polo shirt, not a suit. And most dissonant of all, he was here at her home. She'd never given him this address.

"Brian," she remembered to call him. "What brings you here?"

Despite the casual clothes, he looked grim. "I ran a criminal history for Charles Mull, like you asked."

"Oh." She let the rake fall to the ground. "I'm sorry. I should have told you. Everything's fine. They're back together again."

His eyes narrowed. "And that doesn't worry you?"

She took a step closer. "Why? Did you find something?"

He shook his head. "Except for a speeding ticket thirty years ago, nothing. He's clean."

"Oh," she said on an exhale. She felt relieved but also foolish for having ever suspected Charlie. She should have known better. He was a good man. The best. "Well, thanks anyway for looking—"

"But did you know he was married before?"

"Oh, yes. His daughter, Becky, was at—"

He cut her off again. "Twice?"

She blinked. "No."

"Back in the eighties. In Lebanon. Nadia Khoury was her name."

There was something in Brian's tone. "Was?" she repeated.

"She died. Less than a year later."

Julie's breath caught. "Of what?"

"No cause listed in the records I could get at. It's all kinds of bureaucratic mess over there."

"Oh." Their neighbors across the street were hauling trash bags to the curb, and they gave Julie a wave. A beat passed before she remembered to wave back.

"I thought you'd wanna know that much," Brian said, "if you didn't already."

"I didn't," she said, but the bigger question was whether her mother did. And the biggest question of all was what Nadia had died from.

"I'll keep digging," he said. "Meanwhile, maybe you could talk to the daughter? See what she knows."

Julie hesitated. She'd only ever spoken to Becky at the wedding and then in the briefest exchange of pleasantries.

Brian was watching her. "Unless—you're convinced your mom dreamed up the whole thing?"

"No." She took a breath. "No, I'll call her."

He reached into his pocket. "Here's my card," he said.

"No, you already—"

"I wrote all my other numbers on the back." He handed it to her. "Call me after you talk to her. Or any time."

"I will. And you'll let me know if you find those records?"

"I will. I promise," he said.

She extended her hand. "Thank you, Brian. Thank you so much."

He took her hand and held it in both of his. "Julie," he said.

She watched him drive away while her mind ran through all the possibilities of what this other marriage could mean. It probably meant nothing, she told herself. It was a quick romance in a war-torn country. Nadia could have died from a dozen causes that had nothing to do with Charlie.

She was standing there looking at nothing when a heavy hand landed on her shoulder. She flinched and whirled. Eric was down from the roof. "Who was that?" he said. "Was that the detective? From the hotel?"

"Right. Detective Holley."

"What the fuck did he want?"

"Just following up," she said.

"On what?"

"Um." She couldn't tell him she'd asked for Charlie's criminal history. "On how we came through the hurricane. Whether we were okay."

"What business of that is his?" Eric's face darkened. "Has he been sniffing around you?"

"No!" She laughed. "Of course not."

"Give me a break. You think he's going door-to-door checking on the whole population? He's a county detective. This isn't even his jurisdiction!"

"Come on. He was only being kind."

He scowled. "He was only coming on to you."

"Well, if that's true"—she looped her arms around his neck and gave him a playful smile—"he's wasting his time."

His shoulders were stiff as she kissed him, but after a moment he relaxed and deepened the kiss. After another moment, he reached around and clenched her buttocks and jerked her pelvis up against his. In seconds, the kiss was far too amorous for the front yard. Their neighbors were working across the street. She broke free. "Not here," she whispered.

He tugged her to the door and inside the house. She started for the stairs, but he grabbed her and turned her and pressed her back against the door as he kissed her harder.

He pulled off her clothes, then his, with the quick, deft movements of the surgeon he was. He hoisted her up and entered her, and she wrapped her arms and legs around him and clung to him. The front door rattled with every thrust, and she thought what the neighbors must be thinking, until the whiteout descended and she couldn't think about anything at all.

CHAPTER 23

It wasn't until Sunday afternoon that Eric climbed up the ladder again. That was Julie's first chance to call Becky.

They were stepsisters now, she told herself. There shouldn't be anything weird about calling just to chat. She went into the laundry room and closed the door, but it wasn't until she heard the rhythmic hammering from the roof that she pressed the number in New Hampshire.

"Hi! Becky," she began brightly when a woman answered. "It's Julie. Hoffman. Kate's daughter?"

"Oh," Becky said. "Hi. Is everything okay?"

"It is now," Julie said. "I guess you heard what a hero your dad was in the hurricane."

"No, I haven't talked to him since the wedding. Wait. Was there a hurricane? In Tahiti?"

"No—" Julie realized then: Becky still believed they were away on their honeymoon. "No, it was here in Florida. They ended up not going on that cruise."

"Because of a hurricane?"

"No—" This was getting more and more confused. "That came later."

"Then why didn't they go on their honeymoon? What changed?"

"My mother's mind." Julie laughed as she said it, because she'd just hit upon a segue. "I'm sorry to be the one to tell you what a strong-willed woman your stepmother is. But I guess you're used to stepmothers, right?" She winced as she said it. What a clumsy segue.

"What d'you mean?"

"Your first stepmother? Your dad's second wife? Nadia?"

There was an audible gasp over the line. "He told you about her?"

"No. Well, just in passing."

"I'm shocked. I'm absolutely shocked. He never talks about her."

"Oh. He must have taken her death really hard?"

"I guess." Julie heard an audible sigh. "That whole time was a dark period in his life. He'd seen some combat, and he was having trouble in his unit—some guy owed him money and wouldn't pay up, and on top of that, my mom was hounding him for child support, then he went and had this quickie marriage? And then she died!"

"How sad." Julie struggled for a casual tone. "What caused it?"

"I was just a little girl. Nobody really explained it to me."

Because nobody knew? Julie wondered. *Or because nobody would tell something so horrific to a little girl?*

"He got through it," Becky said. "But he never wanted to talk about it. He shut me down any time I got even close to that time in his life. I can't believe he brought it up to you."

"Well, like I said, it was only a passing mention."

"Still—that sounds good! Like he's happy enough now to come to terms with all that stuff in the past. Thanks to your mom. They are so lucky they found each other."

"Yeah. Such luck," Julie said.

"So what's this about a hurricane?"

THE CALL TRAILED off eventually into awkward stumbles and silences, and finally, *I better let you go.*

It wasn't until Julie rang off that she noticed how strangely quiet the house suddenly seemed. The hammering had stopped. When she opened the laundry room door, Eric was right outside, chugging a glass of water at the kitchen sink.

"Who was that?" he asked, turning.

"Charlie's daughter. Becky."

His eyebrows went up. "Since when do you gab with her?"

"She wanted to know about the hurricane."

"Why didn't she call Charlie?"

"She thinks they're on their honeymoon."

He snorted. "Right. The great pretense." He took another gulp of water and nodded toward the laundry room. "So why'd you close the door?"

She gave a short laugh. "You were making quite a racket up there! How's it coming, by the way?"

"Almost done." He drained the glass and plunked it on the counter.

"Have you talked to Charlie lately?" she asked when he was half-way out the door.

"No. Why?"

"I haven't heard from my mother."

He rolled his eyes. "One, honeymoon, remember? Two, and this is the big one, she's too embarrassed to talk to you after dragging you into her nonsense. She's trying to forget it ever happened. Talking to you just brings it all back."

She scoffed. "So, what, she's never going to talk to me again?"

"We should be so lucky," Eric said, and let the door slam behind him.

She put his glass in the dishwasher. Something was making a rattling sound—the rickety ladder, she worried—but then she saw the source: a small flip phone on the counter, vibrating with an incoming call. She cocked her head, wondering where that phone could have come from. It didn't belong to either of them; they both had smartphones. The rattling stopped by the time she reached for it, and at the same moment, Eric came inside and snatched it off the counter.

"Since when do you have a second phone?" she said.

"Something new the hospital's trying out." He thrust it in his pocket and went back outside.

IT WASN'T UNTIL Julie was at the office the next day that she found an opportunity to report to Brian about her call to Becky. She almost didn't. She'd wrestled with it through the night, and the very idea that Charlie might have killed Nadia seemed more and more ridiculous with each turn. It was only natural that he wouldn't want to talk about it. It was a tragic loss. Reticence didn't equal guilt.

Anyway, they'd established that Charlie didn't have any kind of criminal record. If Nadia had died under suspicious circumstances, there'd have to be some indication somewhere. If Brian couldn't find it, then odds were it didn't exist. And it wasn't like Charlie had any obligation to tell Julie his whole life story. Kate was the only one who needed to know, and he'd probably told her long ago.

Still, it would be nice to confirm that with Kate. It would be nice to confirm anything with her, anything at all, and the fact that she wouldn't answer her phone was what made Julie finally call Brian.

"Okay, so he had money problems," Brian said. "He had a quickie marriage. And she died. What we need to find out is whether his money problems went away."

"How?"

"Call the first wife. Find out if he ever paid the child support."

She couldn't imagine making such a call, asking personal questions of a woman she'd never met. Who would certainly tell her daughter, who would certainly tell her father. Julie would be mortified if Charlie ever found out she was asking such questions. "I can't do that," she said.

"Even to save your mother's life?"

She inhaled sharply. She was stunned that he could say such a thing.

"Jeez, Julie, I'm sorry," he said at once. "I didn't mean to alarm you. It's just—you see a lot of bad stuff in my line of work. It's my job to rule out the worst-case scenario."

She took a deep breath before she spoke again. "The worst-case scenario was only that he'd have Mom committed and take control of her money. That was all I was ever worried about. It wouldn't make any sense for him to kill her. See, he signed a prenup. If Mom dies, all he gets are the house and the boat."

"The house and the boat," Brian repeated.

"That's it."

"No offense, Julie," he said after a moment, "but to us ordinary folk? That much would be a fortune beyond belief."

She winced. He was right. How disconnected from reality could she be to imagine that a twenty-million-dollar mansion was nothing? Tad Ainsworth would have a field day mocking her for that kind of privilege.

"And let me ask you this," Brian said next. "What's he get if they divorce?"

She swallowed hard. "Nothing."

He let the word lie there a moment in stark silence before he spoke again. "All right, then. I still need to rule out the worst-case scenario. But listen, you don't need to call the ex-wife. I'll keep pushing those bureaucrats in Beirut. You put it out of your mind, okay?"

She thanked him and ended the call, but she couldn't put it out of her mind. The seed had been planted.

CHAPTER 24

The honeymoon month was reaching its end. As far as the world was concerned, Kate and Charlie would be flying home on Saturday, and Kate would be back at work on Monday.

Charlie called Saturday morning when Eric and Julie were in the Lambo, heading out to their favorite brunch place. Eric put the call on speaker and slowed enough to listen.

"Hey, buddy," Charlie said. "How'd you like to take the boat out fishing with me tomorrow?"

"You don't want to spend the last day of your honeymoon with Kate?" Eric shot a grin at Julie.

"She wants the day to get her mind back in the game. And I'm itching to get out on the water. Come along and keep me company. Bring a six-pack."

"Okay, thanks!"

"Bright and early, now. Early worm, ya know."

Eric laughed. "You got it."

"Oh, and Kate says Julie should come along, too. Keep her company and update her on what's going on at the office."

"Okay," Julie said. She doubted Kate was much interested in her company, but she'd certainly want an update on the business. At any rate, it would be Julie's first opportunity to talk to her mother since she'd said, *Let's not talk about this now.*

THE ISLAND ROAD was littered with storm debris, and the dune grass was torn and flattened where the floodwaters had reached. But when Eric turned onto the circle drive at La Coquina, everything was immaculate. The garden statues were back in place, the bougainvillea reattached to the trellises, all the mud and grime scrubbed away. Except for the missing palm tree at the end of the drive, there was no sign that a hurricane had ever dared to trespass on Kate Sawyer's property.

It was the same around back. The outdoor furniture was in place, the cushions gleaming clean and bright, the pool uncovered, and the water a crystalline blue. Charlie was already on board the *Half-shell,* and he gave them a big two-armed wave when he spotted them. "Get your ass up here!" he barked in his best drill-sergeant voice. "We're burning daylight!"

Eric laughed and broke into a bounding run down the length of the dock. Julie smiled as she watched him climb aboard, balancing his cooler of beer. He looked so handsome in his shorts and boat shoes, his striped shirt like a French sailor's, his hat like an Australian out-backer's. His skin was glistening from the sunscreen she'd slathered on him, and as the sun rose behind him and its beams radiated around his face, she was reminded of the day she'd met him, how she'd imagined he was a sun god. He looked so happy to be up there with Charlie, so buoyant. Even boyish. His job made him so serious all the time. It was a delight to see him let loose like this and to watch his muscles bunch and ripple as he helped Charlie prepare to cast off.

Luisa ran up behind her, panting. "Your lunch!" she cried, and Eric vaulted down to snag a second cooler from her and scrambled back aboard just as the boat was pushing back from the dock.

"Is Mom up?" Julie asked Luisa when they were gone.

"No, Mr. Mull said she wants to sleep in today. The last day before she goes back to work. Come," Luisa said, heading up the dock. "Have breakfast."

Julie followed dutifully to the kitchen. Ferdy was lingering over his coffee, and old Mexican ballads were playing through the speakers in the ceiling. It was a nice change from the wretchedly tragic arias being constantly broadcast when Julie was last here. Luisa plated up her famous huevos rancheros, and Julie sat down to eat as Ferdy caught his wife around the waist and waltzed her around the kitchen. Julie laughed and applauded, and Luisa pretended to be annoyed.

Everyone was in fine spirits this morning, which had to mean everything was fine in the Sawyer/Mull household. Julie could actually spend the day doing as Charlie had suggested: briefing her mother about developments at work.

Kate still wasn't up when Julie finished breakfast, so she found her swimsuit and went out to do laps in the pool. The water felt deliciously cool, and she let her mind empty with the monotony of the exercise. Swimming had been her sport in high school and college. Or not sport, since she hadn't raced. Her discipline, perhaps, since all she'd done was swim laps. She loved the weightless feeling, the dreamlike mood that came over her as she stroked and breathed, stroked and breathed, flipped at the end of the lane, and stroked and breathed again. It was working now just as it had back in school. All the nervous energy of the past few weeks seemed to burn off, and by the time she hauled herself onto the pool deck, she felt the pleasant euphoria of physical exhaustion.

She toweled off and put on her cover-up and flip-flops and went back to the kitchen, where Luisa was adding soy milk to a cup of coffee. That was the way Kate took it.

"She's finally awake?"

"No, but soon, I think."

"Let me take it up."

Luisa handed her the mug, and Julie carried it up the staircase and down the hall to Kate's bedroom, now Kate and Charlie's. The door was closed, and she knocked. When there was no answer, she knocked again, called, "Mom?," and opened the door.

Kate was asleep, and the room was in shadows. Julie pressed the button to open the curtains, and they parted with a faint electrical whine. Sunlight flooded in and poured a golden glow over the khaki-colored wing chairs and on the peacock dressing gown draped over one of them.

Kate didn't stir. She was wearing a pink sleep mask, and the ivory satin straps of one of her bridal negligees were showing above the covers. One arm trailed off the side of the bed. The other side of the bed looked undisturbed. Charlie must have pulled his covers taut after getting up, a habit from a lifetime in the marines.

"Mom," Julie said, louder. Kate must have been wearing earplugs along with the sleep mask. Julie went over to the bedside and lifted her arm back onto the mattress. Her skin felt strangely cold. "Mom?" she said again. She pushed up the sleep mask, and Kate's eyes stared out at nothing.

Julie let out a single strangled scream before the coffee spilled on her feet and the floor lurched and the room went black. The nightmare reel began to play, and she was there again, walking down the long hallway, glancing in the doorway. The shoes were there again, the toes pointing up. The arm was trailing down. No, wait, the arm was on the bed, the toes were on the floor. No, it was all mixed up, the reel was broken, the colors were exploding, the teal peacock, the black wingtips, the pink sleep mask, the dead blue eyes. The images were swirling, they were out of control, this couldn't be happening again, it couldn't, it couldn't, it couldn't. The ceiling was dropping, the walls were closing in, the air left the room, the air left her lungs, she couldn't breathe.

The floor lurched again and slammed into her, and the film reel broke with a snap, and everything went black.

CHAPTER 25

Julie was swimming laps again, stroke and breathe, stroke and breathe, flip at the end and push off, back and forth, again and again, lap after lap. Until an arm reached down at the end of the lane and grabbed her wrist and started to pull her out of the water. She rose slowly, weightless and willing. It wasn't until her shoulders emerged that the realization landed on her like an anvil—her mother was dead—and she pulled free to sink back under the surface.

But consciousness intruded, even underwater. Her mother was dead. She was dead no matter how deep Julie dove, and when the arm extended again on the next lap, she let herself rise. Her eyes fluttered open into a blaze of light, so glaring she had to squeeze them shut and even then watch the afterglow burn into her eyelids. The image formed: pale gold hair surrounded by a radiance of solar flares. Her Sun King of yore. "Eric," she groaned. But the voice that answered her was too soft and the hand that stroked her face too gentle. Her mind tripped over her confusion, and she fell into the deep again.

The next time she surfaced, it was to sound, not sight. Voices murmuring somewhere nearby. She kept her eyes closed to listen.

"Maybe another dose of Ativan?" the soft voice said.

"Let's wait and see. You're the sister?"

"Sister-in-law, but we're like sisters."

Ah, Julie thought. It wasn't the Sun King. It was the Sun Princess.

"It's just—it's all too much for her," Greta was saying. "You see, her father also committed suicide, and she was the one who found his body, too."

No, wait. That was wrong. Her mother didn't commit suicide. She wouldn't have done that to Julie. She promised she wouldn't. No, she had a stroke. She had a stroke on her wedding night, too. That was what made her imagine Charlie's confession. Alex was wrong when he said she showed no symptoms of stroke. But he was right about one thing: she should have been checked out. She would have been diagnosed. Treated. The next stroke averted. Her life saved.

This was all on Julie. She should have insisted. She should have dragged her mother to the hospital. She'd be alive today if Julie weren't such a passive, insipid, do-nothing. If she had any kind of backbone.

Guilt made her grief so much deeper, all the way to the bottom of her spineless core.

"She's still suffering from PTSD over that, and this time—I'm afraid this might cause a real psychotic break."

No. That wasn't true. Once—only once—when she and Greta were roommates, Julie woke screaming from a nightmare. The incident left Greta shaking so badly that Julie ended up having to console her instead of the other way around. If either of them was suffering from unresolved trauma, it was Greta. Julie needed to tell them so. She needed to assert herself for once. But first she needed to get out of the water. She pulled hard with her arms. She kicked her legs. She burst through. "No," she gasped as she came to the surface.

"Julie. Sweetie."

She opened her eyes. Greta's face was hovering over hers. Her pale gold hair was hanging loose. She wore it in a bun at the nape of her neck when she was on the bench. But it was Sunday. She hadn't come from her courtroom. She must have come from home.

But come to where? Julie turned her head from side to side. White curtains on three sides. A bed with plastic rails. A hospital.

"No," she said again, louder. She struggled to sit up as another face loomed over hers. A man in scrubs—a nurse, a doctor?—was on the other side of the bed. He laid a hand on her shoulder and gently pushed her down while the back of the bed slowly raised her up. "Why am I here?" she asked him.

"Julie. Sweetie," Greta said again. "You've had a terrible shock. You need to rest."

"Did you give me something?" she asked the man.

Greta answered instead. "A little something to calm you down." Then she whispered, "I think another dose?"

"No." Julie sat up all the way. The sheet fell away, and she saw that she was dressed in her swimsuit and beach cover-up. "This is the ER?" she asked the man.

He nodded.

"Your maid found you," Greta said. "She called an ambulance, then me. Julie, sweetie—" She patted her hand. "You were hysterical."

Julie pulled her hand away. "Well, I'm fine now."

Greta spoke over her head to the man in the scrubs. "We should call her therapist."

"I don't have a therapist."

"The one you used to see." Greta spoke slowly, as if addressing a child.

"The one who ended my treatment seven years ago. Where's Eric? I want to go home."

"Um, let me find out for you." Greta tilted her head at the man. "A word?" she said in a whisper.

They disappeared behind the curtains and moved far enough away that Julie couldn't make out their words. She swung her legs over the side of the bed and slid to the floor and padded on bare feet to the edge of the curtains.

"—prepare a petition," Greta was saying.

"For a psych hold?"

"Just seventy-two hours. Long enough to make an assessment."

The man was mumbling. Julie caught only a few phrases. *Harm to herself or others. No sign. Only natural to be shocked.*

"But with her history."

The man cleared his throat and spoke more firmly. "Let me get someone from Behavioral Health down here. While you track down the husband."

Their voices dimmed. They were moving away. Julie looked around for shoes and found her flip-flops in a plastic bag on a shelf under the bed. She slipped them on and searched next for her purse, her phone, but apparently, the ambulance hadn't brought anything else with her. She didn't know how she could call Eric or book an Uber or pay for a cab or even let herself into the house when she got home. For one defeated second she thought about crawling back into bed. But that was what passive, insipid, spineless Julie would have done. The Julie who'd let her mother suffer a fatal stroke rather than risk an unpleasant conversation. No, she'd walk home if she had to. She'd break a window to get in if she had to.

She parted the curtains. A row of other cubicles stretched between her and the door. There were voices behind one of the curtains, but no one was in sight. She crept out to the corridor. Two people in green scrubs speed-walked past her, deep in their own conversation. They were heading to the right. An exit sign glowed neon red to the left. Julie turned that way.

More voices, multiple conversations, and the volume swelled as she reached the door and entered a roomful of unhappy people slumped in chairs or gripping their elbows as they paced the floor. It had to be the ER waiting room.

One man stood out. He was in a suit, on his feet, leaning against the wall near the entrance. He straightened as Julie came through the door and met her eyes with a sad smile. He held up a handbag. Her handbag. Detective Brian Holley had brought her handbag. Her phone, her keys. Tears sprang to her eyes. Tears of relief, of gratitude, a keening stab of grief. By the time she reached him, she was sobbing.

He folded her into his arms. "I'm so sorry, Julie," he murmured. "I am so, so sorry."

She repeated the same words as she wept into his shoulder. "I'm sorry," she choked, humiliated to be crying like this in front of him but unable to make herself stop. "I'm sorry."

"It's all right. You're all right," he said. "Hey." He leaned back to look at her. "You wanna get out of here?"

"Yes, but—" She sniffed. "I should see my mother before I leave."

"I'm sorry. You can't."

She searched his face, then the room. "She's not here?"

"She's here, but they don't allow viewings at the ME's."

She blinked. "The M—the medical examiner? Why is she there?"

"Let me explain in the car."

The car was right outside, parked in an emergency-vehicles spot with a sign displayed on the dash: SARASOTA COUNTY SHERIFF'S OFFICE. OFFICIAL BUSINESS. He opened the passenger door for Julie and trotted around to his side. After he got behind the wheel, he turned to face her. "Suspicious deaths fall under the ME's jurisdiction. That's why they have her."

"No," Julie said. "It wasn't suicide. I know it wasn't. She wouldn't do that to me. Not after—" She swallowed a lump in her throat but still couldn't say the rest.

"Not after what your father did. I know. I read the report. You were only thirteen when you found him. It must have been awful."

She took a ragged breath. "That's how I know this couldn't be suicide. She knows—knew how it would hit me. It was a stroke. It must have been."

"You're right that it wasn't suicide. But it wasn't a stroke, either." His face was grim. "It was murder."

She felt like she was still underwater as she stared at him. Sluggish and so slow to understand. "How?" she finally managed to ask. Her voice sounded strangled in her ears.

"Acute alcohol poisoning."

"No, that can't be." That was how her father had killed himself. By drinking grain alcohol straight from the bottle. The empty bottle was beside him, and vomit was all over him. Her mother's death scene was nothing like that.

"By injection," Brian said.

"What?"

"We found a hypodermic syringe in the room. With traces of alcohol in it. And an injection mark on the inside of her right elbow. The ME's testing her blood alcohol. We'll know soon."

On her right arm. Julie pictured it. That was the arm that was trailing toward the floor. The one that felt so cold.

"And there was a bottle of Everclear stashed in a closet."

"What's that?"

"Ninety-five percent pure alcohol. Can't even buy it in Florida. I think that's what the syringe was loaded with. The lab's running it now, along with the prints on the bottle and the syringe. Julie—" He put his hand on hers. "I'm so sorry. I hope you can forgive me."

"Forgive you?" She squinted at him. "For what?"

"I should've dug harder. I should have gotten the American consul involved. If I'd nailed that down, I might've been able to prevent this."

She was too sluggish. It took another second for the shoe to drop, and when it did, it hit like a bomb. "You think Charlie murdered her!"

"The Everclear was in his closet. And after the other wife . . ." His voice trailed off.

"It can't be true," she said. "What does Charlie say?"

"We're still trying to find him."

She remembered then: the fishing trip. "Oh, right. He took the boat out this morning. My husband went with him."

Brian nodded. "Last sighting, they were headed due west. Straight line to Matamoros."

Matamoros. Mexico? She gaped at him. "You don't think—He's not fleeing?"

He lifted a shoulder. "No response on the marine radio. We got a chopper and three vessels in pursuit now."

"My husband wouldn't—Wait." She dove into her bag for her phone and gave a jolt as it rang in her hand. She looked at the screen. "Oh. My sister-in-law."

"The judge?" Brian said. "Better take it." He started the engine.

Julie nodded, though she answered reluctantly. "Greta—"

"Oh my God! Julie! Where are you? We've been searching everywhere!"

"Greta, I'm fine. I'm with the police right now." She glanced at Brian, who nodded as he pulled out of the hospital parking lot.

"What? No, they shouldn't be questioning you at a time like this. You've had a terrible trauma!"

"I'm fine," she repeated.

"Oh, Julie. You really need to be in bed."

She'd already spent too much time in bed. Brian's dashboard clock showed it was nearly five p.m. It had been eight-thirty a.m. when she'd taken her mother's coffee up. She'd lost the whole day to hysterics and Ativan. She couldn't lose seventy-two hours more in a psychiatric hold.

"No," she told Greta. "I really need to help the police with their investigation."

"Their—what—?"

"I have to go. I'll talk to you later."

Julie disconnected and tapped through to Missed Calls. There were none from Eric, but of course there wouldn't be. He was on the boat and way out of cell range. But en route to Matamoros? That couldn't be right. Charlie always said the best fishing was between Marco Island and Key West. He would have been heading south, not west.

She looked up from her phone. Brian was also heading west, and she started to tell him where to turn when she remembered that he'd already been to her house, the day he told her about Nadia—Charlie's other dead wife. And what had Julie done with that knowledge? She'd made one timid, mealymouthed call to Charlie's daughter, then dropped it.

She should have gone over to the island at once and confronted Charlie, and she should have done it in front of her mother. Kate had a right to know about his secret dead wife, and she had the resources to hire a team in Lebanon to drill down on the death records. She could have thrown Charlie out of the house. She could have hired armed guards. She could have protected herself. Instead, she'd been left totally vulnerable, sharing her home, sharing her bed, with the man who may have murdered her.

If it was true. It couldn't be true.

Brian spun the wheel and turned into her driveway. "I need to ask you some questions," he said on the doorstep as she fumbled with the key. "If you feel up to it?"

"Yes, of course," she said, though she didn't. "Come in."

He followed her inside. His shoes scuffed across the bare concrete floor, but if he noticed, he was kind enough not to mention it. Just as he was kind enough not to notice her beach tunic and flip-flops. "Let me run upstairs and change first?" she said.

"Sure. Take your time."

She took a shower, too, and when the water was spraying at full volume, she leaned her forehead against the tile wall and let herself cry. Her mother was dead, and it was all her fault, and she couldn't have said which of those facts was tearing her apart the most. The guilt or the grief, each one compounding the other. Whether it was a stroke or whether it was murder, it was all her fault. Either way, it could have been prevented if not for her inertia. Her passivity. Her utter gutlessness.

The Dynamic Duo was now nothing but a static solo. Julie had lived her whole life in the shadow of her mother. *You need to get out of your mother's shadow,* Eric always said, Greta always said. But they didn't understand: when the sun died, the shadow didn't disappear. No, that was when real darkness descended.

CHAPTER 26

Brian wasn't in the living room, where she'd left him. An aroma was coming from the kitchen. He was at the sink, and on the table was a bowl of tomato soup next to a grilled cheese sandwich. It was her favorite childhood meal, and tears swam in her eyes again.

"I hope you don't mind." He looked at her anxiously. "I thought you'd be hungry."

"No, it's great. Thank you," she choked out as she sat down. Kate had never been a normal mother, but she could play the part from time to time, and one of her favorite acts was to make Julie this exact meal on a chilly Saturday. Those Saturdays grew further apart as Kate's business grew, and now that Julie thought about it, she recalled that it was actually Luisa who last served her this meal.

"Oh! I need to call Mom's housekeeper." She reached for her phone.

"Hold off until I take your statement," Brian said. "So your recollection doesn't get tangled up with hers."

Julie didn't think that was likely, but she put the phone down, and while he washed and dried the pans at the sink, she sipped her soup and nibbled at her sandwich. When she was done, he washed those dishes, too, before he finally sat down across from her. He took a small notebook from the inside pocket of his suit jacket. "If you'd just go over the timeline for me," he prompted her.

She told him everything she remembered, from Charlie's call Saturday morning up to the moment she fell to the floor at her mother's bedside.

He listened without comment until she was done, then he went back and asked questions to fill in the details. What time did Charlie call on Saturday? Had he ever invited Eric fishing before? Did Eric seem surprised? Was it unusual for Eric not to already have plans for Sunday?

Actually, yes, she thought, they usually filled up their weekends days in advance. But—

"What are you suggesting?" she said. "That Charlie and Eric had already planned the fishing trip?"

Brian looked up from his notebook. "Not at all. Just trying to paint the whole picture. Wondering if there was anything unusual going on."

"The hurricane," she said. "We've been spending the last couple weekends at home, dealing with the hurricane damage." She waved an arm at the bare concrete floor in the next room.

He nodded. "About the fishing invitation. You weren't included?"

"No, I don't much like fishing. But Charlie told me to come along and spend the day with my mother."

Brian looked up sharply at that.

"What?" she said.

"Maybe he wanted you to find the body."

"No." She put her hand over her mouth. That couldn't be true. He wouldn't do that to her. If any of this was true.

"Maybe not," Brian conceded. He flipped a page in his notebook. "How'd they meet, anyway? Your mom and Mr. Mull. DMV shows him with a Tampa address."

"They were high school sweethearts," she said. "Reunited after fifty years." Fresh tears came to her eyes as she told the story, just as she'd cried during Charlie's wedding speech. It was so romantic then and so tragic now. Tragic for a woman to die only a month after her wedding. A thousand times more tragic if she died at the hands of her husband. If it was true. Julie couldn't believe it was true.

"When did all this happen?" Brian asked. "The Lamborghini, the dinner party?"

She remembered exactly, and after he wrote down the dates, he took her back to the events of that morning. Arriving at La Coquina. Finding Charlie already on the boat, ready to cast off, urging Eric to hurry. "And your mother was still in bed?"

She nodded. "Luisa—the housekeeper—told me she was sleeping in."

He peered at her. "Is that exactly what she told you?"

She cast her mind back. "No, well, she said that Charlie told her to let Mom sleep in."

He nodded and wrote that down. "How much time passed before you found her?"

Julie stopped to think. She and Eric had arrived at about seven, then she'd had breakfast and swum laps. "An hour and a half," she said.

He looked like he was calculating something, and she was about to ask what when his phone rang. He looked at the screen. "Sorry. I have to take this." He got up and went out to the mudroom and spoke in a low voice. "Okay," she heard him say. "Got a time?"

He returned to the kitchen table. His face was grim. "That was the ME. We got a BAC and a TOD."

"What?"

"Blood alcohol content and time of death."

"Okay." She was clenching her hands in her lap.

"BAC of point-four."

She tried to remember how the numbers worked. For DUI, it was .08. "You mean point-oh-four," she clarified.

He shook his head. "Point-four. Almost five times the legal limit. Definitely lethal."

"Oh, God." She buried her face in her hands. So it wasn't a stroke. A stroke would have been swift. One stabbing pain and it was all over. But alcohol poisoning—

"No, listen," he said, as if he knew what she was thinking. "It wouldn't be like when your dad died. It didn't go through her stomach, so she didn't throw up, she didn't stagger around or anything like that. It went right into her bloodstream. It would have suppressed her breathing and her heartbeat almost instantly. I swear, Julie, it would have been quick. And TOD was between midnight and three. She could have been asleep already. She never even knew what happened."

Julie took a shaky breath and nodded.

His phone rang again. "God, I'm sorry. I gotta take this one, too."

He went to the mudroom again. She stayed where she was, trying not to visualize it. Her mother asleep in her bridal negligee, the sleep mask over her eyes, blocking out the light as Charlie filled the peptide syringe with alcohol and crept across the room to jab it into her arm.

No. She shook her head. It couldn't be true. The Charlie she knew couldn't have done that, not to anyone but certainly not the woman he adored.

Brian returned to the kitchen. He didn't sit down. "That was the lab," he said. "They confirmed the solution in the syringe was Everclear, a hundred and ninety proof. And they identified the prints on the bottle and the syringe. Only one set. Same on both."

She looked up at him, waiting.

"Charles Mull."

It was true. She stared at him, and the silence stretched out between them, trembling like a wire pulled too taut.

A burst of music snapped the silence apart. Her phone, playing "I've Got You Under My Skin." She answered at once.

"Julie!" Eric shouted, so loud that Brian could hear him, too. "What the fuck is going on?"

CHAPTER 27

Brian wanted her to ride with him, but she insisted on following in her own car. Eric would need a ride home, too, and she knew he'd refuse to get into Brian's car.

"You sure you're okay to drive?" Brian said, hesitating in her driveway.

He didn't even know about the Ativan that might be in her system. "I'm fine," she told him.

She drove carefully as he led her east through town, beyond the incorporated city limits, almost to the interstate. He drove five miles under the speed limit and kept darting glances in his mirror to check on her, and it took more than thirty minutes before they arrived at the three-story hulk of a building that housed the sheriff's office.

He pointed her where to park and took her inside, through security, upstairs, and down a long corridor to Criminal Investigations. A row of chairs lined one wall along the corridor, next to a desk where a woman in half-frame glasses was sitting.

"Where's Eric?" Julie asked. She'd thought he would be waiting here for her to drive him home.

"Must be in Interview," Brian said. "Have a seat and I'll go find out." He gave Julie's hand a parting squeeze before he took off down the hall.

She sank onto the cracked vinyl upholstery of the chair. She kept turning her head one way and then the other, scanning the corridor for a glimpse of Eric. She was desperate to find him, desperate for him to hold her and comfort her and say, *I'm so sorry, babe*. He hadn't said that on the phone. He must not have known then. All he'd said was that the *Half-shell* had been boarded and he and Charlie detained and brought here. *Shanghaied* was the word he'd used. Charlie had already set a course back to Cascara, Eric told her, when they were hailed by two skiffs and boarded by men flashing badges. One of them commandeered the helm while others forced Charlie to sit at the stern and Eric at the bow and still others conducted a search of the boat. *Like we were drug smugglers or something,* Eric had ranted. The cops didn't explain, they didn't answer questions, and they didn't take the boat back to Cascara. Instead, they drove it to a marina where deputies were waiting in patrol cars to bring them here.

They'd seized their phones, he'd told her, but it was his phone he'd called from. That had to mean his interview was over. He was free to go. So where was he?

After she rooted in her bag for her own phone, the woman at the desk cleared her throat loudly and pointed to a sign on the wall. NO CELL PHONE USE. Julie dropped the phone back in her bag.

During the drive, she'd tried hard to keep her mind blank, to think about nothing but Brian's taillights. But her mind must have been working in the background, because now, sitting here, it was all coming together. She finally understood the calculating look on her mother's face at the moment when she first saw Charlie after the hurricane. She finally understood the fearful look on his face as he stood there waiting by the kayak. The moment before Kate shouted *My hero* and pretended everything was fine, everything was wonderful.

Julie's mind kept spinning, and all the details whirled into place. Kate had a plan, and the joyous reunion was part of it. Her long walks on the beach had seemed aimless, but she must have been plotting the whole time. She knew that if she filed for divorce only days after the wedding, it would give ammunition to Charlie's petition for guardianship. Lenore Greggson had told her that, and she'd obviously taken it to heart. She must have decided that the longer she could pretend to keep the marriage going, the less that would be a problem. That was the reason for her cry of *My hero,* the faux honeymoon. It was all a sham, put on for the benefit of anyone watching for signs of her incompetence. For Charlie's benefit, too, to lull him into complacency until she jerked the rug out from under him and filed for divorce.

But Charlie was on to her. His gaslighting plan wasn't working, and he figured out that she was just biding her time until she could divorce him. The prenup assured that divorce would leave him with nothing. So he decided to grab what he could. The house and the boat. Like Brian said, that much alone was a fortune, and that was what he'd get if she died.

Kate might be a genius, but there was a fatal flaw in her plan. She thought the worst Charlie could do was have her declared incompetent. She never imagined he would kill her.

Because she didn't know about Nadia.

Because Julie never told her.

Charlie's gaslighting plan actually did work, Julie realized. He'd succeeded in gaslighting her.

She doubled over, clutching her ribs as the realization hit her. She felt sick. Guilt and grief swirled together and left her dizzy and so nauseated she was afraid she might vomit.

The woman at the desk seemed to have the same fear. She glared at Julie over the rims of her glasses, as if warning her not to even think about it.

Julie straightened and took a few slow deep breaths. She had one consolation: Eric had fallen for Charlie's act, too. She remembered how excited he'd been to spend the day out on the water with him, how boyishly he'd laughed when Charlie shouted, *Get your ass up here.* If Charlie had charmed his way into becoming a replacement for Julie's dead father, he'd done the same thing to Eric, presenting himself as a new and improved stand-in for Eric's gambling deadbeat dad.

Eric was going to be crushed by this news, Julie thought. He'd be almost as grief-stricken as she was.

IT WAS ALMOST an hour later before he finally appeared, emerging from the doorway of a room down the hall.

"Eric!" she cried, jumping to her feet in relief.

His eyes met hers and moved past her to the end of the corridor. "Where is he?"

"Who?"

"Miller. The lawyer. Have you seen him?"

"Who?" she asked again.

He didn't answer. He took off down the hall, and she hurried past the scowling woman at the desk as he disappeared around a corner.

A voice behind her cried, "Julie!"

She whirled. Luisa and Ferdy were coming down the other end of the hall, both wearing their Sunday church clothes. Julie ran to Luisa, into her hug.

"Oh, my poor Julie, I am so sorry," Luisa murmured, squeezing her tight while Ferdy awkwardly patted her shoulder. "Your poor mother. I am so, so sorry!"

"What happened after—? I don't even know what happened."

They sat in a huddle on the chairs against the wall, close enough for their knees to touch, while Luisa related all that had happened that morning at La Coquina. She'd heard Julie's scream and run upstairs to find her in a dead faint on the floor and Kate—

"Dead," Julie finished for her when she couldn't quite say the word.

Luisa nodded. She'd called 911 and yelled for Ferdy, and the two of them had managed to rouse Julie and hoist her to a chair.

"I don't remember that."

"No." Luisa shook her head sadly. "Your eyes, they were—" She trailed off. As perfect as her English was, it failed her now.

She continued. The sheriff's deputies had arrived and, close behind them, an ambulance. The EMTs carried Julie out on a stretcher, and when Luisa tried to get into the ambulance with her, the deputies stopped her. She didn't want Julie to be alone at the hospital, so she called Charlie, then Eric, and when they didn't answer, she found Greta's number and called her.

A detective arrived next, and after asking them a few questions, he took their phones and told them to wait in their apartment. Hours passed. The whole day. From their front window, they watched cars and vans come and go. They could hear footsteps and voices all through the house, and the sound of furniture moving, doors opening and closing. They saw another stretcher being carried out and lifted into another ambulance. That one held—Luisa faltered and looked to Ferdy.

"A body bag," Julie whispered.

"*Sí,*" he said, the first word he'd spoken.

They watched other vans pull into the circle drive, news vans with the names of TV stations on their side panels. The police made them leave, then closed the gates to the courtyard and stretched yellow tape across the driveway entrance to keep them from coming back.

Finally, late in the afternoon, a detective—a different one—said they needed to go to the sheriff's office and give their statements.

A deputy drove them here and put them in separate rooms, and one detective asked Luisa questions, and another—a Spanish speaker—asked Ferdy questions, then finally gave their phones back and said they were free to go.

Ferdy said something to Luisa, who explained, "Our truck is back at the house."

"I have my car," Julie said. "I'll take you home."

"We were so worried about you," Luisa said. "But we could not call anyone or do anything." She searched Julie's face with anxious eyes. "You are all right?"

"I'm okay," she said.

"Julie." Luisa picked up her hand and held it gently. "She did not kill herself. She would not do that, I promise you."

"I know," Julie said. "It wasn't suicide. It was murder."

"What?" Luisa froze a moment before her eyes darted to Ferdy.

"Charlie killed her."

Luisa reared back. Suddenly she looked terrified.

"No, don't worry," Julie said. "He can't hurt you or anyone else. They already have him in custody. And they have all the evidence they need to charge him."

Luisa looked again to Ferdy, who stared at her, blinking wildly. "What evidence?" Her voice shook.

"He used her peptide syringe to inject her with pure alcohol. They have his fingerprints on the needle and the bottle of Everclear."

"Everclear," Luisa repeated. "From the pantry."

"No, it was in Charlie's closet."

Luisa pressed her hands against her face, then pressed them together, prayerlike, against her lips. "Julie, I—"

Ferdy grabbed one of his wife's hands and squeezed it.

"What?" Julie asked.

"There you are!" Eric called from down the hall. "Come on. Miller's out. We need to talk."

"Who?" Julie threw a confused look at Luisa and Ferdy. By the time she looked back, Eric had disappeared around the corner of the corridor. She got up and hurried that way.

He was standing beside a door. He waved her into a small conference room. A man stood up as she entered and reached a hand across the table. "You're the daughter? Harrison Miller, how do you do." The man had silver hair and a matching goatee and the kind of deep bronze tan that spoke of hours out on the water with melanoma just over the horizon. He wore a well-tailored charcoal suit, crisp white shirt, red silk tie.

Eric closed the door behind him, and when the two men sat down, Julie fumbled to pull out a chair and join them at the table.

"Harry's down from Tampa," Eric said. "This is too big for a Sarasota lawyer. Greta polled her colleagues on the criminal bench, and they all agreed we should hire Harry."

Julie was slowly beginning to understand. "You're a criminal defense attorney?"

The man smiled, a brilliant flash of gleaming white. "Best in the state, so they tell me."

A terrible fear seized her. Eric had been aboard the boat, but that didn't mean he was aiding and abetting Charlie's flight, not without more. "They're not charging you?" she gasped.

"Me? Of course not! Harry's going to represent Charlie."

"Subject to terms and conditions," Miller said. "Which we need to discuss."

Julie tried to send a question to Eric through wide eyes and raised eyebrows. *What is he talking about?*

Eric talked past her. "You've spoken with him, right?"

"Briefly," the lawyer said. "And briefly with the lead detective. I'm not going to sugarcoat this. It looks bad."

"He's innocent," Eric said.

Julie's head swiveled. She stared at him.

"So he maintains," Miller said. "All he did was what he did every night. Pick up a prefilled syringe of some kind of cosmetic serum and inject it into her thigh. Said good night, went to bed, woke up early, and went fishing."

Eric nodded.

"Trouble is, so far the forensics paint a different picture."

"Preliminary forensics," Eric said. "It was a rush job. Which leads to sloppy science. Happens all the time when you put a rush order on labs."

Miller nodded. "That's probably our first line of defense."

"Okay, then." Eric leaned back and folded his arms. "Let's get going."

Miller held up a hand. His palm looked almost startlingly white against the deep walnut of the rest of his skin. "First things first. My office will email you my standard retainer agreement. And I'll need a certified check for five hundred thousand dollars."

Eric's breath hitched. Beside him, Julie was scarcely breathing at all. "That much?" Eric said finally.

Miller shrugged. "It's a big case. A tough case. There'll be lots of media attention. We'll need a PR team to handle that. We'll need expert witnesses to challenge the science. We'll need a forensic accountant to look at her finances. His, too. We'll need a jury selection expert to help us figure out who hates billionaires versus who hates ex-military. All that's just off the top of my head, before we even start thinking about trial prep."

Eric exhaled, then nodded slowly. "We'll need some time to pull it together."

Miller nodded, too. "Arraignment's tomorrow. I'll do that much on the fly. But I can't invest any more time after that without the retainer in the bank. And if I'm successful on bail, you'll need to factor that into the equation."

"Jesus," Eric said.

Miller stood and extended his hand over the table, and after a beat, Eric got up and shook it. Julie didn't stand, and she didn't react as Miller turned his two-tone hand her way. He shrugged and went to the door.

"I've got your email," he said. "We'll shoot you that retainer agreement tonight."

"Okay. Thanks."

Miller left the room, and Eric closed the door after him. He turned to Julie. "We'll go to the bank first thing. There's gotta be some creative financing we can do here. You ought to be able to borrow against your expectancy."

"My—what?" For a second she didn't understand what he meant. But then it dawned on her in a flash of white-hot fury. "Wait. You want to use my mother's money to defend the man who killed her?" She shot to her feet.

"She killed herself! C'mon, Julie. Use your brain!"

"Use yours!" she fired back. "His fingerprints are on everything!"

She knocked against him on her path to the door, and he grabbed her by both arms, squeezing her biceps hard. "They're setting him up! Can't you see that?"

"Let me go," she said, twisting against his grip. "I have to drive Luisa and Ferdy home."

"He's innocent! We have to help him!"

"Let me go," she said again through clenched teeth. "If I scream here—"

He dropped his hands at once, and she turned and wrenched the door open.

"Wait," he said. "I need a ride, too."

"Call an Uber," she hurled over her shoulder.

CHAPTER 28

Luisa and Ferdy were quiet during the drive to Cascara Key. They sat in the backseat of Julie's car, and whenever she glanced up to the mirror, she always found them staring straight ahead with big, haunted eyes. Kate's death obviously hit them hard. They'd worked for her—lived with her, too—for twenty-five years. For the last fifteen of those years, they'd spent more time with her, day in and day out, than Julie had. And her death would effect a bigger change in their lives than in Julie's. They'd lost their livelihood.

La Coquina was ablaze with lights when she turned into the circle drive. The police must have left every light on in the place. Outside, the landscape uplights were setting the crime scene tape aglow.

"Come inside," Luisa said when the car rolled to a stop outside the tape. "I will make you something to eat."

Julie shook her head. She didn't feel like eating. And she didn't know if she'd ever feel like going back into that house.

Luisa hesitated. "You will be all right?"

"I'll be fine. You two get some rest."

Ferdy held Luisa by the elbow as they ducked under the tape and trudged around to the side entrance. After they were inside, the lights switched off throughout the house in waves, like a rolling blackout.

Julie drove back to the mainland and her own house. It stood in darkness, which told her the first thing she wanted to know: Eric wasn't home yet.

Inside, she checked her messages. He hadn't called, but Greta had, twice. Jack Trotter had called, too. He never did outside office hours, which made her wonder.

She went to the study, opened her laptop, and navigated to the *Herald-Tribune* website. There it was—the headline: *Kate Sawyer, Real Estate Baroness, Found Dead in Sarasota Home.* It made the national news, too. *Kate Sawyer, Florida-Based Developer, Dead.* Below that, the subhead read: *Authorities Call Death Suspicious.* Kate's stock publicity headshot appeared with the caption: *Called a Force of Nature by Friends and Critics Alike.*

It must be true, Julie thought, if it was on the Internet. She barked a laugh that quickly turned into a sob until she put her fist to her mouth and stopped it.

SHE WAS WIDE awake but in bed when she heard a strange car in the driveway, a door slamming, a key turning in the front door lock.

Eric's shoes scuffed across the concrete slab, then softer steps sounded on the stairs with the perpetual creak on the fifth step. She knew what would happen next. It was what he did every time they had a fight. He wouldn't speak, even if she was obviously awake. He'd use the bathroom, then get stiffly into bed and lie there a rigid foot away from her. Until sometime during the night, when he'd roll over and make love to her, fiercely at first, then slowly and softly. They'd spend the rest of the night wrapped in each other's arms and never mention their fight again. Leaving the issue unresolved forever.

She lay there now, waiting for him and wondering if she had enough resolve to do anything differently this time.

His tall silhouette loomed in the doorway. She closed her eyes and listened to him move. He wasn't going into the bathroom first. Nor did he go around to his side of the bed. He came to her side, and she braced herself.

He dropped to his knees on the floor beside her. "Julie," he whispered. "I am such an ass. I am so sorry. Your mother died, and you found her, and I didn't even think to tell you how sorry I am. I am such an idiot. My poor love. What you must be going through, and all I could talk about was lawyers and money. You must fucking hate me right now."

She opened her eyes. "No, Eric—"

He took her hand. "Of course you don't want to use your mother's money. I never should have brought it up. We probably can't even do it legally." He pressed his lips to the back of her hand. "Don't give it another thought, okay? Try to forget I was such an ass."

"Eric—"

"Shh." He turned her hand over and kissed her palm. "The important thing is that you get all the rest and support you need. And love. 'Cause I love you, Julie. You know that, right? I love you so damn much." He got up from the floor and kissed her on the forehead, both cheeks, and finally, her lips.

She shook her head and broke the kiss. "But what about the lawyer and the money?"

"I have another solution." He bent his head to her breast.

"What solution?" She put both hands on his jaw and tilted his face up.

"We'll borrow against our house. It's worth at least twice that. Three times."

"A mortgage."

"Right." He pushed up her sleepshirt and rolled on top of her.

She lay unmoving under him. She was remembering how hard she'd campaigned to buy her dream house and how firm he'd been in his refusal. He couldn't abide the idea of debt or a mortgage.

She twisted free. "Not tonight," she said, rolling away. "I mean, my mother died today."

"Oh." He sounded stunned. She'd never denied him. Not once. It was a second before he added, in his calm bedside voice, "Of course. I understand completely." He patted her on the back. "Get some sleep."

CHAPTER 29

Monday was surgery day. Eric got up early, and Julie lay in bed with her eyes closed until he was out of the house. She showered and dressed for work, but she wasn't sure if she should go. She wasn't sure what she was supposed to do.

What did the bereaved normally do the day following the death of a loved one? She doubted they went to the office.

She drank her coffee at the kitchen table and scrolled through the contacts on her phone. There were a few cousins back in Massachusetts, but apart from the annual exchange of Christmas cards, neither she nor her mother had any regular contact with them. They weren't going to make the trip to Florida for a funeral.

There were hundreds of people who would. Kate's Rolodex was full of friends and colleagues, and a good starting point would be the guest list for the wedding. Julie had their names and contact information on an Excel spreadsheet. But to call all those people would take hours, maybe days. She wondered if a mass email would be in bad taste. Then she wondered what she would even say in the email. That the marriage they'd all celebrated last month had ended rather badly?

No. She decided to confine the email to the funeral arrangements. Which meant that first she had to arrange it, starting, she supposed, with a call to the funeral home. But she didn't know which one.

She had all of Brian Holley's numbers in her contacts now. She called his cell.

"Julie," he answered, and the background noise told her he was in his car. "I was going to call you. I looked for you last night, but you were already gone."

"Yes, well, I was tired, I guess."

"Sure. Sure. That's why I didn't call this morning. I thought you'd wanna sleep in today."

"No, I'm up. I was wondering where my mother is?" When she realized how that sounded, she added, "Her body, I mean."

"At the ME's, like I told you."

"Still?"

"Yeah, well, they have to do the postmortem and make an official determination of the cause of death. That's routine in every suspicious death."

"Oh." She'd assumed the blood alcohol test was the end of it. She got up from the table to stand in front of the kitchen window. "When will they be done?"

"They won't even start for a couple weeks. I'm afraid that's routine, too."

"Oh."

"You're thinking about a funeral. I understand. Some people go ahead and have a memorial service while they're waiting. Most people wait for the body to be released."

"Oh. Well, I guess I'll wait."

"I'm glad you called. I have an update for you."

She stood up straight. "Yes?"

"That bottle of Everclear. Mull bought it in Georgia back in February. We have the credit card records."

February, she thought. Three months before the wedding. When her mother was almost giddy with love and excitement. "You think he was planning this way back then?"

"As a fallback, maybe. He went to some trouble, anyway, driving out of state to get it."

Dimly, she recalled Charlie making a trip out of state last winter. Some kind of marine reunion or ceremony, possibly in South Carolina.

"—be at the arraignment?" Brian was saying.

"What?"

"Eleven o'clock at the courthouse."

"Do I have to be there?" She didn't know if she could bear to look at Charlie today. Or ever.

"Not at all. I'll report back." He cleared his throat. "Listen, Julie—"

Another call was coming in on her phone. She looked at the screen. It was Jack Trotter. "Brian, I have to go. Call me later?"

"You bet."

She connected the incoming call. "Jack?"

"Oh, God, Julie. Is it true?"

"I'm afraid so."

"How? I mean, what happened?"

She hesitated. The truth would be out soon enough, but it seemed she should protect her mother from it as long as she could. Kate would be so humiliated for anyone to know this was how her story-book romance had ended. "It's under investigation," she said.

"I don't know what—I mean, folks are asking. The employees. The contractors. The banks. There were reporters outside when I came in this morning. What do I tell them?"

"Nothing," she said at once, like a reflex. But she wasn't sure that was the right call. KS Development was a big enterprise, affecting a great many lives and livelihoods. The death of its CEO would affect them, too. They had a right to know. "Nothing to the reporters," she said. "I'll come in and talk to the staff. Then you and I can sit down and put together an email to all of our business partners."

"Good." Jack sounded relieved. But he must have felt compelled to add, "Are you sure you're up to this, Julie? Coming in and—everything."

She wasn't sure at all. "It's what she'd want me to do," she said. That much she was sure of. "Oh, and Jack," she added, "beef up security at the entrance."

THE GUARDS WERE there when she arrived. They kept the reporters at bay by blocking both the sidewalk entrance and the ramp into the parking garage. Jack must have described her car to them, because they waved her through when she arrived. She parked underground and rode the keyed elevator up to the KS Development offices. But instead of getting off on her own floor, she continued up to the penthouse level.

She stepped off into a swell of silence. Her mother's was the only office on this floor. The rest of the space was occupied by a small auditorium and an exhibition space. This was where KS entertained guests and displayed models of their projects. This was where, Julie supposed, they would hold the memorial service.

There was no one up here now. Kate's secretary had been reassigned downstairs during the duration of the honeymoon month. Julie went past her desk and into Kate's private office. Thirty feet of glass opened onto the terrace and a breathtaking view of the bay, but Kate's desk was turned deliberately, resolutely, the other way.

Julie sat down in the high-backed leather chair behind the enormous desk. The three computer monitors were dark, and the surface of the desk was clear. Not a single sheet of paper. Not even a paper clip, and that void made Julie feel her mother's death like a sharp pain. It was never this way in life. She always had contracts in neat stacks, spreadsheets arrayed on the monitors, blueprints unscrolled across the desk.

In thirty minutes, the small auditorium across the hall would be filled with employees wondering what had happened and what would happen next. Julie was the one who was supposed to tell them, but she was wondering, too. She had no idea what she was going to say to them.

She shifted her weight in the seat. She imagined she could feel the contours of her mother's body in the desk chair. This had been her throne, and like everything else in her orbit, it had molded itself to her. Julie turned her gaze slowly through the office. It was decorated much the same as La Coquina, sparingly, with clean, modern lines. There were no knickknacks or family photos. Instead, the walls were hung with photos of the biggest and best of her projects. On the shelves was an array of crystal statuettes and gold trophies and silver plaques, commemorations of Kate's many awards and honors.

Julie went over to study the inscriptions, hoping to find inspiration in the words written there by some foundation or chamber of commerce or industry group. *Visionary* cropped up a few times. *Leader. Groundbreaker.* No, that was far too literal.

Trailblazer.

Her phone rang. It was Brian, calling to report on the arraignment, as he'd promised. She walked over to the windows. "Is it over?"

"Short and sweet. He pleaded not guilty, no surprise there, then his lawyer—Harrison Miller, he's this big wheel up in Tampa—applied for bail. And it was denied." Smug satisfaction sounded in his voice.

"Really?"

"He's facing the death penalty, and he was apprehended ninety miles out to sea. Classic flight risk."

"No." She'd been gazing out the window, but as she shook her head, she saw her own reflection in the glass. "That doesn't make any sense. If it was this carefully planned murder, why would he flee? And he wouldn't take Eric with him."

"He must've panicked afterward. Happens all the time. No matter how clever they think they were, when they see the actual body, they go into panic mode."

"Okay," she said doubtfully.

"And as far as your husband goes, well, who knows? He was there, by the way."

"Yes, I know."

"No, I mean at the arraignment. Sitting right behind the defense table."

Her eyes bugged out in her reflection. Eric had surgeries this morning. He would have had to cancel the OR and the anesthesiologist, not to mention all those patients who'd spent weeks waiting for a surgical date, who'd spent last week in pre-op testing, and who'd spent last night sleeplessly worrying about today's surgery. She couldn't believe he would do such a thing.

"I have to go," Brian said. "We'll talk later, okay?"

"No, wait—" But at that moment, she heard the elevator chime with the first arrivals of staff. They were filing into the auditorium, waiting for her.

CHAPTER 30

The auditorium seated thirty. Every seat was filled, and a dozen late arrivals leaned against the back wall. Another dozen appeared in Zoom windows on the giant screen at the back of the stage. A lectern stood center front on the stage, and Jack went to it to call the meeting to order and remind the remote callers to keep themselves muted.

"You've all heard the sad news by now," he said into the microphone. "The devastating news, really. I'm sure you have a lot of questions. Let me turn the meeting over to our general counsel, Julie Hoffman. And for anyone who doesn't already know it, that's Julie Sawyer Hoffman, Kate's daughter."

He stepped away from the lectern, and Julie crossed the stage to take his place as he withdrew to the wings. There was a smattering of inappropriate applause, quickly stifled. She looked out over the faces. Most of these people were the clerical employees of the company— the accountants and bookkeepers, the secretaries and mail clerks. On the screen behind her were the site managers and project supervisors.

She searched for an opening phrase. Not *Good morning,* when it so obviously wasn't. *Thank you?* For what, exactly?

She dispensed with an opening. "As most of you have probably heard, Kate Sawyer was murdered in her home early yesterday morning."

They all knew it already. Still, there were a few gasps and murmurs from the audience.

"Her husband, Charles Mull, has been charged with her murder."

The gasps were louder this time. They'd heard the rumors, but this was the first confirmation.

"This morning he entered a plea of not guilty. He's being held without bond at the Sarasota County Jail."

She tried to think of a closing phrase. Maybe a simple *thank you* now? She hesitated. She'd done all that Jack had asked her to do, but she wondered if she should say a few words about her mother. This wasn't a memorial service, though. She wasn't delivering a eulogy.

She looked out at the live audience and back at the screen. Kate had handpicked most of these employees and personally trained quite a few of them. Even though she never fraternized with the help, she did value them. So did Julie, who knew and liked almost all of them. Now she had to wonder how many of them would be here in a month or a year. She knew there was often a mass exodus after a founder's death.

She thought back to the engravings on the awards in Kate's office. One of the inscriptions loomed large in her mind, and suddenly, she knew what she ought to say.

She ducked her head to the microphone. "Kate Sawyer built this company from nothing into the giant it is today. She had her admirers, she had her critics. People have called her many things, good and bad. Visionary and villainess. Leader and lightning rod. A force of nature. The destroyer of nature."

A few people groaned in protest, and Julie held up a halting hand. "I know, I know. But here's the one name no one could argue with. Trailblazer. She accomplished things that few women of her generation had ever done before. She carved paths that no one ever thought she could.

"Here's the thing about trailblazing. The trail's being blazed so that others can follow. Kate didn't block that trail when she died.

She didn't close that door. She left it wide open for the rest of us to follow.

"So I'm asking all of you to come with me through that door and down that trail. To keep this company alive. No." She stopped and shook her head. "Not just alive. Flourishing. Growing by leaps and bounds. Her legacy isn't what she's already built. It's what she built the potential for. And I hope and trust that you'll all stick with me—with me and Jack—as we take this company to places maybe even Kate never dreamed of."

Again there came a smattering of applause, followed by an awkward silence as the clappers seemed to realize that even though it was a rallying cry, applause still wasn't appropriate.

"But let's talk about the places Kate did dream about. The projects that are already underway and the ones that are in the early planning stages. Let's start with Jacksonville. Eighty percent of the residential units sold, and we've barely broken ground. And late last week we signed retail leases with Cartier and Carolina Herrera."

Julie ticked off similar aspects of half a dozen KS projects. She'd worked on each of these deals, and although she'd never arranged them into anything approaching a speech, it seemed to come to her easily enough. The four-sentence talk she'd started with had morphed into a twenty-minute speech.

"In closing, let me say that the tragic news that brought us here today is a matter for the authorities. There's nothing we can or should do to influence or control it. But there is something we can and should control. All of us together, and that's the future of this company.

"I want to thank all of you," she said. "Not for being here this morning but for everything you did for KS Development before this morning. All the hard work and talent and loyalty you've given this company. Because I hope and trust that every one of you will continue to give that same hard work and talent and loyalty to this company after today, too, and into the future as far as any of us can see it. That's how I hope to honor my mother's legacy, and I hope you'll all join me."

She turned from the lectern. Jack Trotter was standing in the wings with a strange look on his face.

"What's wrong?" she asked when she reached him.

"Nothing," he said, startled. "I just—well, you surprised me, that's all."

She brushed past him toward the exit. "Meet me in my office. We'll work on that email. Ten minutes," she added over her shoulder.

The elevator bank was milling with the employees heading back to work, so Julie took the stairs down to her office, and on the way her phone pinged in the stairwell with an alert. A text from Eric, so loud it echoed inside the concrete walls. Meet me at the bank. 3 pm appt with mortgage officer.

CHAPTER 31

The flowers started to arrive that afternoon, arrangements and sprays and wreaths, some addressed to the company, some to Julie, most from people doing business with KS Development in some form or another. The florist delivery vans had to jockey with the news vans for parking spaces. One enterprising reporter brought her own flowers and tried to get into the building under the guise of making another delivery. It would have worked, too, if the same reporter hadn't already been turned away by the same security guard a few hours earlier.

The phones were ringing nonstop throughout the office. Some were legitimate business calls; many were condolence and curiosity calls; and the rest were journalists seeking an angle, an update, and best of all, a quote, from anyone.

Brian Holley called at three o'clock. "Heads up," he said. "Detectives Long and Russo are on their way to interview you."

"What? Why?"

"You're the victim's daughter and the one who found the body. Obviously, they need your statement."

"No, I mean, I thought this was your case. And you already took my statement."

"We work in teams," he said. "And follow-up interviews are routine."

"Okay, but what are they going to ask me?"

"Same things we went over yesterday. Don't be nervous. Just tell them what you told me. It'll be fine."

"Okay."

"One thing, though. Don't mention anything about the second wife. Nadia."

"Why not?" That detail struck Julie as pretty relevant.

"We-ell—" He sounded a bit sheepish. "That digging you asked me to do? It was all off-book. Unofficial. You know, a personal favor—"

"I understand," she said at once. The last thing she wanted to do was get him in trouble when all he was trying to do was help her.

"Thanks, Julie," he said. "The circumstances of Nadia's death will be confirmed officially soon enough. Through regular channels."

"Got it," she said.

ERIC CALLED FIVE minutes later. "Hey, babe. You running late?"

"The police are here. I have to give a statement."

"Oh, fuck. Tell them to come back later. You don't need to be at their beck and call."

"Eric. They're investigating my mother's murder."

"They're investigating her death," he snapped.

She didn't answer.

"Okay, listen," he said more softly, in his humor-Julie voice. "I'll do all the preliminary paperwork, and you just get here as fast as you can to sign."

"Can't talk," she said, and disconnected.

THE DETECTIVES ARRIVED an hour later. Normally, Julie would have met them in a conference room, but today she decided to have them brought to her office and to greet them from behind her desk. This was what her mother always did, and Julie could understand why the moment she resumed her seat. It was as if she'd marked her territory and declared who was in control.

The two men were older than Brian by at least a decade. Detective Long was Black, tall, and lean. Russo was white and carrying a bay-window belly over a low-slung belt. Both were solicitous, thanking her for seeing them and apologizing for disturbing her at a time like this.

They asked the same questions that Brian had, just as he'd predicted. The fishing invitation. Yesterday's timeline. Her discovery of her mother's body. But there were a few new wrinkles. When had she last spoken to her mother? She knew the date exactly. The day after the hurricane. Their eyebrows raised a bit. "That long?" Russo asked. "Was that unusual?" Long asked.

"Yes, but see, they were on their honeymoon. I wanted to give them some privacy."

"Yes, about that." Long consulted his notebook. "We have a report from Tampa PD about an incident on their wedding night?"

Julie clenched her fists below the sight line of her desk. "Yes?"

"Can you tell us in your own words what happened?"

She spun a quarter turn in her chair. "My understanding is that Charlie told my mother that he'd committed the Tylenol murders in Chicago back in the eighties. She reported that to the authorities."

"Who established that he had an alibi."

"Right."

"And he denied that he'd ever made any such confession."

"Right," she said again.

The detectives gazed at her in silence. She knew this trick. Lawyers did it all the time. Stare silently, and the witness will eventually feel the need to fill the silence and blurt out something useful. Julie maintained her silence, and it was Detective Russo who ultimately felt the need to fill it.

"What do you think really happened?"

Julie spun back to face them head-on. "Exactly what I just said. He told my mother he'd committed a crime that in fact he couldn't have."

"Why do you think he'd do that?"

"I think he hoped to make me and others question my mother's mental competence so that he could take control of her affairs."

Detective Long gave her a sidewise look, his eyes narrowed. "If you honestly thought that, why'd you leave her alone with him all that time?"

She squared her shoulders. "First, because my mother was perfectly capable of making her own decisions. Second, because I thought that was the worst he could do. I never thought he would hurt her. Or—God—kill her."

"But now you do."

"Because now he did."

There was another silence, and again Julie did nothing to fill it. Detective Russo flipped a page in his notebook. "I understand your father committed suicide."

She took a sharp breath. That wasn't a question, so she didn't have to answer it. She pressed her palms against her thighs and breathed slowly in and out. Here was another advantage of sitting behind her desk: they couldn't see what her hands were doing.

"That must have been devastating to a little girl," Long said.

She gave a half shrug to acknowledge the obviousness of the statement.

"And to your mother, too, I expect."

Now she gave a full shrug. "She mourned him, of course. But it hardly set her back. I mean, in the twenty years since then, she built all this." She swept an arm to take in the office and everything beyond it.

"Yeah, about all this," Russo said. "And all the rest of your mother's estate. We hear that Mull's not getting it?"

"That's correct. He gets the house on Cascara Key and the boat, and that's all per the terms of their prenup."

"So all this will be yours." Russo swept an arm as she had.

"No."

The eyebrows shot up on both detectives' faces.

"Her will makes specific requests to a few beneficiaries, including me, but the company and everything else goes to her alma mater."

Russo let out a low whistle. "That's some gift."

"You wouldn't happen to have a copy of that will?" Long leaned forward. "Or the prenup?"

"Of course." Julie turned to her computer and located the email her mother had sent her after the signing session at the lawyer's. Attached to it were PDFs of the prenup and of the new will Kate had signed the same day. Julie printed out both documents and handed the pages to them over her desk. "You'll note," she said, "in the event of divorce, Charlie gets nothing."

Long looked up from the pages. "Do you have any reason to think your mother was contemplating divorce?"

Julie hesitated. "I believe she gave it some consideration after that incident in Tampa. After his false confession."

"But instead, she spent a month alone with him out on Cascara?"

"I guess she wanted to give him another chance."

Russo lifted a shaggy eyebrow. "Or maybe she was doubting herself about that so-called confession."

Julie almost laughed. "My mother never doubted herself in her life."

THE INTERVIEW WOUND down over the next ten minutes. A few details were filled in. The names of Kate's lawyers and the doctor who prescribed her peptide injections, the name and address of Charlie's daughter, the incorporation details of KS Development, the key person insurance policy that the company had taken out on Kate. Finally, the detectives folded their notebooks and tucked them away, and Julie left the shelter of her desk to show them to the elevator.

When she returned to her office, she closed the door and collapsed in her desk chair, utterly drained. She felt like she'd been performing mental gymnastics throughout the whole interview. *Just tell the truth,* Brian had said, but the truth wasn't that straightforward. There were nuances and angles and different interpretations of the same events.

But some facts, she reminded herself, were spinproof. These facts. Kate had a lethal level of alcohol in her system, and Charlie's were the only fingerprints on the syringe and the bottle. There was no nuance to it. He'd murdered her.

THE LAMBORGHINI WASN'T in the garage when Julie arrived home that evening. At four Eric had texted: Never mind. Loan officer can't wait any longer. At five another text: Still with cops? Have to work 2nite. Be late.

She could guess why he had to work late. He had surgeries to reschedule and, she hoped, apologies to offer after blowing off his whole day's appointments to spend the morning in court and the afternoon at the bank.

Inside on the kitchen table was a multi-page document with SIGN HERE sticky tabs on the margins. *Residential Home Equity Loan Application* was the heading. Eric had already filled in all the fields, including Julie's social security number, employer, and income. All that was left blank was her signature, and for one bitter moment she wondered why he hadn't just filled that in, too.

She stopped and stared at another field that he'd filled in. *Loan amount: $700,000.*

She went to the kitchen window and stared out into the black night for a long time. She made a sandwich and loaded the dishwasher and put out the trash. All her nightly tidy-up-before-bed chores. Then she ripped the loan application in half and left it on the table and went upstairs.

CHAPTER 32

It was almost midnight before she heard the Lamborghini. It announced its arrival two blocks away in a high-pitched guttural whine that was twice as loud as any normal car engine. Although there was some mechanical rationale for it, she'd read that the real reason for the noise level was that Lambo owners liked it to sound that way. They wanted to turn heads as they roared down the street. *Look at me,* they proclaimed. *I've arrived.* Blocks before they actually arrived.

She turned off the bedside lamp before Eric made the turn onto their street. He pulled into the garage, and she heard him fumbling with the house key, cursing under his breath until the door opened. His footsteps sounded inside, crossing to the kitchen.

There was a long silence before his feet pounded on the stairs. She rolled to her side and squeezed her eyes shut.

"Julie," he said from their bedroom doorway.

She feigned sleep.

"Can we talk about this?"

She didn't answer.

"Come on. I know you're awake."

She held her breath.

"Real fucking mature," he muttered.

She opened her eyes at that. The room was dark, but she could make out his silhouette against the light from the hallway. She fixed it with a baleful stare.

"I get it, okay?" he said. He came into the room. "But come on—Miller is going to walk if we don't get him his retainer."

"He's not the only lawyer in Florida," Julie said.

"Yeah, but he's the best. Besides, any lawyer's gonna want some kind of retainer."

"Here's the solution." She sat up straight. "Sell your car!"

His silhouette froze. "I can't."

"If you care more about the car than—"

"It would lose half its value!"

"Then let Charlie pay the retainer himself! He must have savings."

Eric shook his head. "Not after last month. He paid off his daughter's mortgage—kind of a reverse wedding gift. It wiped him out."

Her eyes narrowed. "You're saying he's completely broke?"

"Until he gets La Coquina, yeah. Which he won't get unless he can defend himself against this bullshit—"

She cut him off. "So he's indigent."

Eric cocked his head in the dark, puzzled. "Yeah . . ."

"Which means he gets a public defender. There." She folded her arms and leaned back against the headboard. "Problem solved."

"Oh, sure. Some night-school rookie to handle the biggest murder trial this state has ever seen."

She shrugged. "If it's that big a deal, Miller should do it for free, just for the publicity."

"You're being an idiot."

She threw the covers back and scrambled out of bed, heading for the door. He grabbed her before she got there. "Julie. Stop. Come on. Can't we talk about this rationally, like civilized adults?"

"Okay," she said, pulling free. "Let's be rational. What's the rationale for the extra two hundred thousand?"

His eyes shifted. "I had to build in a cushion. In case it runs over."

"Okay," she said again. "And how are we rationally going to repay a loan this size?"

"Charlie'll pay us back."

"Indigent Charlie?" she taunted.

Eric rolled his eyes. "He won't be indigent after he gets the house. He'll be able to borrow or sell, whatever."

"Not if he's convicted."

He threw his hands up. "Jesus Christ."

"Rational people weigh all possible outcomes. Including the worst-case scenario. What if Charlie's convicted and we have this enormous mortgage against our house? With a balloon payment due in two years, did I read that right? So what do we do? Let the bank take our house?"

"Julie. Julie." He put his hands on her shoulders and ducked down to look her in the eye. He spoke slowly, as if trying to calm an excitable animal. "By that time, you'll have your inheritance. Seven hundred grand will be a drop in the bucket."

She felt her stomach lurch. Her face froze as she stared at him. This was a conversation she'd been putting off for all the years they'd been together. She'd managed to dodge it last night at the sheriff's office, but now she'd talked herself into a corner she couldn't escape from. She bit her lip and looked up at him with eyes full of dread.

His head tilted back. "What?"

"Eric, I—I'm only getting two hundred and fifty thousand from my mother's estate."

"What?" he said again.

"She wanted to leave me just enough to get through a year or two of unemployment if the new owners of the company cut me loose."

He shook his head. He still wasn't following. "The new owners?"

"Harvard," Julie said. "The entire residual estate goes to the Harvard Radcliffe Institute."

He groped behind him for the edge of the bed and sat down hard. "You're telling me—you're saying—" He faltered. "Your mother fucking disinherited you!"

She clasped her hands. "Not quite. She left me two hundred and fifty thousand."

"This is because of me, isn't it? Because she hated me."

"No! It was nothing like that. She just doesn't—didn't—believe in intergenerational wealth. Neither do I! I didn't do anything to deserve her money. It would be the ultimate nepotism if I got it."

He snorted. "As opposed to the nepotism that got you your current job? Gimme a fucking break." He heaved himself off the bed and paced across the room. "I know what she really didn't believe in. Me! She didn't want me to get anywhere near her precious money."

"No, Eric, it wasn't you, I promise! These were—these were always the terms of her will."

He stopped abruptly, then wheeled on her. "Wait. You're telling me you knew all along you weren't getting anything? Before we even got married? And you never mentioned it!"

"Why would I mention it?" she shouted. "Unless you were only marrying me for my mother's money!"

"No! Fuck!" He raked his hands through his hair. "Because married people tell each other these things. Why wouldn't you mention it? Because you thought I was only marrying you for your money? I mean, damn it, Julie!" He spun away from her. "How insecure are you?"

His words roared in her ears, and her mouth trembled as she tried to form her own words to hurl back. But as the echo of his shout faded into ripples, she heard something else. The scuff of shoe leather against bare concrete.

"Eric!" she hissed, and when he turned, she widened her eyes at him. "Somebody's downstairs!"

He went still, listening hard. After a moment the scuff sounded again, and his eyes widened, too. He lunged for his nightstand as she lunged for hers. She grabbed up her phone, and when she turned around, he had a gun in his hand.

"Eric, no!" she whispered. "Don't go down there!"

"Wait here," he whispered. He ejected the magazine and checked it and snapped it back in.

"Eric, no! I'm calling 911."

"No, don't!" he hissed. "Let me check it out first."

He toed off his shoes and disappeared into the hallway.

CHAPTER 33

The phone glowed in Julie's trembling hands, and her fingers shook as she tapped the numbers.

"911. What's your emergency?"

"Someone broke into our house," Julie whispered hoarsely. "He's here now. We can hear him moving downstairs."

She whispered her name and address in halting syllables, listening between each breath for sounds of the intruder. She could hear Eric's footsteps on the stairs, and she was terrified for him. Homeowners with guns were always the ones who ended up getting shot, either by the intruder or by their own ineptness. Eric wasn't experienced with guns. He bought the pistol and put it in his nightstand, and that was the end of it. She choked on a sob as the operator asked her to repeat her address.

"Stay on the line," the operator said.

She heard something then. A shout. Eric's voice. "Get the fuck out of my—"

A different voice cut him off, and her skin crawled at the sound of it. There was no doubt now. A man had broken into their house, and Eric was confronting him, and this was going to end in something awful.

"My husband's gone down there," she whispered.

"Sarasota PD is two minutes away."

"Hey!"

That was Eric's voice, and a sob burst out of Julie's throat.

"Is there someplace safe you can go?" the operator asked. "Into a closet or the bathroom?"

The other voice sounded again from downstairs. It was too low for her to make out the words but not too low for her to know it wasn't Eric's.

She crept out of the bedroom into the hallway and leaned over the railing, squinting hard into the darkness. There was no one on the stairs or in the front hall, and she couldn't see beyond that.

That voice sounded again. From the dining room, she thought. The next voice was unmistakably Eric's. "Fuck you!" he said.

Then both of them were shouting. Hurling obscenities. *Fuck you* and *You think you can fuck with us.*

She jumped as something crashed. A lamp or a bowl shattering on the concrete floor. It boomed like a blast of dynamite, and the reverberations rang through the house.

She was trembling violently now. She kept the phone clamped against her ear and trailed her other hand along the railing until she reached the top of the staircase. She slid one bare foot down to the first step, then the other.

From the dining room, she heard a grunt and an *ooof!*, and she was terrified that the next sound would be the roar of a gunshot.

"Are you someplace safe?" the operator was asking her.

"Yes," she whispered, and she slid her foot down to the next step. She didn't know what she could possibly do to defuse the situation, but Eric's gun was only going to escalate it. She had to do something.

She crept down the next three stairs. From there, she could lean over the banister and see partway into the dining room. It was in darkness, but she could make out shapes.

Two tall men, and she couldn't tell which one was Eric.

She inched down the rest of the stairs to the front hall. A few more steps would take her to the living room, and from there she'd have a clear view into the dining room.

"Police!" came a booming voice behind her, and a pounding on the front door, so hard it rattled the hinges.

"Shit!" said a voice that sounded, impossibly, like Eric's.

Julie wheeled and hit the light switch. The back door slammed as she flung the front door open. Two uniformed officers stood on the doorstep. "Julie Hoffman?" one of them shouted.

"Ye-es," she stammered. She pointed to the dining room. Eric had a hand on the table and was hauling himself up from the floor.

The cops crowded through the doorway, past Julie, and into the living room.

"Off-Officers," Eric said, panting hard as he stood upright. "Sorry. False alarm."

"You reported an intruder?"

"No, my—my wife must have—Julie, honey?" Eric called to her. "Julie, did you call the police?"

She came into the living room with the phone in her hand. "Yes, I—" She realized the operator was still on the line. "It's okay. The police are here," she said, and hurried to disconnect. "Yes," she said again. "I heard an intruder."

The cops turned and eyed her, and she was suddenly aware that she was wearing nothing but a long T-shirt. She grabbed a throw from the sofa and tugged it over her shoulders.

"Sorry," Eric said with a strange chuckle that sounded like he was clearing his throat. "She must've heard me stumbling around in the dark. I knocked over a vase. Sorry, honey," he said to Julie. "Didn't mean to scare you. I worked late tonight," he said to the cops. "She must have been startled out of sleep. Honey, were you asleep?"

She blinked at him.

"You cut yourself," one of the cops said.

Eric touched a hand to his forehead and stared at the blood on his fingers. "Must've banged it on something. Like I said, I was stumbling around in the dark. Trying not to wake my wife by turning on the lights."

"You mind if we take a look around?"

"That's not necessary. Like I said—"

"Yes. Please," Julie said. "Look around. The back door's that way." She pointed through the kitchen.

Eric shot her a heated look as the officers made their way to the mudroom. "I told you not to call," he whispered.

"Why did you lie?" she whispered back. She looked up at the gash on his forehead. "You're bleeding. He cut you."

He gave a quick shake of his head, a signal to be quiet.

"Looks like somebody did break in," one of the cops called out. "There's a pane smashed in this door here."

"No, that happened during the hurricane," Eric called back. "I haven't gotten around to fixing it yet. That's probably what's made my wife so skittish tonight. Imagining things."

Julie's eyes bulged at him.

"Honestly, Officers," he went on. "There's no trouble here. Well, I broke a vase, so I guess I'm in trouble. Right, honey?" He made that weird chuckling sound again. "Really, really sorry to waste your time."

The two men trooped back into the living room. "If you're sure—"

"Absolutely. All good." Eric stuck out his hand at the first cop. "I'm Eric Hoffman, by the way."

"Dr. Eric Hoffman?" the second cop said, and when Eric nodded, the cop broke into a grin. "Hey, you did my dad's ACL last year. Donald Moody?"

"You're kidding! How's Donald doing? Any trouble with that knee?"

"Nope. It's like new. A miracle, he tells folks."

"Glad to hear it. You tell him I said hi."

"I sure will."

"You wanna have that cut looked at," one of the cops said as Eric showed them to the door, then laughed at himself. "As if I need to tell that to a doctor!"

"I will. Thanks," Eric said, laughing, too, as he opened the door.

Brian Holley stood on the threshold, one hand raised to knock, the other holding up his badge. The two cops snapped to attention. "Detective," they said and stepped out of his way.

"Mrs. Hoffman, you okay?" Brian said while Eric threw a wild questioning look at Julie. "I got a report of an intruder?"

Julie clutched the throw around her shoulders like an old woman's shawl. "We're okay?" She couldn't keep the question out of her voice.

"It's all clear," one of the patrol cops said, and Brian pulled them both into a brief whispered conference on the doorstep before he sent them on their way. He turned back to Julie. "You sure you're okay?"

"Wait a minute." Eric jabbed a finger at Brian. "You're with the County Sheriff's Office, right? We're in the city. So what are you doing here?"

"I was in the vicinity," Brian said. "I thought I'd check it out."

"This isn't your jurisdiction."

"Eric." Julie tried to shush him.

He ignored her. "You got no business—"

Brian cut him off. "Given your close connection to a capital case currently being handled by my office, any police activity here is my business."

Eric ignored that, too. "You were here the other week," he said hotly. "Sniffing around my wife!"

"Eric!" Julie stepped in front of him.

He leaned around her, jabbing that finger at Brian. "You keep away from her, you hear me?"

"We're fine, Detective," Julie said, reaching for the door. "But thank you for checking."

Brian eyed Eric as he stepped outside. "You let me know if you need anything," he said to Julie.

She closed the door and turned and stared at Eric. She felt angry and baffled and terrified all at once, but at that moment the aftershocks of terror won out, and she collapsed into his arms. The throw fell to the floor, and they held each other tight, breathing in broken little hitches. "It's okay, you're okay," he murmured into her hair. "You're okay."

That was enough to remind her that he wasn't. She leaned back and looked at his forehead. Serrated lines of blood dripped from the cut. "Here. Sit down."

She pulled him to the couch and ran for the first-aid kit in the mudroom. As she cleaned the wound with antiseptic wipes, he put his hands on her hips, and after she pressed the bandage in place, he pulled her onto his lap and wrapped his arms around her.

"I'm sorry," he said softly.

She wasn't sure what he was apologizing for. "Why did you lie? Somebody did break in."

"I didn't want to get him in trouble."

"You knew him?"

He sighed. "He's the son of a patient. A woman I lost on the table. It was an anesthesiology issue, but the kid doesn't know the difference. He blames me."

"You never mentioned it."

"No, I don't like to talk about it. Especially knowing how hard it hit the son. Poor guy's out of his mind with grief."

"Then you should have told the police. If he's out of his mind—"

"No, I think he scared himself this time. This was the wake-up call he needed. He won't bother us again." He kissed her forehead, then her lips. "I promise."

She let her breath out slowly and nodded. She looked around. "Where's the gun?"

"Oh." He looked around, too. "I didn't want the cops asking questions. I put it in the drawer in the sideboard." He hugged her tighter. "Babe, I'm so sorry about what I said." He pointed his chin up the stairs, and now she knew that was what he was apologizing for—their big blowout. "You know I didn't mean it," he said.

"I know."

"It's not that I care about the money. It's just that you kept it secret from me."

"I'm sorry," she said. "I should have told you. But it wasn't because I thought you married me for an inheritance. I promise I never thought that."

"What, then? Why didn't you tell me?"

She bit her lip. "Because—Eric, I'm so sorry, but you were right. She thought if she left the money to me, you'd end up controlling it. I didn't tell you because I kept hoping you two could get along. I was afraid that would never happen if you knew how hateful she could be."

For a moment he stared at her without speaking. Then he threw his head back and hooted with laughter. "Julie—babe—I knew that the day I met her!"

She didn't know whether to laugh or to cry. Mostly, she just felt relieved. Relieved that they were safe, that the intruder was gone, that their quarrel was over. She let out her own weak laugh.

Eric kissed her again, harder this time, then deeper, then he was laying her out on the sofa and pushing up her sleepshirt. The adrenaline must have still been pumping through his veins, because he was rock-hard when she reached for him, and the fight ended the way their fights always did, in the age-old way their bodies could agree even when they couldn't.

JULIE WOKE WHEN the first fingers of morning light started to creep through the living room windows. They were on the couch, limbs tangled together, naked and sweat-sticky. She worked her arms and legs free and found her T-shirt on the floor and went to the mudroom for a broom and dustpan. She picked up the big shards of crystal from the dining room floor and swept up the smaller bits and dumped it all in the kitchen trash.

When she came back to the dining room, she could see that Eric was still asleep in the living room. She eased open the drawer of the sideboard. The table linens lay crisp and folded inside, the candles tucked in beside them, a punch bowl ladle at the back. No gun.

She looked on the table, under the table, all around the room, then she searched the kitchen, too. The gun was gone.

The intruder—the patient's son, mad with grief, full of blame—he had it now.

CHAPTER 34

Three days later, Brian met Julie in the supermarket parking lot. He wouldn't come to her office anymore because, he said, people would start asking questions, and of course he couldn't come to her house. So they'd been meeting in parking lots like this one.

He pulled his car alongside hers, driver's window to driver's window, like they were both cops conferring behind a highway billboard. He passed over a tall Starbucks cup, and she peeled back the lid and took a sip. Half-caf latte. By now he knew how she took it.

"I can't find any record," Brian said. "If there was any OR death involving your husband, it's been swept under the rug."

"It was the anesthesiologist's fault. Maybe it's indexed under that doctor's name?"

He shook his head. "I can't find it."

She sagged back against the headrest. "That boy's out there looking for revenge. With a gun! And there's nothing we can do about it?"

"You could ask your husband for his name."

She knew what Eric would say: *I told you, I don't like to talk about it.*

Brian hesitated. His next words were tentative. "You think he made it up?"

"No!" She flashed him a look. "Somebody definitely broke in. I heard him!"

"Somebody else, I'm saying. Somebody he doesn't want you or the police to know about."

"Who? Why?"

"Has he been getting any strange calls lately? Keeping any strange hours?"

"He's a doctor," she said. "His hours are always strange." But she was thinking about calls. That flip phone on the kitchen counter that he'd snatched up and pocketed before she could look at it. All the times he'd ducked away to take a call and stood with his back turned, his shoulders hunched, speaking in a low voice. *Maintaining patient privacy,* he said whenever she asked about it.

Her own phone rang at that moment. She glanced at it in its holder on the dash and looked away for a second before her eyes shot back to the screen. "Oh my God," she whispered, as if the caller could hear her even before she answered. "It's Charlie's daughter."

Brian's eyes gleamed with interest. "Put her on speaker. Let's see what she has to say."

Julie couldn't help cringing as she tapped the screen to connect. "Becky?" she said uncertainly.

"Julie. It's Becky. Oh, wait, you knew that. Sorry." The woman let out a nervous giggle before she went on in a rush. "And I am. So sorry, I mean, about your mom, and I'm sorry I waited this long to call you. I didn't know what to say, and I didn't even know if you'd want to hear from me."

"No, Becky. It's fine."

Brian leaned out of his car window, both arms folded on the door. He cocked his head to listen.

"Well, I am just so sorry for your loss. Your mom was so beautiful. And smart. She was a real classy lady, you know?"

"Yes."

"Wait, am I on speaker?"

"Yes, I—I'm in the car."

"Oh, okay. Anyway, I know we only met the once, but I wanted you to know I'm thinking about you, and I'm so sorry for your loss."

"Thank you."

"And I wanted to tell you how much my dad loved her. He never stopped. Even when I was a kid, he used to talk about her. He called her the one who got away. I swear to God, Julie, there's no way he did what they're saying. There's just no frickin' way."

"Um—" Julie looked desperately to Brian, who gave her a nod to keep talking. "Well, it is hard to believe." She was still holding her coffee, and she hurried to put it in the cupholder before she spilled it.

"I hope you don't believe it, is what I'm saying. I think that's what Dad's worrying about most of all. That you'll buy into this."

"You've talked to him?"

"Sure. On the phone, then they let us set up these video calls. He looks absolutely wrecked. And not because he's in jail. Because he lost the love of his life. And like I said, he's worried what you might be thinking."

Brian spread his hands, and Julie took that as a signal to hedge. "I don't know what to think," she said.

"The only injection he ever gave her was in the thigh with that cosmetic stuff. He said you'd know that 'cause you used to do the same."

"Sometimes."

"And that bottle of Everclear? Your mom asked him to buy it when he was up at Parris Island last spring. He thought she was planning to make a batch of limoncello."

"Huh." Julie couldn't imagine her mother ever making her own liqueur.

"So you see, there's an innocent explanation for everything!"

"Uh-huh. Except for the fingerprints."

"Yeah, that's gotta be a lab mix-up. Eric says that happens a lot."

"Eric? My husband?" Julie exclaimed as Brian's eyebrows shot up. "You talked to him?"

"He called me. Didn't he tell you? He wanted me to come down there, but I can't get off work, not without a good excuse, and I don't want to tell my boss—Well, anyway, I can't get off."

"No, he didn't mention . . ." Julie's voice trailed off.

"He's been such a help to Dad. He almost got him that big-time lawyer. But I guess you heard. Dad's only got a public defender now."

"Oh, but they're excellent. They'll give him a first-rate defense." Julie had no idea if that was true.

"Well, I hope so. Losing Kate and then being accused of killing her? I can't imagine anything more awful. It's like those moms whose babies die and the cops decide she musta done it. It's like, hasn't the poor woman suffered enough? You know?"

"Right," Julie said. Brian drew a circle in the air, a signal that she took to mean *wrap it up*. "Anyway, Becky, I have another call. But thank you for calling. I appreciate it."

"Oh. Well, bye."

Julie punched the button to disconnect and flopped back against the headrest. She felt like she'd just run a race. Or, more accurately, walked a tightrope.

"Interesting," Brian said. "What she said about Eric."

She rolled her head to look at him.

"We've been looking into Mull's finances, including his sales records at the car dealership. That car your husband's driving. You know who bought it?"

She sat up, squinting. "He did. I told you. That's how he met Charlie."

"Nope. The car was purchased by a company called PLE, LLC. Cash purchase of two hundred and thirty-five thousand. Then the title was assigned to Eric for a dollar."

"PLE?"

"It's a shell owned by a chain of other shells that ends in the Caymans."

"No—"

"Only verifiable human in the whole thing is one of the incorporators. Charles Mull."

"Charlie?" She shook her head in confusion. "What are you saying?"

Brian shrugged. "We need to drill down some more. But it looks like Mull set up a dummy company to buy the car. Then he gave it to Eric."

"For a *dollar*?"

"Maybe for his help in getting at your mom's money."

Julie shook her head again, but this time in firm denial. "No. There's gotta be some tax reason for setting it up that way. Eric must have funneled the purchase price through the LLC, and Charlie helped him set it up. It might be a tax dodge, but that's all."

"Maybe so." Brian started his engine. "Windowpane okay in your back door?"

"Yes—" Then she realized. "Brian! Was that you?" It had been fixed by the time she got home the day after the break-in. She'd assumed Eric had called someone. He must have assumed that she had. "You didn't need to do that!"

"Patrol division's doing nighttime drive-bys, but I'd feel better if you got a security system."

"Brian." She didn't know what to say. "Thank you. Thank you so much. For everything."

JULIE DROVE TO the office and rode the elevator to the penthouse. She'd taken to working out of her mother's office from time to time. It was quieter up there, and she could avoid all the furtive glances from well-meaning coworkers watching to see how she was holding up. She didn't want her emotions to be on display for them any more than for the photographers outside. Up here she could work alone.

Except that a man was waiting there when she stepped off the elevator. He rose to his feet as she lurched to a stop. He wore a dark suit with a white shirt and blue tie; his face was clean-shaven and his hair neatly combed. It took a moment for her to recognize him. "Tad Ainsworth?" she blurted.

"Sorry. Your receptionist said I should wait here."

That would be Amy, with whom he'd flirted so shamelessly on his last visit. Successfully, it seemed.

"I'm sorry to barge in like this," he said. "I came straight from court." That explained the disguise he was wearing and the briefcase he was carrying. "Is this a bad time?"

She brushed past him. "A bad time, and in very bad taste if you're here to hit me up for two million dollars again." She kept walking.

"No. I wouldn't do—Julie, I'm here about Charlie Mull."

She spun around in astonishment. "What do you have to do with Charlie Mull?"

"I've just been appointed by Judge Shoemaker to represent him."

That astonished her even more. "No, the public defender—"

"Recused himself."

"What? Why?"

"Apparently, your mother was a big donor on his last electoral campaign. He thinks he has a conflict."

That was as astonishing as all the rest. Her mother donated to candidates who could be of use to her. She had no use for the public defender.

"But I'll recuse myself, too," Tad said. "If that's what you want. That's why I'm here. To see how you feel about it."

She didn't know how she felt, beyond wildly confused. "You're not even a criminal defense lawyer."

"I do my share. I'm on the roster for court appointments." He shrugged. "Anything to pay the bills."

She didn't know what to say. What to think. A pair of chairs stood outside her mother's office, and she sank into one of them.

Tad's face changed. "God, Julie, I'm sorry." He took a step toward her. "I didn't even offer you my condolences. I'm really sorry."

She nodded mutely.

"And I hope you know—when I called her an SOB? That was just political posturing. I didn't mean it."

She wasn't following. SOB? Then she remembered. He wanted to call his foundation Save Our Bay, SOB, but that was who he was fighting against. A weak laugh escaped her, and she waved at the other chair. He perched on it, his briefcase at his feet.

"What did you tell Judge Shoemaker?" she asked.

"That I needed to run my own conflicts. He gave me an hour. That's why I showed up like this."

"Why would I be a conflict?"

"Because we were colleagues once—"

She scoffed. "For two weeks back in law school."

"And because we're friends now."

"Us? Friends?"

"Well, sure. I mean, we rescued that baby together—"

"Hey!" she said with put-on indignation. "I rescued that baby."

He leaned toward her with an earnest look on his face. "I know you're dealing with a lot right now, and I won't take the case if it makes things any harder for you. Whatever we are to each other."

She gazed at him a moment. "You don't even specialize in criminal defense. This could be a death penalty case."

"I have a plan for that. I'll handle all the preliminaries and gather all the evidence. Then I'll package the case and shop it around to some A-list defense lawyers. Get somebody to take it on pro bono."

"You really think that'll work?"

"Oh, I can be pretty persuasive."

She knew that was true when it came to twenty-two-year-old receptionists. She wasn't so sure otherwise. But it was hardly her job to ensure that her mother's murderer had competent counsel. She stood. "Go ahead," she said. "Tell the judge you'll take the case." She held out her hand as he stood, too. "And I wish you bad luck with it."

He laughed and shook his head as he shook her hand.

CHAPTER 35

Julie spoke to Luisa a few times that week and was struck by how anxious she sounded. It wasn't like Luisa to worry about anything. She'd always managed the household and every crisis that arose in it with unflappable calm and quiet efficiency. Now she seemed to fret over every minor task. Should she cancel the pool cleaner? The police had damaged the pantry door and some dresser drawers during their search; should she have them repaired? A week ago, she would have made those decisions on her own. Now she was asking Julie.

So when she asked Julie to please come to lunch on Sunday, Julie steeled herself and said yes.

Eric had a tennis match Sunday morning, and as soon as he left for the club, Julie got in her car and headed for Cascara Key.

It had been a week since she'd last made this trip—less than a week—but it felt like a lifetime. It was as if Kate had the power to stop time, but now that she was gone, time was rushing to catch up, playing like a hyperspeed video. The whole landscape of the universe seemed altered, and it was almost a surprise to find the bridge to the island exactly where it always was, the narrow road the same, and La Coquina itself completely unchanged except for the fallen palm tree, now cut up and hauled away.

Julie parked in the drive and crossed the courtyard. This was where the wedding guests had dined and danced that night and where Charlie had made his confession of abiding love. His first confession that night, and all of it a ruse.

The front door was locked. She was about to ring the bell when she heard *"Hola!"* and saw Ferdy beckoning to her from the far side of the house. She followed him there and around to the back door, where Luisa was waiting. "We use only the kitchen," she explained as Julie came in and gave her a hug.

"Did the police tell you that? To stay out of the rest of the house?"

"No, but—" She spread her hands. "Who could we ask?"

Julie could see her dilemma. It wasn't Kate's house anymore, and it wasn't Charlie's yet, or ever. Luisa and Ferdy must have felt like they were living in limbo-land.

Luisa had made fish tacos for lunch, and they each topped them the way they liked and carried their plates outside to the terrace. A breeze was blowing across the bay, and the water was lapping softly against the pilings of the dock. But the end of the dock looked eerily empty. The *Half-shell* was in the impound lot at the police marina. Also still in limbo.

Luisa and Ferdy wanted to know about the funeral arrangements, and Julie explained about the medical examiner and the postmortem and the weeks-long delay until the body could be released. They wanted to know about Charlie next, and Julie explained what she could—the charges, his plea, his court-appointed counsel.

"And the court trial—when is that?"

"No date's been set yet, but it's months away. Probably a year."

Luisa's eyes went wide. "So long!" She said something to Ferdy in Spanish, and he nodded grimly as he ate.

Luisa hadn't eaten at all, though she held a fork in her hand and moved the shredded cabbage from side to side on her plate. She looked out over the bay, then over at Julie, then away again before she spoke. "It is really true? That he did this thing? For certain?"

"Only the jury can say," Julie said. "But the evidence is irrefutable."

That was a word Ferdy didn't know, and when he looked to his wife for a translation, Julie hurried to amend. "Undeniable. Overwhelming. He had a clear motive and an obvious opportunity. And the means. The alcohol. The needle."

Luisa dropped her fork with a clatter against the glass-topped table.

"And apparently," Julie added in a lower voice, "he had some financial shenanigans going on."

Ferdy looked to Luisa again for a translation, but her gaze was somewhere else.

"Fraud," Julie supplied.

"Ah." He reached for his wife's hand and gave it a squeeze, and after a moment she picked up her fork and started to eat.

Julie helped clear the dishes to the kitchen, and after Luisa shooed her away from the sink, she ventured out into the main part of the house and did a full circuit of the first floor. Earlier, Luisa had described the mess the police had left it in after their search, but there was no sign of any disarray now. Luisa had restored everything to the way it should be.

Down here, at least. Julie stopped at the foot of the stairs and slowly moved her gaze upward, step by step. Her feet followed even more slowly, and she gripped the banister like a child learning to walk until she reached the second-floor landing. The door to her mother's bedroom was closed, just as it had been last Sunday morning. Julie put her hand on the knob and took a big breath. She swung the door in.

This room was also in perfect order, and after a moment she realized that she was, too. Her pulse wasn't racing, she wasn't struggling to breathe. She was standing upright with not even a hand on the doorjamb to steady her.

She closed her eyes just to be sure, but the nightmare reel didn't play. She didn't see her father's shoes pointing upward. She didn't see her mother's arm trailing off the bed. She didn't feel like her mind was trying to burrow down into her belly. None of those old feelings were there. All she felt was what she should feel. Sadness and loss.

She walked deeper into the room, the newly redecorated room in a color the designer might have called putty or linen or smoke but was obviously khaki. A palette Kate must have selected to please her old soldier/new husband. One of the many things she'd done to please him. She had turned her life upside down and inside out for him, this boy from her youth come back to her. Her hero. Her killer.

Suddenly, Julie felt something more than sadness and loss. She felt hate. She hated Charlie with a heat she'd never felt. He'd killed her mother's body, that was certain, but even before that, he'd killed her soul. That night in the bridal suite in Tampa when Kate had learned that his confession couldn't be true, when she'd realized who he was and what he was after, her spirit had died that night. Those long drifting beach walks in her pale linen tunics? That wasn't the Madwoman of Cascara Key. That was the ghost of Kate Sawyer.

He'd killed something in Julie, too. She'd laughed at his jokes and craved his affection. Beamed at his praise and encouragement. Imagined she loved him. It was exactly as Kate said: Charlie knew that was the way to get to her. Poor little Julie, so starved for fatherly attention. She'd been such an easy mark. He'd killed that part of her, and she was glad of it. She'd never be anyone's easy mark again.

When she returned to the kitchen, Luisa and Ferdy were sitting at the table with their hands clasped and their foreheads touching. They broke apart when she came in. She laughed and was about to make some lame joke, like *Get a room,* when she saw Luisa frantically wiping tears from her face.

"What? What's wrong?"

Neither one answered her. A folded newspaper lay on the table between them, and when Julie came closer, she saw the page turned to the classified ads, with inked circles around some of the ads. Job listings on one side. Apartments for rent on the other.

She felt a sick jolt as she realized: Luisa and Ferdy had held the same jobs for twenty-five years, and lived in the homes that went with them. That life had ended with Kate's. Now they thought they were not only unemployed but homeless.

"Oh my God," Julie said, and sat down with a hard thump in a chair beside them. "Mom didn't tell you? About her will?" Their blank faces told her they had no idea what she was talking about. "Oh my God," she said again. "Mom provided for you in her will. She left you the conch house down in Key West—she remembered you had family down there—and cash of two hundred and fifty thousand dollars."

Their faces remained blank. They didn't seem to understand or believe her, so she said it again. "The Key West house—you remember, you've been there—that's going to be yours, along with a quarter of a million dollars. I know that might not be enough to retire on, but maybe you can pick up some part-time work down there. Or you can sell the house and invest the money. Whatever you want."

Ferdy did a slow blink and turned to Luisa, who was shaking her head in wonderment. "I cannot believe it," she said. "She did this for us?"

"She loved you." Julie gave an apologetic shrug. "In her way."

Luisa was still shaking her head, but she turned to Ferdy and repeated everything in Spanish. He blinked more rapidly as he listened. Then he turned to Julie and spoke one of the few sentences he'd ever spoken to her in English. "This is true?"

She smiled. "This is true."

They exploded into laughter and tears and hugs, and Julie left them to celebrate in private.

It occurred to her that she was going to lose the beach access she'd enjoyed all the years since her mother had built La Coquina. The house would soon belong to the Harvard Radcliffe Institute, whose trustees would probably sell it to some billionaire hedge fund manager. She decided to go for one last ocean swim while she could.

She changed into her suit and went out to the beach. The waters in the Gulf were a pale shimmering turquoise, so clear she could watch her toes sparkle against the sea floor as she waded deeper and deeper until she finally closed her eyes and plunged in.

CHAPTER 36

It was after six by the time Julie crossed the bridge back to the mainland. She didn't have anything prepared for dinner, and Eric hadn't suggested going out, so she stopped downtown for some Thai takeout before driving home.

She was surprised to see Alex's car parked at the curb in front of the house. She pulled into the driveway, and the moment she stepped out of her own car, she could smell meat grilling in the backyard. Apparently, Eric had invited Greta and Alex to a cookout.

Julie went in the front door and through to the kitchen to put the takeout bag in the refrigerator, then she went upstairs to change and to comb out her beach-blown hair. The guest room window overlooked the patio, and she went there first to see what Greta was wearing so she could decide what to wear herself.

The window was open, and Julie had a clear view of the gathering. Eric was flipping burgers at the grill, and Greta was tucked up against Alex on the love seat. She was dressed casually, in capris and a golf shirt.

"It's like she's turned into a different person," Eric was saying to them. "Arguing over every little thing. Contradicting everything I say. I don't even know who she is anymore."

Julie caught her breath and shrank back behind the curtain.

"Give her a break," Greta was saying. "She just lost her mother. She's in trauma. Again. She should be back in therapy. At a minimum, she should be resting at home. Not going to the office every day like nothing happened."

Alex cleared his throat. "One of my patients told me she gave a speech to the whole office on Monday. It was supposed to be a memorial, I guess, but it ended up sounding like a campaign speech. Like she's gunning to take over the company."

"See?" Eric said. "It's like she had a personality transplant the minute her mother died."

"This is all classic avoidance behavior," Greta said. "She was never able to process her father's death, and now, with her mother's? She might be heading for an actual breakdown. Seriously, Eric, you need to get her into treatment."

"She won't go."

"You need to persuade her."

"I'm telling you, she's not that girl anymore. She fights me on everything."

"Well—" Greta hesitated. "You could petition for a temporary guardianship and get her into a residential program."

"Temporary? That's a thing?"

"You'd make all the decisions for her until she's herself again."

"Huh."

"Those burgers about done?" Alex said.

Julie backed away from the window and sat down on the edge of the bed and waited for her heart to slow. Eric was actually considering it. She'd heard it in his voice, in that thoughtful *huh*. That one syllable told her everything he was thinking. It was the way he sounded every time an exciting new idea came to him. He could petition one of his sister's colleagues on the bench to name him the temporary guardian of Julie's affairs. Once he was appointed guardian, he could sign the mortgage papers on her behalf. He wouldn't need her consent anymore. And that wasn't the end of it. Acting as court-appointed guardian of Kate's only natural heir, he'd have standing to contest the will. If the will were set aside, Julie would end up with nearly everything. Which Eric would then control.

It was her mother's worst fear realized.

Julie tried to tell herself she was being paranoid. This was her mother's conspiracy mongering at work. Eric, Greta, and Alex couldn't really be scheming to get the money. Greta was simply sounding her old alarms about Julie's mental health, and Eric was intrigued by the idea of a temporary guardianship. It was probably nothing more than that. It didn't mean he'd ever go through with it.

Still.

Julie changed and crept down the stairs and outside to her car.

A minute later, she tiptoed back and snagged the takeout bag from the refrigerator.

THERE WERE NO security guards at the office on a Sunday night, but no press, either, and she was able to enter the garage without incident. She took the elevator up to her floor, and the doors opened on darkness. No one was at work, not at this hour on a weekend. The entire floor was eerily quiet.

She made her way to her office without switching on the lights and lowered the blinds before she turned on the tiny lamp at her desk. No one watching the building would be able to track that she was at work.

She was being paranoid again, but she kept thinking about Alex's comment that she was gunning for her mother's job. A patient had told him, he'd said. *Who?* she wondered. Her email to the company's business partners had gone out over Jack Trotter's signature, so it couldn't have been an outsider who was spreading that rumor. It had to be a KS employee, someone who'd attended Monday's meeting in the auditorium.

It could have been Jack himself. She remembered the unsettled look on his face when she left the lectern after her speech. Maybe he was worried that she was going to supplant him in the company hierarchy. Maybe he was worried that she might even oust him. He didn't know yet that she wouldn't be inheriting the business. He didn't know that even her own mother assumed she'd lose her job after Harvard took ownership.

As she ate the pad Thai cold at her desk, she had a crazy thought. No, not crazy. She wasn't crazy, no matter what Greta might think. A fanciful thought, perhaps. Why not make the most of whatever time she had left at KS and confound Jack and everyone else at the same time?

She went to the supply room for some empty boxes and packed up the contents of her desk, her credenza, and most of her bookshelves. Five elevator trips later, Kate's penthouse office suite was now Julie's. Tomorrow morning she'd have her assistant move up to the secretarial station outside the door. Everyone would assume it was official—that Julie was the heir apparent to her mother's empire.

It would be the worst kind of nepotism. She'd done nothing to deserve it, and everyone would be entitled to resent her for it. Soon enough they'd know it was a lie, but in the meantime she'd spend a few weeks thinking about the possibilities. What she might have done with this company if given the chance. Despite what she'd said in her speech, she wouldn't want to follow the trail blazed by Kate. She'd want to chart some course of her own. Take the company in a whole new direction. She leaned way back in her mother's chair and let a dozen different ideas unfold in her mind.

Abruptly, she shook her head and sat up straight again. These were ridiculous thoughts for her to be entertaining. It was almost as if Eric were right that she'd had a personality transplant.

Which made her thoughts circle back, inevitably, to Greta's suggestion of guardianship and Eric's too revealing *Huh*.

She was being paranoid again, she realized. She had to be on guard against bizarre conspiracy theories. Such as Brian Holley's theory that Charlie had given Eric that car in exchange for Eric's help in his scheme. From now on Julie would deal in facts only.

There was one fact that ought to be easy enough to determine. Whether and how much Eric paid for the car.

She connected her laptop to her mother's monitors and logged into her joint checking account with Eric. She went to the Bill Pay page and looked for automatic payments to VIP Motorcars of Tampa, but there weren't any. They seldom wrote paper checks anymore, but that must have been how Eric made his monthly payments. She switched to the page listing checks paid out of the account. Again, nothing to VIP Motorcars. Some other company could have made the car loan, so next she searched for any regular monthly payments to a name she didn't already know. There weren't any.

She stared at the account page, mystified. Eric couldn't have paid the full purchase price for the car. They didn't have that kind of cash. He made good money, excellent money, but whatever savings they didn't spend on their house, he spent on his office furnishings and equipment. There was almost nothing in reserve. She'd never questioned him about how he was paying for the Lamborghini; she'd simply assumed that he'd been willing to put aside his aversion to debt where his dream car was concerned. But if he had a car loan, he wasn't making any payments on it, at least not out of this account.

She logged into their savings account next and looked for a big disbursement during the month he'd bought the car. Nothing. Then during the month before and the month after. Again nothing.

Eric had a separate business account for his practice. He must be making the monthly payments out of that account. The taxman would have something to say about that, but as long as Eric repaid it from their personal account, it ought to be okay.

But she couldn't find any money flowing from their personal accounts to his business account. And there was no reduction in the regular monthly amounts he transferred from his business account to their personal account.

She hesitated. She'd never logged into his business account. There was never any reason to. But she clicked on it now and tried the same username and passcode they used for their personal accounts. She held her breath.

The page opened.

She leaned close and scrolled through pages of payroll records and vendor payments and insurance receipts. But she found nothing that could have been a disguised payment for a Lamborghini, not a lump sum, not a down payment, not monthly installments.

She couldn't escape the obvious any longer. Eric hadn't paid for that car. Someone or something had given him a car priced at a quarter of a million dollars.

The only remaining question was what he'd given them in return.

JULIE WENT TO work on Monday morning in a fog. There were fires to put out, a labor action in Fort Lauderdale, a major tenant default in Orlando. There were calls she had to take, which led to calls she had to make, but through it all, the questions dogged her: *Why did someone give Eric that car, and what did he have to do for it?*

She'd worried she was being paranoid when she imagined that he was trying to take control of her mother's money. But it was a whole different level of paranoia to imagine that he'd conspired to kill Kate. It was impossible to imagine. He hated Kate, he always had, but he wouldn't—not for a car, even a car worth that much.

But for all of Kate's wealth? Until recently, he'd believed Julie stood to inherit everything. Was the car nothing but a down payment toward the real fortune?

She couldn't believe she was thinking these thoughts. She must be losing her mind.

It was a moment before she noticed that the intercom line was buzzing on her phone. She pressed the button to answer.

"Julie?" her assistant said. "Franklin Foster's on line one."

"Who?"

"Franklin Foster. He said he's your mother's lawyer?"

"Oh. Right." He was Lenore Greggson's partner, the estate lawyer. Julie connected the call.

"Julie. First off, my deepest condolences."

She wondered how many times he had to speak those words in the course of a workweek. "Thank you, Frank," she said dully.

"I realize there's no death certificate, not until the ME signs off. So the will can't be probated yet. But I think we should meet anyway to discuss the terms of your mother's will. There're things you need to know."

"Oh, I already know the terms, Frank. In fact, I have a copy."

"She executed a new will."

"Yes, I know. Right before the wedding."

"No," he said. "Two weeks ago."

CHAPTER 37

The meeting was set for Wednesday morning in the offices of Foster & Greggson and would include what Foster called *all interested parties.*

Luisa called Julie in a panic Monday afternoon. She and Ferdy had received the same invitation and didn't know what it could mean. They were afraid they were being evicted from their garage apartment at La Coquina.

"No, no, nothing like that," Julie tried to assure her. "It's just to explain how Mom left her property."

"Oh! You mean to explain how she left us the conch house?"

"Yes," Julie said, and prayed that the new will hadn't removed that bequest. It would devastate Luisa and Ferdy to think they were getting that property only to have it snatched away. She never should have told them the provisions of the earlier will. She should have known that nothing was ever final until probate.

But she still couldn't believe it. Why would Kate execute a new will a mere three weeks after the last one? It couldn't have anything to do with her suspicions about Charlie, because his inheritance was already set by the terms of the prenup. Under Florida law, a will couldn't contradict the terms of a prenup.

Late in the afternoon Jack Trotter came up to the penthouse to tell Julie that he'd been invited to the meeting, too, and to ask if she knew why. She didn't. He wasn't named in any of her mother's earlier wills. But he was a valuable employee, and it would be nice if Kate had remembered him in this newest one.

The bigger surprise awaited Julie at home that night. She was pulling a head of lettuce from the refrigerator when Eric came in the back door, smacked her on the lips, and said, "You'll never guess who called me today. Franklin Foster."

She nearly bobbled the lettuce. "Why?"

"To invite me to that meeting you were probably going to tell me about tonight. About Kate's new will."

"I was, but I mean, why you?"

"Apparently, I'm an interested party." He winked. "Wouldn't it be something if she secretly loved me and left me everything?" He laughed all the way upstairs.

ERIC CANCELED HIS Wednesday-morning appointments, and they drove there, largely in silence. He'd stopped asking what she knew, and she'd stopped telling him, *Nothing*. "Well, at least we know it won't be bad news," he'd said finally. "Because she couldn't treat you any worse than she did in the last will."

Foster & Greggson was a boutique firm specializing in what Julie liked to call actual human law—marriage, divorce, adoption, death—as opposed to the business law she did, which was only about money. Not that human law wasn't usually about money, too. Today, for instance.

The firm occupied its own building just off Main Street downtown, a two-story art deco structure with dedicated parking spaces out front. Eric drove past Ferdy's truck and Jack Trotter's Mercedes and parked the way he always parked the Lamborghini, straddling the line so that it took up two spaces. A bicycle was chained to the lamppost in front of the building. They walked past it and into the lobby.

Foster's assistant was there to greet them. The staircase was right in front of them, but she rang for the elevator and ushered them inside, and they rode up one floor. She led them down the corridor to a set of double doors that opened on a large conference room. Franklin Foster stood up from the head of the table. He was all in gray—hair, suit, and foulard tie. Even his face had a grayish cast. "Julie. And you must be Eric? Come in. Have a seat." He waved to the two vacant seats to his right.

Julie sat down beside him and looked at the others around the table. Jack, across from her, gave her a nod. Luisa and Ferdy looked overwhelmed, like they were trying to shrink into their chairs, and she gave them a little smile of encouragement. Beside them at the foot of the table was Foster's partner, Lenore Greggson. She looked coolly professional, as always, in a dark suit and pearls.

Someone else sat beside her, on the other side of Eric. Julie rolled her chair back to see who it was. Her jaw dropped.

Tad Ainsworth caught her eye and gave a bewildered shrug, as if to say he didn't have a clue why he was there, either.

"Let's begin, shall we?" Foster said. He introduced everyone around the table by name and explained that Lenore was sitting in because of her involvement in the prenuptial agreement signed by Mr. and Mrs. Mull. He then spoke solemnly and at length about how it was his privilege to represent Mrs. Mull and how tragic her death was.

Mrs. Mull? It rankled Julie every time he said it. Kate would hate to be called that now. Julie hated to hear her called that. But the mention of the name made her wonder if it was why Tad had been included in this meeting. He was Charlie's lawyer. But he'd been appointed only to represent him in the criminal case; he wasn't his lawyer for all purposes. It didn't make any sense.

Now Foster was talking about Mrs. Mull's recent decision to make a new will and her visit to the office two weeks ago to sign it in the presence of witnesses. "I can assure you," he said, "that all the formalities of execution were observed."

He then explained that the will couldn't be probated until the resolution of certain other matters. Julie supposed it would be in bad taste to say *Until her corpse is sliced open and her organs removed and weighed and examined under a microscope.* The image made her shudder. She shook her head to shut it out and turned her attention back to Foster.

"Nonetheless," he was saying, "there are certain provisions, certain conditions, that are, let us say, unusual, and as to which some of you may wish to seek your own counsel." He looked directly at Julie as he said that. "That's why I asked all of—"

"What provisions and conditions?" Eric cut in.

Foster breathed in sharply through his nostrils, obviously perturbed at the interruption. "My secretary will give you each a copy as you leave here today. Meanwhile, let me summarize the salient points.

"First," he began. "She names as her executor Mr. John Trotter."

He nodded at Jack, who looked pleasantly surprised. Julie was surprised, too. Kate's earlier wills had named her bank's trust department as executor.

"The will gives Mr. Trotter full powers and authorizes him to receive the full statutory commission." Foster looked pointedly at Jack. "For estates this size, that's one point five percent."

Julie was doing the math in her head, and she could see by the look on his face that Jack, a numbers guy, had gotten there first. He looked like he'd been struck by a two-by-four. He'd be getting almost an eight-figure commission. He'd be a millionaire many times over.

"But there's a condition," Foster told him. "You can be sworn in as executor only after you resign your position at KS Development."

Jack was still seeing stars and didn't react, but Julie was flummoxed. Jack was important to the successful management of the company. Critical now that Kate was gone. "Why would she ever want that?" she asked.

Foster shook his head as if to say *ours is not to question why.* "Next we have a specific bequest to her widower, Charles Francis Mull. He is to receive the title to a vessel known as the *Half-shell,* registration number provided, et cetera, and that certain real property located on the northern end of Cascara Key in Sarasota County known as La Coquina, legal description provided, et cetera, together with all furnishings and fixtures and appurtenances. My partner, Mrs. Greggson, will speak to this matter."

Lenore sat up straighter in her chair at the foot of the table. "The bequest to Mr. Mull complies with what the parties agreed to in their prenuptial contract. It's my view that the prenup and this provision of the will are fully enforceable as written." She sat back and folded her hands. Her part in the show was done.

"With one caveat," Foster said, holding up a forefinger. "As I believe we all know, Mr. Mull has been charged with the homicide of Mrs. Mull. If he is in fact found to have unlawfully and intentionally killed the decedent, then Florida law bars him from receiving anything from the decedent's estate."

That Florida law was the Slayer's Act, Julie recalled.

"If he's convicted, you mean," Eric said.

"He may wish to seek his own counsel on that point," Foster said. "But my understanding of the law is that a conviction isn't necessarily required. If it can be proved by a preponderance of the evidence, by anyone, that he killed her, then he would not be entitled to receive."

He didn't look at Tad Ainsworth for that point, but Julie realized that had to be the reason Tad was included here today: so that he could advise Charlie on the application of the Slayer's Act.

"Moving on," Foster said. "The next specific bequest. To Mr. and Mrs. Barrera." He nodded at Luisa and Ferdy. "Namely, the sum of two hundred and fifty thousand dollars, plus certain real estate located in Key West, Florida, together with all furniture, fixtures, and appurtenances."

Julie's eyes closed in relief that her mother hadn't cut them out. Across the table, Ferdy was looking a little confused by *appurtenances* but Luisa whispered something to him, her eyes shining, and his face split wide in a grin.

"And then the final point," Foster said. "The entire residual estate, after payment of all taxes, liabilities, commissions, and specific bequests, goes to Mrs. Mull's daughter, Julie Sawyer Hoffman."

She gaped at him. Beside her, Eric made a startled sound like a hiccup and squeezed her hand hard under the table. She barely felt it. "I don't—that can't—I don't understand. She was leaving it all to Harvard. She always said so."

"Julie, babe." Eric took her by the chin and turned her face to his. "She changed her mind." His eyes shone into hers. "She remembered how much she loved you and how much you deserve this."

Foster cleared his throat. "The residual estate, as I'm sure you know, consists of all the other real property, including the apartment in New York and the cottage in Bar Harbor. The Cascara Key house, too, if it comes to that. Along with all her personal effects, jewelry, et cetera. Her investment portfolio. And all the shares of KS Development, Inc."

Julie was shaking her head. "I don't understand. She didn't—she always told me—"

"She changed her mind," Eric said again. "She saw sense."

"There is a condition."

All eyes turned back to Foster.

He hesitated. "This is the principal reason I asked you here today. This is a point on which you may wish to seek your own legal advice. Courts have routinely struck down these kinds of conditions. Trying to control one's heirs from beyond the grave is generally frowned upon, especially in matters like this. I so advised Mrs. Mull, but of course, she was entitled to provide any condition she so wished. Just as you may be entitled to challenge that condition."

"What is it?" Eric demanded. "What's the condition?"

Foster looked even more somber as he turned his gaze upon them. "That Julie be divorced from you."

Somebody gasped, and there was a moment of utter silence in the room before Eric slammed his fist down on the table. "Bullshit!" he shouted. "She can't do that!"

Foster spread his hands. "As I said, the courts frown upon it—"

"You're damn right we're going to contest it!"

"Eric, please. Not now." Julie felt numb all over. She was shocked, yet at the same time it all made sense to her. This was the only way Kate would ever leave her fortune to Julie—if Eric were out of the picture.

"In that regard," Foster said, "the will goes on to provide that if that condition should be invalidated for any reason, then the entire residual estate goes to a nonprofit corporation known as Save Our Shores, Inc. Represented here today by, I believe, its president? Mr. Ainsworth."

Now Julie understood why Tad was here. She didn't look at him, she couldn't move, but she could hear him take in a sharp breath. At the same time, she was hearing an echo of her mother's voice: *Promise me. You have to promise me you'd never give him any money.* This was Kate's failsafe. Her way of guaranteeing that Julie would have to divorce Eric.

"This is all bullshit," Eric said. "We'll contest that condition. We'll contest the whole fucking will!"

Foster blanched at the language, but he pulled himself up and soldiered on. "Two points in that regard. First, Julie is the only one who can contest it. As the only natural heir, she alone has standing."

"But it's my—"

"Second," Foster cut Eric off. He wasn't countenancing any more interruptions. "If this will is invalidated on whatever grounds, it would restore the prior will. Which leaves the entire residue to the Harvard Radcliffe Institute."

Eric stared at Foster in horror before he collapsed back in his chair. "She's fucked us," he said. "She's totally fucked us."

At the other end of the table, Lenore Greggson rose and, as unobtrusively as possible, exited the room. Tad Ainsworth was practically on her heels as he left. Luisa and Ferdy looked at each other, then at Julie. Luisa mouthed the question, *Can we go?*

Julie nodded, and they hurried out of the room, too.

"One question," Jack Trotter said, rising to his feet. "The earlier will, am I named as executor in that one, too?"

"No, that would be Sterling Bank and Trust."

"I see." He looked at Julie, gave a weak little shrug, and left the room.

The three of them sat alone at the table. Eric slumped low, his jaw working furiously; Julie beside him, biting her lip, nails digging into her palms; Foster steepling his hands as he regarded the two of them. After a moment he pushed his chair back and got to his feet. "Julie, if I might have a private word?"

Eric came to life at that. "Anything you have to say, you can say to both of us."

Julie thought, *Hey, that's supposed to be my line.* And maybe she would have actually spoken it if he hadn't preempted her. "No," she said as she stood. "You wait here."

Eric looked up at her with an expression torn between betrayal and outrage. She turned away. Foster was holding the door open for her. His assistant stood outside, handing out copies of the will. Julie took one and followed Foster down the hall to his office. He closed the door and went to his desk but didn't bother sitting down. He opened a drawer and took out a small flip box covered in blue velvet. "Your mother asked me to give this to you in private in the event of her death." He handed it to her.

Julie opened it expecting an heirloom ring, her grandmother's wedding band, perhaps. Instead it held a thumb drive. She looked up at him.

"It's a video, I believe," he said.

"Have you watched it?"

"No. Nor have I copied it to any of my devices. She was quite emphatic that it was for your eyes only."

Julie closed the lid and tucked the box into her handbag.

He walked her to the door. "I know this new will comes as a surprise to you. And as I stated, there are issues. But let me say this much: I think your mother knew what she wanted."

"She always did," Julie said.

She made her way back to the conference room. Eric would demand to know what that private meeting was all about, and she was thinking about what to tell him when he burst out of the room. In the five minutes they'd been apart, his demeanor had completely changed. He looked almost exultant as he grabbed her hand and reeled her in for a kiss. "What?" she said.

"Wait till we get to the car."

Outside, Jack's Mercedes and Ferdy's truck were already gone. So was the bicycle that she now knew was Tad's. The Lamborghini stood alone, a hot orange flame glowing in the late-morning sun. Eric opened the passenger door for Julie, unusual chivalry, and trotted around to jump in behind the wheel.

"What?" she said again.

He let out his breath in a long, satisfied sigh. "She tried to screw us over. She thought she fenced us in." He leaned over and kissed her again. "But we're getting the last laugh. We're going to screw her over!"

"What are you talking about?"

"We're going to get divorced. Then, as soon as the estate's settled and all the money's yours, we'll get married again." He started the engine and stomped on the gas a couple times just to hear it roar. "Simple as that!"

Julie's head whipped back as he peeled off down the street.

CHAPTER 38

Julie started to cry the moment her mother's face flickered to life on the screen.

She hadn't expected to, not while she was still seething over Kate's conniving manipulation, her high-handed power grab, her need to control everything even from the grave. But when her face appeared on the computer screen, larger than life, a force of nature in this unnatural moment, Julie couldn't stop the tears from falling.

"Hello, Julie," Kate said as the image sputtered and resolved. "Darling Duo. If you're watching this, I must be dead. But don't I look mahvelous?" She brought her palms up to frame her face like a child posing in an old Sears portrait studio.

In fact, she didn't look marvelous at all. She looked tired, though that could have been the poor lighting and camera angle. It was obvious she'd shot the video on her phone. She could have hired a professional videographer—she could have hired a Hollywood director to film this if she'd wanted—but no, she'd done it herself with her cell phone on a makeshift tripod. It was mounted too low: Julie was seeing too much of her nostrils—or, rather, nostril. One side of her face was in shadow. Kate must have filmed it in the early morning, when the sun was streaming in the east-facing windows of her office at La Coquina. The right side of her face was overlit; the left side was dark.

Julie was watching the video on her mother's computer monitor in the penthouse office at KS. Eric had rounds at the hospital, so he'd dropped her off at the house after they left Foster's office. *We'll celebrate tonight,* he'd told her with a wink and a grin. As soon as he was out of sight, she'd gotten in her car and come here.

"You're probably wondering about the latest changes to my will," Kate said from the screen.

Wondering? Try furious, Julie thought, and wiped away her tears.

"So let me explain. Harvard doesn't need my money. They have the world's largest endowment, and at the same time they're charging those kids seventy-five thousand dollars a year to go there. What do they need my money for?

"And then I started to think about what they'd do with the company. They'd hire some MBA who'd make the most conservative, stodgy decisions imaginable. I didn't build my company by being conservative and stodgy. I did it by taking risks. That's the only way to accomplish anything. You have to take risks.

"Darling Duo. I want you to take risks. Be bold.

"That's why I booted Jack Trotter. He's a good man, he's been a steady hand on the till, but let's face it—he's basically a bean counter. He'd fight you every time you tried to do something daring and innovative and exciting. Plus, his male ego probably wouldn't abide having you as his boss. He'd undermine you at every turn, and you don't need that. You've had enough of that in your life.

"So I threw him a bone—a big bone. He'll do a fine job of settling the estate, then he'll take his commission and go off and play golf somewhere, and you won't have to worry about him anymore.

"Okay." Kate sat up a little straighter and took a deep breath. "Here's the part that may rankle a bit. You have to divorce Eric before you get any of this. Because he'd take charge of it all. You know he would. He'd control the company the same way he controls you."

Kate held up a palm. "I know what you're thinking. That I should butt out of your marriage. That I have no right to condition your inheritance on divorce. But here's the thing. You're going to get divorced eventually. You know you are, when the sex starts to fade and he loses that hold on you. So why not go ahead and cut him loose now?

"And here's what else you're thinking. Who am I to talk about Eric holding you down when I've done the same or worse to you your whole life? And maybe that's true. But here's the other thing"—Kate paused, and her face contorted into a strange smile—"I'm dead now, so I can't do it anymore!"

She cackled a laugh. "You're free of me, so be free of him, too. Take over the company. Do amazing things! Be innovative! Be bold! Be dynamic! You have it in you. I know you do.

"One last point: you promised me you'd never give any money to that cute boy at Greenpeace or whatever. Remember? During the hurricane? You promised.

"Okay. That's it. I love you. Make me proud."

Kate's face blurred as she suddenly leaned toward the camera. "Now how do I turn this damn thing—Oh, hello, darling. I was just telling Julie about the new will."

Charlie's voice sounded—"Hey, sweetie! Tell your hubby to call"—before the recording ended.

Julie stared into the void of the blank screen. A heartbeat. That was all it took, the briefest millisecond, for all her anger against her mother to veer in one direction and aim like a heat-seeking missile at Charlie. *Darling. Sweetie.* Her hatred for him burned so hot it boiled and bubbled and steamed until a miasma filled the room. This man who had bamboozled the shrewdest woman on the planet. Who had snuffed out the heart and soul and life of the one and only Kate Sawyer.

Julie's train of thought screeched to a halt. *Wait. Charlie knew about the new will?* Did he tell her *hubby*? That would explain why Eric first proposed to borrow against her inheritance—not because he assumed she'd be getting the money but because he knew she was. His outburst at the lawyer's office—*this is all bullshit*—was that all just theater? So no one would suspect that he already knew the terms of the will? He must have known about the divorce condition. He'd already planned how to get around it.

Julie's mind was churning. The layers were peeling back. Why did Kate change her will? Because Charlie convinced her to? She could hear him say it in his jovial voice. *Harvard doesn't need your money, why not leave it to your sweetheart of a daughter?* Was that the plan all along, his and Eric's? If Charlie failed at gaslighting Kate and making himself her guardian, then change the target to Julie and get Eric appointed as her guardian, with Charlie hovering by for the split.

She could hear her mother's voice, too. *For God's sake, Julie, he knows he could never manipulate me. It's you he's gaslighting.*

Julie. The dupe, the sucker, the easy target.

And it would be so easy to make a convincing case for her incompetence. Simply trigger her PTSD by arranging for a second traumatic discovery. She could hear Charlie's oh-so-casual invitation. *You come over, too, sweetie.* That was the whole reason for the fishing trip. Charlie wasn't fleeing. He was inventing a pretext for Julie to be there alone so that she'd be the one to find her mother's body.

The facts were spinning so fast and wild inside her brain that she could almost feel them battering against her skull. Her head felt like it might explode if she didn't let some of these thoughts out.

But who to talk to? Not Eric. Obviously. And not her best friend, either. Again her mother's voice: *Who brought Charlie back into my life? And who's related to a probate judge and a neurologist?* Greta and Alex might not be part of the conspiracy, but they were certainly Eric's allies.

No, there was only one person she could turn to.

She reached for the phone.

CHAPTER 39

Brian was waiting in the parking lot of the big mall by the interstate. Julie pulled into the space beside his, and this time he got out of his car and into hers.

The words started to spill out of her even before he pulled the door shut. "It's true, what you said. I've been through all the bank accounts. Eric never paid for that car. Somebody gave it to him, and it must have been Charlie, and it wasn't just to get him to arrange the reunion with my mother, because Charlie could have called her on his own any time he wanted. It had to be for something much bigger than that. It must have been to get Eric to help with Charlie's plan. His long-range plan."

"Which was?"

"To get control of her money. One of two ways. First by convincing her and the rest of us that she'd lost her mind so he could petition for guardianship. When that wasn't working, or wasn't working fast enough, he switched gears. He killed her and arranged it so I'd look like I was the one losing my mind and Eric would be appointed guardian, and he and Charlie would split the money."

She'd spoken too fast. Her chest was heaving. She paused long enough to draw in a big breath before she went on.

"Obviously, they didn't plan for Charlie to be arrested. He must have screwed up somehow—with the fingerprints, I guess? And Eric's been desperate ever since to get him off. He wanted to hire this lawyer, Harrison Miller, and he wanted to borrow against my inheritance, then against our house, to pay the retainer. And when

I said no, that's when he started talking about having me declared incompetent so he could take charge of the money. But that was their plan all along, it must have been!"

She finished with a final sputtering gasp, her eyes squeezed shut and her hands clenching the steering wheel in a white-knuckle grip.

Brian was quiet, and when he spoke, it was calmly, in a voice of caution. "Okay, let's not jump the gun here. Let's not assume the worst. Eric might only be an unwitting accomplice. Maybe Mull gave him the car just to get in his good graces. So he'd be sure of his loyalty when the shit hit the fan. It doesn't necessarily mean he's a coconspirator." He paused. "There's only one way to find out."

She opened her eyes and looked at him.

"You need to confront him with what you know and see what he admits to."

"Oh, God." Her palms were so sweaty they slid against the steering wheel. She wiped them on her skirt. "I don't know. I'm not sure . . ."

"Julie, this is your mother's killer we're talking about. You need to know how deep in your husband might be. Do it. Don't put it off. Do it tonight. I'll be nearby. You need me, call or text, and I'll be there in two minutes."

"I don't even know how to begin."

"Try to stay calm. Stick to the facts. Tell him what you know, and see if he'll come clean. Do it in the kitchen or the bedroom. In my experience, that's where most heart-to-heart conversations take place between couples."

"Does it have to be tonight?"

"Well, you tell me," Brian said. "How much longer can you live with him, not knowing if he played any part in your mother's murder?"

ERIC TEXTED THAT he'd be late and not to worry about dinner; he'd made a restaurant reservation. He added a heart emoji.

The kitchen or the bedroom, Brian had advised. That was where the truth would come out. In Julie's experience, the bedroom was where the truth was shoved aside and forgotten, so she waited for Eric in the kitchen. She sat with her hands clenched in her lap, staring at her phone on the table. She could feel herself breathing too fast. *Stay calm,* Brian had told her. She needed to calm down.

She opened a bottle of wine and poured herself a glass and drank it on her feet, too fast. She sat back down. She stared at the phone, waiting for another text from Eric. Almost hoping that he'd been held up: *Sorry, babe, won't be home till late.* Then she could put this off to some other night.

When a sound finally came, it wasn't a ping from her phone. It was the car, that strident whine that suddenly reminded her of a dentist's drill. She heard the garage door open with its own whine and close again with a clatter. She heard the solid thud of the car door closing, then all she could hear was a high-pitched ringing in her ears and her own heart pounding in her chest.

He came in the back door, dropped his briefcase in the mudroom, and hung his jacket on a hook. He usually came home in scrubs, but tonight he was wearing the suit he'd worn to Foster's office that morning. He came into the kitchen loosening his tie.

"Hey, babe!" He kissed the top of her head with a loud smack. "I made a reservation at that steak house. Hyde Park. Nine o'clock. Why don't you run upstairs and put on something sexy?"

She clenched her hands around her empty wineglass. "What are we celebrating? Our divorce or my mother's murder?"

He rolled his eyes, as if to say *Here we go again.* "You're upset about the divorce. Well, me, too! But she didn't leave us with any other choice. Unless you want that vegan tree hugger to get everything. Which, trust me, is the last thing your mother would want."

"Sit down. We need to talk."

He eyed her glass. "Have you been drinking?"

"We need to talk," she said again.

"Look, it's just a piece of paper. No one will ever know. And we'll get married again the minute the estate's settled. Someplace romantic. Venice. Santorini. Whatever you want."

He wouldn't sit down, so she stood up. "Eric, I know about the car."

"What car?"

"The car that should have cost us a quarter of a million. That you seem to have gotten for the bargain price of one dollar."

He blinked. "Okay, I don't know where you're getting this—"

"I saw the records. Or, rather, the absence of records. You never paid for that car."

His mouth tightened. He took a step toward her. "You went snooping—"

"Don't you dare turn this against me!"

She wasn't nervous anymore. She wasn't reluctant anymore, not after he'd tried to palm off a barefaced lie. She took a step closer to him and jabbed a finger at his chest. "I know Charlie gave it to you. What I want to know is what you promised him in return!"

He stared at her for a beat. "What?" He threw his head back and hooted. "Charlie! Like he ever had that kind of money! He was living on nothing but his pension and an occasional commission. There's no way he could afford to give me that car!"

"Fine. Then he stole it. Or cooked the books or something, I don't know. But I know the purchase was made by some LLC and that Charlie signed the incorporation papers."

Eric turned to the sink and filled a glass of water. "He witnessed some signatures there at the dealership." He took a swallow. "That's all."

"Whose signatures?" she asked, and in a burst of clarity, she finally understood all of it. "It wasn't just you and Charlie, was it? There's somebody else behind all this. Somebody pulling your strings."

"Behind all what? You're not making any sense!" He took another gulp of water.

"Somebody who bankrolled Charlie at the start. Who figured out a way for them to reel you in. That's who broke in here the other night. Or one of their henchmen. They wanted to make sure you were sticking to the program. That you were going to follow through with your part."

"My part in what? What the fuck are you talking about?"

"The plot to murder my mother and take control of her fortune."

The glass slipped through his fingers and shattered against the tile floor. He looked down at the shards of glass, then lifted his eyes to Julie. "Jesus Christ," he said. "You honestly think that? That I conspired to kill your mother?"

"It's the only explanation!"

He looked again at the broken glass winking in the glare of the overhead light. When his eyes came up, they were hollow. "Except it's not," he said. He shuffled to the table, his shoes crunching through the glass, and sank onto a chair. "Julie, I have to tell you something."

"What?" Suddenly, she was afraid again.

"The car was a gift," he said. "Or a pay-off or a bribe or a loan. Take your pick. From Darryl Keener."

"Who?" The name rang only a distant bell.

"Paula's husband. Her partner in the pain management clinic. Or not even from Darryl, exactly. From the people he works for." Eric let out a bitter laugh. "The people I used to work for. Who won't let me stop."

"What kind of work?"

He buried his face in his hands. "Writing prescriptions. For patients I never saw. Who were just names on a list they gave me."

The confession washed over her like warm water. It was better, a thousand times better, than what she'd been imagining. What Brian Holley had convinced her to imagine. Eric wasn't working with Charlie. He was never part of a plot to kill her mother. She was so relieved that the coil of anxiety in her chest started to unwind.

"Wait." The coil tightened again. "Prescriptions for what?"

His voice was hollow when he finally answered her. "Oxy."

"Oh my God!" She clapped her hands to her face. "Eric!"

"At least it wasn't fentanyl," he said weakly.

"Why would you do such a thing?" she cried.

When he looked up at her, his face was wet. "You know about my old man's gambling. What you don't know is he funded most of it by embezzling from his boss. He always thought he'd win enough to pay it back, but of course he never did. His boss found out and was going to blow the whistle on him if he didn't pay it back."

"So you paid it?"

"I had to find a way, or he would've gone to prison."

"So you went to Paula." Julie couldn't keep the edge of jealousy out of her voice.

He shook his head. "My mom told her. They stayed close after we broke up, even after she married Darryl. Mom told her the whole story, and Paula and Darryl came to me with the solution. There were people they knew who could front the money for me. All I had to do in return was write a few prescriptions.

"So we made restitution to Dad's boss, and I wrote enough scrips to work off my debt—"

"*Work?*" Julie said archly.

He made a face, acknowledging the dig. "Anyway, I kept Dad safe and got him into a program—and well." He shrugged. "You know the rest."

"I don't know where the car came in."

"Right." He stared at his hands on the table. "Like I said. They don't want me to stop. It was always this carrot-and-stick thing. *Stop and we'll leak your name to the feds. Keep going and here's this car you've always wanted.*"

"So they hooked you up with Charlie. He was part of this."

"No. No! I met Charlie on my own. I had my eye on the car, and I was trying to figure out how to make the money work when they kind of swooped in. Charlie did the paperwork. That's all. He doesn't know who they are. He thinks the whole setup was some kind of tax dodge."

"And you went along with it. You accepted the car."

His head drooped. "I thought I could pay them back over time. But they didn't want installment payments. They want the full purchase price. Or they want prescriptions."

Her eyes opened wide. "So you're still part of it?" She shuddered as she realized something else. "That's what the burner phone's for. So you can communicate with your—your criminal network."

"I tried to stop. I swear. I let them know that if I go down, I know enough names to take them down with me. Mutual assured destruction, right? It's been months since I wrote the last scrip. I thought I was done. Until—"

"They sent that guy here! The one who took your gun! To—what? Intimidate you?"

"To remind me. That they know where I live." He looked at her with his hollow eyes. "Where my wife lives."

A chill rippled down her spine. "That's why you added the extra money to the mortgage application. You were going to pay them off out of that."

He nodded miserably.

"Oh, Eric. Why didn't you do that from the start?"

"What?"

"Borrow against the house. You could have repaid your dad's boss out of that. You didn't need to get involved with these horrible people."

He didn't answer. He picked up the wine bottle and went out to the patio to drink in the dark.

JULIE WAS IN bed by the time he came inside. She heard his footsteps on the stairs, then crossing the landing. But his feet stopped at the doorway and stayed there. She imagined that he was watching her, but when she opened her eyes, he was staring at the floor. With a sigh, she pulled back the covers, and he hurried to slide into bed beside her.

"We'll get through this, right?" he whispered. "Somehow?"

She was silent a long time before she whispered back. "Somehow."

CHAPTER 40

She expected Brian to check in, to find out how last night's heart-to-heart had gone, and she spent some time at the office the next day debating what to tell him. Not the truth, obviously. But she had to come up with something, something innocuous, to keep him from digging any deeper into Eric's acquisition of the car. She needed a story that would be embarrassing without being criminal, bad enough that Eric would've kept it from her but not so bad that he'd go to prison. She decided on a wealthy patient, an older woman who was so grateful to him and more than a little too fond, who sent him extravagant gifts that he regularly returned, but when she dangled the Lambo keys in front of him, he just couldn't say no.

She waited all morning for Brian to call, and when she couldn't wait any longer, she called him.

"Julie. What's up?"

She gave a baffled look to the phone. *What's up? Like yesterday's conversation in the parking lot never took place?* "I thought you'd want to know. I had my showdown with Eric last night."

"Oh, right." He sounded distracted, and she could hear other voices in the room with him. Obviously, she'd called at a bad time. "How'd it go?"

"Turns out it was nothing to worry about. So thanks for hearing me out, but you can chalk this up to my overactive imagination."

"Good. Glad to hear it." Somebody said something to him. "Hold on," he said to Julie. He must have muted his phone, because the line was silent for a moment until he returned. "Hey, do you have plans tonight?"

"No. Do we need to talk? Is there news about Charlie's case?"

"No. Nothing like that. Listen, I gotta go."

"Okay."

The line went dead.

That was strange, she thought. She put her phone down, but a minute later, it pinged. She had a text from an unknown number: Can't talk on the phone. Meet me at Starbucks downtown near the library?

Brian was texting from some other phone. He couldn't talk with other people in the room.

When? she texted back.

I'm there now.

She grabbed her bag and hurried to the elevator and down to the lobby of the building. She was out on the sidewalk when a third text landed from the same number.

Btw, this is Tad.

Tad? She lurched to a stop and frowned at the screen. So they were texting buddies now? And how did he have her cell phone number, anyway?

The answer came to her pretty fast. Amy in reception had struck again.

She considered standing him up and returning to work. But she was already outside. She decided she might as well hear what he had to say.

Tad was waiting at one of the outdoor tables on the sidewalk, and he stood up as she approached. He was back in his native garb today, cargo shorts and a T-shirt with a logo that read: THERE IS NO PLANET B.

"Thanks for meeting me," he said. "Can I get you something to drink?"

His plant-based eco water bottle was on the table in front of him. Of course he wouldn't buy a drink in a single-use disposable cup. She shook her head and sat down.

"I wanted to apologize for the way I bolted out of that meeting yesterday," he said as he sat down beside her. "Your mother's will kind of knocked me on my ass."

"I know the feeling."

"And I won't lie. It got my head spinning, too. I was up most of the night thinking about what SOS could do with that kind of money. It would be a total game changer." He leaned closer, and she could see the dark circles under his eyes, even though the eyes themselves were shining. "The things we could do with KS Development? Green building, and clean energy, and stormwater management. Rain-capture cooling. Sustainable farming on all that acreage in the middle of the state. Maybe even carbon farming."

She didn't know what carbon farming was, but from the look on Tad's face, it must have been pretty exciting.

"Buutt." He drew the word out. "It's pretty obvious that she named SOS as a contingent beneficiary only to pressure you into divorcing your husband. And the last thing I want to do is get in the middle of your family drama. Sooo." He drew that word out, too. "As soon as the will is probated, I'm going to file a disclaimer and take the contingent bequest off the table."

She sat back and regarded him a moment. It was a thoughtful gesture but an empty one. "Have you thought about what happens if you disclaim and I don't divorce Eric? Because I have."

"If neither of us is entitled to receive the property?" His eyes clouded. "It goes to the state of Florida."

"Exactly. And I assume you wouldn't want to see that happen."

He shuddered. "With this administration?" He took a long drink of whatever was in his water bottle. "God, she really boxed you in, didn't she?"

She shrugged. "Damned if I do, damned if I don't."

He winced a smile. "And I thought I had family drama."

"No one beats us," she said. "Speaking of—" Now she leaned close. "I hope by now you've convinced Charlie to change his plea."

He let out a short laugh. "That would be a privileged communication."

"Ah. So you have discussed it."

He laughed again, but in the next moment he looked chagrined. "Sorry. I shouldn't laugh about your mother's death. Even if you're the one making me laugh."

She shrugged, conceding the point, accepting his apology.

"Listen," he said, "there's no reason for you to care about my opinion, but I think the guy's innocent. I believe him."

She scoffed.

"He's a broken man, Julie. He doesn't care what happens to him. He's lost the love of his life. That's what he keeps saying. *I've lost the love of my life.*"

"Yes, he's very good," she said. "He fooled me, too."

"I'm seriously worried about him. I've even put in a request for suicide watch. I mean, this on top of his medical history and the loss of his last wife—"

"Wait. What?" She sat up straight. "You know about Nadia's death?"

"Sure. I have all the records."

"And you don't find that the least bit strange? That his previous wife also died under suspicious circumstances?"

"What's suspicious about childbirth?"

Her face froze. "Childbirth?"

He nodded. "It really hit him hard. He was in a military hospital in Germany at the time—"

She remembered something about that. "Recovering from a gunshot wound. He was shot in Beirut."

"No. Well, yes, but the wound was superficial. He was there for PTSD. The doctors chalked it up to the accumulation of combat experiences. Anyway, something snapped. He was in the hospital for a month. And then he gets word that his wife and baby son are dead? It really hit him hard. Now, on top of that, to lose the love of his life? I mean, Julie, I really do believe—"

He broke off as a young woman in blue jeans and a blazer approached their table.

"Excuse me. I'm sorry to interrupt." She had a phone in one hand and a manila envelope in the other.

"Yes?" Tad said.

She turned away from him. "Julie Hoffman?"

Julie groaned. She'd hoped these journalistic ambushes were over. "I have no comment."

The young woman slapped the envelope onto the table. "You've been served." She snapped a photo with her phone and turned on her heel and left.

Tad half rose from his chair as if he meant to follow her, but she was already out of sight. He turned back to Julie. "What was that about?"

Julie opened the flap on the envelope and slid out the document inside. She read the heading on the first page: *Petition for Dissolution of Marriage* . . .

That was as far as she got before the words blurred. Eric had filed for divorce.

Now she understood why he'd come home late last night wearing a suit. He'd been meeting with a divorce lawyer. He must have made a beeline from Franklin Foster's office to this other lawyer's office. He was filing for divorce with or without her. She blinked to clear her vision long enough to confirm it. *Eric Karl Hoffman, Petitioner, versus Julie Sawyer Hoffman, Respondent.* It was him against her.

Tad's hand was on her shoulder. "Oh, God, Julie. I am so sorry."

She slid the petition back in the envelope and stood up. "No problem," she said thickly. "The good news is you don't have to bother filing that disclaimer anymore. My mother's condition has been satisfied."

She stumbled her way through the tables to the street with the envelope clutched between her trembling fingers. With the single document inside it, she'd become two things she never thought she'd be: divorced and obscenely rich.

CHAPTER 41

Two dozen red roses were delivered to her office that afternoon, and another two dozen were on the dining room table when she got home that night. The card on the office bouquet read, *Marry me.* The card at home said, *Please?*

It shouldn't hurt so much. Divorce was the logical solution. She knew it was. It was the only way they'd be able to pay off the people who had such a hold on Eric. But it was the fact that he'd done it without her. Unilaterally. Sometimes it seemed that every decision they'd ever made was really his own unilateral decision. Without her consultation or consent. Now he'd decided they would remarry. But there was a difference. He could divorce her without her consent, but he couldn't marry her without it.

She was standing in the dining room with the card in her hand when Eric came out of the kitchen. "I know we're not celebrating anything." He had both arms raised like he was surrendering. "So I didn't make a reservation anywhere. But I don't want you to have to cook tonight, so I ordered in. Seared grouper from Duval's. Is that okay?"

"Fine." She didn't mean to bite out the word, but that was the way it came.

He sighed. "You're not happy."

She turned on him. "Are you?"

"I will be, if you can forgive me and get past this."

She tucked the card back inside the bouquet. "I'm going to go up and change."

"Shall I pour us some wine?"

"Fine," she said again, a little softer this time.

He returned to the kitchen, and she headed for the stairs. She was in the front hall when the doorbell rang. Through the sidelight, she could see a dark van in the driveway. The Duval's delivery was here already. She stopped and opened the door.

Two men in windbreakers stood on the doorstep. Neither one held a food delivery bag. "DEA," they both yelled. They held up IDs hanging from lanyards around their necks. "We have a warrant to search these premises and a warrant for the arrest of Eric Hoffman."

"What? What for? What is this?"

They thrust a sheaf of papers at her and stepped around her into the house.

"What is this? I don't understand."

Those two men were followed by a stream of other men and women wearing similar windbreakers and lanyards. They fanned out through the house while Julie stood rooted by the door, clutching the papers to her chest.

Eric came out of the kitchen. He held a wine bottle in one hand and a corkscrew in the other. He froze as the first two men strode toward him.

"Eric Hoffman, you are under arrest for conspiracy to dispense and distribute narcotics."

Eric locked eyes with Julie as they took the bottle and corkscrew from him and snapped handcuffs on his wrists. They droned the Miranda warning at him, and he never took his eyes off Julie the whole time. They marched him to the front door where Julie still stood frozen.

"You bitch," Eric ground out as he passed her. "You fucking bitch."

"No! Eric! I didn't do this!" She stumbled out the door after him. "Eric, I swear, I didn't do this!"

He didn't look at her again as the men opened the back doors of the van and put him inside.

Julie stood in the middle of the front yard and looked around in a daze. There were cars and vans parked in the driveway and at the curb. More men and women stood at the open doors of their vehicles, conferring with one another or talking on the phone or into their car radios. Across the street, the neighbors were gathering, craning their necks and whispering in huddles.

Julie swept her eyes through the crowd, past all the strange and terrifying faces, until her gaze landed on one familiar face. Brian Holley. He stood by the curb with a phone to his ear. He could explain this, she thought, and she half raised a hand in greeting.

His back went stiff, and he pivoted away and spoke into the phone with his shoulders hunched.

An engine started up behind her, and she whirled to see the van holding Eric back out of the driveway. It rolled slowly down the street. All the neighbors turned to watch it go.

Julie went back inside. Agents were overturning sofa cushions in the living room and opening sideboard drawers in the dining room. Red roses were strewn across the dining room table, and their petals dripped onto the concrete floor. In the kitchen a man stood on a stepladder to unscrew a lightbulb from the ceiling fixture, while others rummaged through the cabinets. She looked up, puzzled, as the man on the ladder reached into the light fixture. He came out with a tiny black disc.

"Electronic surveillance of oral communications was authorized by District Judge Pauletti last week," another man said, coming up beside Julie. "Here's a copy of the order." He handed her a document, and she clasped it to her chest along with all the rest.

Have a heart-to-heart, Brian had told her. *Make it tonight. The kitchen or the bedroom is best.*

Because that was where the bugs were planted.

She'd played right into his hands. She'd delivered Eric's confession on a silver platter.

She went out the back door to the patio and looked up Harrison Miller's number on her phone. She reached his service, and he called back minutes later from the nineteenth hole of his golf club. They struck a quick agreement on his retainer, and by the time they finished, he was already in his car and heading to wherever Eric was being held.

Julie went back inside for the bottle of wine.

THE SEARCH TEAM was inside for hours. Julie waited on the patio, rocking on the glider as night fell over the neighborhood. She drained the bottle and listened to the sounds of children playing. Later she heard parents calling them inside to bed. She could hear the splash of water in a nearby pool as someone went for a nighttime swim. Later, the nocturnal birds stirred awake, and she heard their chirps and caws and the rattling cry of a limpkin. Then came the chorus of cicadas, their mating songs buzzing like electronic static.

All the lights were on inside the house. She smoothed out the sheaf of documents she'd been given and read them by the glow from the kitchen windows. Shadows passed over the pages as the agents moved about inside, and she had to wait for them to move again before she could continue reading. But eventually, she read everything.

She learned that the team now swarming over her house was a joint task force of the Drug Enforcement Administration, the Florida Department of Law Enforcement, and the Sarasota County Sheriff's Office. She learned that Eric was one of several area physicians suspected of opioid trafficking. Included among them were Paula and her husband. The search warrant authorized the search of Eric's home. A separate warrant authorized the search of his office. The warrants authorized the seizure of all computers and cell phones, and the surveillance order authorized the installation of listening devices in his office telephone system, as well as the installation of listening devices in his home.

The darkness deepened. Outdoor lights started to blink off around the neighborhood, and the blue glow of TVs and computers took their place. Doors were closed and locked. The upstairs lights switched off in her own house, and she could hear the thud of car doors closing on the street, the low growl of engines as the cars slowly drove away.

The back door swung open, and Brian Holley came out on the patio. He was carrying the food delivery from Duval's.

"It's cold now," he said when she looked up at him. "You want me to warm it up in the microwave?"

"You set me up," she said.

He put the bag on the table beside her. "I set him up."

It was almost funny now, she thought bitterly, how Eric had accused Brian of sniffing after her. It was Eric's scent he'd been following the whole time. "The night we met," she said. "That first night at the hotel. My mother never called the sheriff."

"No. Tampa PD alerted me."

"You came because you knew she was Eric's mother-in-law."

His shoulder barely lifted in a shrug. "I saw an opportunity."

"You were on the task force all along. That was your case. Not my mother's murder. You were never part of that investigation."

Another half-hearted shrug. "That's Long and Russo's case."

"But you showed up at the ER. You brought me home and pretended to take my statement."

"I saw an opportunity," he said again.

"Opportunities everywhere. Like the opportunity to bug the house. That broken windowpane made it so convenient for you. You didn't even have to pick the lock." Sarcasm grated through her voice as she added, "And it was so kind of you to replace the pane when you were done."

"We had a court order."

"All that kindness. It was all a ploy to make me trust you. You manipulated me. You planted all those ideas in my head about Charlie. That he'd killed Nadia when you knew she died in childbirth."

Brian gave a faint nod.

"But it was never even about Charlie! It was always about Eric. All the seeds of suspicion you planted. That Charlie gave him the car. That he was helping Charlie flee. Then all that sympathy you showed me. All that helpfulness. Charlie wasn't the one gaslighting me. You were. The whole time."

"It's my job."

"Oh, then it's all okay. Go ahead and make me suspect my husband of conspiracy to commit murder!"

He bristled at that. "What about all the opioid deaths he is responsible for? You should have suspected him of that."

She glared at him, though the accusation simmered. All the unexplained phone calls, the burner phone, the car she knew they couldn't afford. She'd never questioned any of it, she'd been so in thrall to Eric. So cowed by him.

Brian shifted his weight. "If there's nothing else—"

She scoffed.

"—I wanted you to know we're taking the car. Seizure's authorized when it represents the proceeds of a crime."

"Good riddance," she said as he went back inside. To him and the car.

A few minutes later, she heard the roar of the engine starting in the garage, then its distinctive whine as it raced down the street. Even cops couldn't help themselves in that car. The Lamborghini, auto of choice for doctors and drug dealers. Who were sometimes one and the same.

CHAPTER 42

Reporters and photographers swarmed the house the next morning. Julie had barely slept during the night and was already late for work when she saw them out there. Cars and vans were parked at the curb and cameras set up on the sidewalk. One intrepid journalist ventured all the way up to the front door to peer in through the pane.

Julie closed all the curtains and called the office to say she'd be working from home today.

Her next call was to the loan officer at the bank, to borrow enough money to pay Harrison Miller's retainer. No mortgage would be required, the banker told her cheerfully. Word that she was inheriting Kate Sawyer's fortune must have leaked out of Foster's office and reached the banker's ears. Her signature on a promissory note was good enough. The fact that she was married to an alleged drug trafficker didn't seem to matter. Perhaps word of the divorce filing had also reached his ears. At any rate, the loan documents were drawn up, she signed electronically, and the money was wired to Miller's office. He called to acknowledge receipt and to tell her that Eric would be released on his own recognizance that morning.

Julie's next call was to Lenore Greggson. She could have shopped for her own divorce attorney, but she decided she might as well inherit her mother's lawyer along with everything else. Anyway, this was going to be quick and easy. She instructed Lenore to file a response consenting to Eric's petition and ceding all marital property to him. With no property disputes or child custody issues to resolve, the divorce would be final in thirty days.

Next she called the on-site administrator at one of the downtown condominium towers built and now managed by KS Development. Yes, there was a furnished apartment available, he told her. Sixteenth floor facing the bay, two bedrooms, two and a half baths. He was starting to describe the kitchen appliances when she said, "Yes, I'll take it."

"Start date?"

"Today."

"End date?"

"Can we leave that open?" She didn't know how long it would take her to find a new home. She didn't even know where to look.

SHE WAS IN the kitchen eating cold grouper when she heard an excited burst of voices from the front lawn. The reporters were shouting over one another, lobbing questions that were too garbled to make out. She stiffened. Eric was home.

A minute later his key turned in the front-door lock. Julie didn't move from the kitchen table. He could come and find her if he wanted.

The door opened and closed. But the footsteps that crossed the front hall didn't sound like Eric's. They made a clicking sound across the concrete floor, like high heels.

A reporter, she thought, who was breaching their walls along with the boundaries of ethical journalism. "Hey!" she shouted, rushing out from the kitchen.

She was only half right. It was a woman wearing heels. But not an intruder.

"Greta!" she said, relieved.

Greta was at the bottom of the stairs. "Eric sent me," she said, her lips pulled tight. "To pack a bag for him. He's staying with us."

Julie flinched a bit at her tone. "He doesn't need to. I'm moving out today. And I've relinquished the house to him."

Greta's eyes narrowed. "Fine. But he can't come here while those reporters are out there." She lifted her chin. "Or while you're in here."

That stung. "Greta, he has to believe—you all have to believe—I didn't do this. I didn't tell a soul what he confessed to me. They had the place bugged."

"Oh, we know," Greta said. "We all know how it happened. How you were suckered into this sting operation. That's what makes him so angry. That you could be so fucking stupid."

Heat raced up from Julie's chest to the roots of her hair. "I know. I'm sorry."

Greta rolled her eyes. "An apology? Like that's going to help him avoid jail time or get his medical license back?"

"He lost his license?"

"As a condition of his release. He may not do time, but his reputation is shot. His livelihood is gone. All those years of training. All that talent and skill. Lost."

"I'm sorry," Julie said again.

"And our parents! Who's going to pay for their retirement community now? I can't afford those fees. Not on my salary. If I can even keep my salary. You've ruined my career, too, you realize that? I'll never be appointed to a higher office now. I probably won't even be reelected to the one I hold. Not when my brother's accused of being a drug trafficker."

"He is a drug trafficker," Julie said quietly.

"He did it for our father!" Greta cried. "In my book, that makes him a hero."

"At first he did it for your father. But he kept doing it for the car. Which makes him—" Julie searched for the right word. *Corrupt. Venal. Pathetic.*

"Shut up," Greta said, sparing her from having to choose. She spun to the door and grabbed the knob and spoke her final words with her back to Julie. "I wish I never introduced you two. It was supposed to be this brilliant match! What a coup for our family to be part of the Sawyer dynasty. But it was the worst thing that could have happened. You've ruined all of us." She wrenched the door open. "I wish I never even met you."

The reporters' voices erupted again outside, but Julie barely heard them. Greta's words had taken up all the room in her head. She stood and stared at the closed door with tears stinging her eyes. Her best friend wished they'd never met. She'd ruined all their lives. Because she was so fucking stupid. So gullible. So easy to gaslight. Every accusation roared inside her mind, and she felt the weight of every single one crushing her.

But another voice was able to penetrate all that din. Her own. Yes, it told her, yes, she'd been stupid. But Eric had been stupid first. He was stupid to think that it made any sense to commit a crime to cover up his father's crime. Stupid to accept an extravagant gift from known criminals and think he could simply send them monthly payments and they'd all be square. It was his stupidity that started this, not hers, and his fault that his life was ruined. Not hers.

She went upstairs and started packing.

LATE IN THE afternoon, there was a new clamor out front. Not voices this time but car doors opening and closing, trunk lids falling shut. Julie went to the front bedroom window and peered around the edge of the curtain. The press brigade was breaking camp.

She peeked out the other side of the window and saw why. Two men in suits were standing on the sidewalk with their hands on their hips in a menacing posture. One man was tall, lean, and Black; the other was white and heavyset. Detectives Long and Russo. They stood and glowered at the reporters and photographers until they all left.

Julie ran downstairs and was there when the bell rang.

"Detectives?" she said as she opened the door.

"I know this is a bad time, but can we come in?"

They obviously knew about Eric. They must have been on the task force, too, along with everyone else in Florida law enforcement. "I don't have anything to say about that," she said. "You should contact Harrison Miller."

Long's brow wrinkled. "Your husband's lawyer?"

"No, this is about your mother," Russo said. "Her postmortem is done."

"Oh!" Julie held the door wide. "I'm sorry. Yes, please come in."

She showed them to the living room, invited them to sit, which they did, and offered them something to drink, which they declined. Their grave expressions worried her. She wondered if the case against Charlie had somehow fallen apart.

"It wasn't alcohol poisoning?" she blurted.

They both looked surprised by her outburst. It was Long who spoke first. "No, it was. The ME definitely ruled that as the cause of death. He's issued the death certificate, too, and released the body. So you can start making your arrangements."

"Oh. Good. Thank you." She realized this was basically a condolence call. That was why they wore those funereal faces.

"We're here because the prosecutor asked us to circle back and follow up on a few points."

Circle back and follow up. Those were classic hem-and-haws. "What points? What do you need?"

Russo consulted his notebook. "We understand you lived with your mother out on Cascara during that first week after the wedding."

"Yes. So?"

"During that time, did you observe any unusual behavior?"

"Yes, but I explained that. She realized what Charlie was up to. She was heartbroken."

"Any forgetfulness? Confusion?"

Those sounded like terms Eric might have fed them, all part of his grand theory that Kate had dementia. "No," she said.

"Any trembling in her hands or changes in her gait? Or changes in her vision or hearing that you noticed?"

Now it sounded like Greta's theory about a brain tumor. Julie turned her stare from Long to Russo and back. "What's this got to do with my mother's murder? The cause of death was alcohol poisoning. You said so yourself."

Long cleared his throat. "The ME found some, um, anomalies in your mother's brain."

Julie sat back, blinking hard. "What does that mean? What kind of anomalies?"

Detective Long opened a folder and passed her a document. "Here's a copy of the report. On the fourth page, you'll see a reference to an intracerebral hemorrhage."

Julie flipped pages, but she couldn't get there fast enough. "What's that?"

"A brain bleed," Russo said.

"Caused by the alcohol poisoning?"

They shook their heads. "A ruptured aneurysm," Long said. "A preexisting rupture. And probably a long-preexisting aneurysm."

She scanned the pages. They were full of numbers and charts and terms she didn't understand.

"If you look at page five, the ME believes this aneurysm was likely the result of a blow to the head many years before. The vessel ballooned but didn't rupture until recently. And it didn't rupture entirely. It was a slow bleed, probably over the last few weeks of her life, and it would have caused those things we mentioned earlier. Forgetfulness, confusion, changes in gait or vision or hearing. Hallucinations."

They hadn't mentioned hallucinations earlier. They were trying to sneak it in, and now she understood where they were going. She folded her arms. "Okay, this is that ridiculous idea that she injected herself. But we know that didn't happen. Because the only fingerprints on the syringe and the bottle were Charlie's!"

"Right." Russo shifted from one buttock to the other in his chair. "We wanted to circle back to that, too. When you found your mother's body—I'm sorry to put you through this, but we need to know exactly what you saw when you entered her room."

She threw up her hands. "I saw my mother's corpse!"

"Yes, besides that."

"Well, considering I fainted, I wasn't really observing much, you know?" She knew how she sounded, like a bratty teenager. She didn't care.

"We understand." Long was taking over, like a relief pitcher. Julie was scoring too many hits against Russo. "The first responders to the scene reported that the curtains in the room were open."

"Right." That detail came back to her. "I did that. They were closed when I came in the room."

He nodded, like: *Now we're getting somewhere.* "And that your mother had a sleep mask on her forehead."

"No." She remembered that now, too. "It was over her eyes. I pushed it up when I couldn't get her to wake up."

He nodded again. "They said that the other side of the bed didn't appear to have been slept in."

"Charlie was already up. He smoothed out the covers on his side."

"So you observed that, too?"

Julie looked at him and didn't answer.

"The room directly across the hall—the search team reported that there was an unmade bed in that room."

"If you say so. I didn't go in there."

"Mull says that's where he slept."

"It would be easy enough to go in there and mess up the covers. Is that what he's trying to use as his alibi? That he wasn't there? But you have his fingerprints!" She felt frustrated by the number of times she had to remind them of this fact.

"Right. Think back. Try to remember as best you can. Did you see a pair of latex gloves anywhere in the room?"

Julie stared at them. So this was their theory. That after Charlie retired to the other room, Kate put on a pair of latex gloves, refilled her peptide syringe with pure alcohol, injected herself in the arm, and disposed of the gloves. "No," Julie said. Her voice was like shards of ice. She tossed the postmortem report on the coffee table. "There were no latex gloves."

The two men looked at each other. Russo closed his notebook and heaved himself to his feet. Long rose more fluidly. "That's everything the state attorney asked us to run down. So we'll leave it at that."

She pressed her lips together and nodded. She didn't get up.

"We'll see ourselves out," Russo said.

JULIE SAT THERE long after they were gone. She knew it must have been Eric who'd concocted this ridiculous, slanderous notion. He fed the idea to Charlie, who fed it to his inexperienced, court-appointed lawyer, who ran with it to the prosecutor. Julie was furious at all of them. It wasn't horrible enough that her mother was a murder victim—now they had to make her out to be the murderer, too. It was insult piled upon grievous injury, and she hated them for it. Every last one of them. But mostly Eric.

She looked at the clock. It was almost five. The press brigade had been chased off and probably wouldn't come back tonight. Which meant Eric might arrive soon. She didn't want to be here when he did.

She hurried upstairs and finished packing a week's worth of clothes and toiletries. She ran downstairs for her laptop and phone charger and added them to the suitcase. She threw the postmortem report in there, too. What else? She stood with her hands on her hips and surveyed her surroundings. She'd come back for the rest of her clothes in a few days, but other than that? The furniture, the linens, her wedding china and crystal? That was all marital property that belonged to Eric now. She didn't want any of it.

She was zipping up a compartment in the suitcase when her rings caught on the lining. She stopped and considered them. She wore a simple platinum wedding band that hadn't been off her finger in four years. On top of that she wore a diamond solitaire. Nothing flashy: Eric had bought it back in the days when he refused to go into debt. Before he was happy to borrow a quarter-million-dollar car from drug traffickers. She slid both rings off her finger and tucked them into an empty ring box she found in her jewelry drawer. She placed the rings on top of Eric's chest of drawers where he'd be sure to find them and, in due course, sell them.

The rest of her jewelry wasn't worth much. She emptied the drawer into the suitcase and slammed it shut.

CHAPTER 43

The condo manager was there to meet Julie when she arrived at her new quarters. He insisted on giving her a tour and showing her how the appliances worked and where the thermostat was. "And the pièce de résistance!" He pushed a button, and a translucent screen rose from the floor to disappear into the ceiling. Behind it was a wall of glass overlooking the marina and, beyond it, the bay.

The space reminded her of every high-end corporate apartment she'd ever seen—clean, luxe, generic. The decor was minimalist, the colors neutral.

When he finally left, she wheeled her bag to the bedroom and hung her clothes in the vast walk-in closet. They looked lonely there, only five hangers on a ten-foot rod. She put her cosmetic bag in a bathroom so clean and white it could have been a sterile room in a laboratory. A desk stood against the window wall in the bedroom, positioned to take in that view that everyone seemed to be vying for in the downtown real estate market. A view that had built much of her mother's fortune. She put her laptop on the desk and plugged it in.

She stood at the window a long time, watching the boats slide in and out of their berths. She watched the tourists as they moved along the bayfront, walking, running, biking. From the sixteenth floor, they looked like colonies of tiny ants on the march, though sometimes the mass of bodies bunched and swelled and formed shapes that reminded her of the murmuration of starlings. Insects or birds or people, they all moved and lived and breathed in groups—families, clubs, teams.

For the first time, it occurred to her that she didn't belong to any group anymore. Not to any duo, dynamic or otherwise. In the space of a week, she'd lost her mother, her husband, and her best friend. Now her home.

Back when she interned for the nonprofit during law school, there was a great debate roiling over whether to use the label *homeless* or *unhoused* to refer to the people they were advocating for. *Homeless* was considered derogatory, while *unhoused* suggested a basic human right to shelter that these people were being deprived of. Now Julie saw it a different way. She wasn't unhoused—she had this spectacular luxury apartment, after all. But she was homeless.

She wheeled the chair up to the desk and opened her laptop. She connected to Wi-Fi and searched the real estate websites for a new home. For location, she put in her current zip code. She wanted to stay close to downtown and the office. She also wanted something in a settled neighborhood, with shade trees and sidewalks. She selected the other search parameters almost without thinking. Single-family home, three-plus bedrooms, two-plus baths, waterfront. It wasn't until she added *gazebo* to her search that she realized what she was describing: her dream house from years ago, the cheery yellow cottage that they couldn't afford without a mortgage.

Of course it didn't appear in the search results. It was too much to hope for that her dream house would be on the market at the exact moment when she was. She wished she could just go knock on their door and make an offer, but she knew better than most people that real estate didn't work that way. She scrolled through the listings. Nothing appealed.

She gave up and returned to the living room. There was no color anywhere in this apartment, nothing but cream and beige and white, and suddenly, she was reminded of the bridal suite at the hotel where everything first went wrong.

She went back to the wall of windows. Dusk was sinking in, and headlights switching on, and tiki torches blazing up in the bayfront bistros. She was looking through the glass, but slowly, gradually, she was looking only at the glass and seeing nothing. She was remembering things—things that happened during the week after the wedding. Memories the detectives had jarred loose in their questioning that afternoon. How her mother summoned her to do the peptide injection every night because her own hands had become too unsteady. How she blasted her opera music at such a volume that the vibrations could be felt throughout the house. How she meandered up and down the beach, drifting like flotsam from the dunes to the surf. How she even forgot that Julie had been living with her that whole week.

Julie shook her head and turned away from the view. All of that was caused by nothing more than her mother's emotional state: she'd just learned that the love of her life was scheming to get her money. That would knock anyone out of sync.

She pulled the postmortem report out of her bag and read it from cover to cover. Then she went back to the desk in the bedroom and googled *aneurysms* and *intracerebral hemorrhages* and every other unfamiliar term in the report.

She went to WebMD and read about all the causes and symptoms of a ruptured aneurysm. Aneurysms, she learned, were usually caused by a traumatic brain injury, i.e., a blow to the head. Her mother had never sustained an injury like that, not during Julie's lifetime.

But before her lifetime? She flashed on the fairy-tale story her mother liked to tell her, the same one that Charlie had regaled the wedding guests with: her mother tumbling down the concrete steps of a football stadium. Okay, so she did have a head injury once. But it resulted only in a mild concussion. At least that was what the doctors said at the time.

Unruptured aneurysms showed no symptoms and could go undetected for years, she learned from WebMD. When they did rupture, it was usually due to a spike in blood pressure brought on by heavy lifting or strong emotions.

Anger was the example the website gave. Not utter joy, which was the only emotion her mother was feeling that night.

The first symptom of rupture was usually a sudden severe headache. A thunderclap, they called it.

At that, something brushed Julie's memory, but she batted it aside and read on.

The symptoms that followed were all the ones that Long and Russo had quizzed her about that afternoon. They must have cribbed their questions from the same website. They could have called it *Intracerebral Hemorrhages for Dummies.*

Wait. Here was a symptom the detectives hadn't mentioned: numbness or paralysis of the face, particularly on one side.

Well, she could cross that one off easily enough. Her mother's face was flawlessly beautiful to the end. Artificially enhanced and preserved, perhaps, but nonetheless perfect. Kate may have looked tired in the video she'd recorded for Julie, but there was nothing frozen or asymmetrical about her face.

Not that Julie could see, anyway. She remembered the strange lighting. Half of Kate's face had been in shadow.

She sat back and thought about that for a minute, then got up and rummaged through the clutter of jewelry in her suitcase in search of the little velvet box that Franklin Foster had given her. She found it and took out the thumb drive and inserted it into the port on her laptop. She started the video and sat back and watched with the sound off.

Yes, Kate's face was as flawless as ever. Her skin was smooth and dewy, her eyes—or eye, at least—wide open, and her lips curving in a perfect smile.

But it was strange how she'd positioned herself, with the light on one side of her face only. Julie paused the video, fiddled with the brightness control, and pressed play again. Now the right side of her face was overlit. She looked washed out, while the left side of her face—

Julie skidded the chair back so fast that the casters screeched against the marble floor. She stared at the image on the laptop screen. The left side of her mother's face drooped like a wilted flower.

IT DIDN'T MEAN anything, she told herself as she paced from room to room and window to window. Maybe her mother did suffer some kind of brain bleed before she died. Even so, that wasn't the cause of her death. The cause was alcohol poisoning. The medical examiner was steadfast on that point. He attached no causative significance to the fact that she might have also been experiencing a bleed in her brain.

So this didn't change a thing. Charlie injected that lethal dose. His were the only fingerprints on the syringe. Even if Kate wasn't in her right mind, she couldn't possibly have injected herself and left no prints on the syringe.

Unless she wore latex gloves.

THE SUN WAS setting as Julie crossed the drawbridge to Cascara Key. It blazed like a fireball as it rolled down into the sea, and the stab of pain in her retinas dislodged the memory she'd been reaching for earlier. That night in the hotel suite, her mother had complained of a splitting headache.

Julie turned north and drove with her left eye closed against the splinters of sun glare. A few house lights winked on as she drove along the narrow road, but many of the mansions were dark. The season was over. Their owners were in Newport or Bar Harbor now.

She hadn't called ahead and didn't know if Luisa and Ferdy were still in residence. She'd meant to call them after the meeting in Foster's office, but too much had happened, and she'd forgotten. For all she knew, they'd gone to Key West to inspect their new house.

But as soon as she turned into the circle drive at La Coquina, she could see that the lights were on in their apartment over the garage. A moment later, the sconces flanking the entrance flashed on, and by the time Julie had parked and reached the front door, Luisa was opening it with her arms spread wide.

"Julie, are you all right?" she cried as Julie bent to hug her. "We just heard about Dr. Hoffman. It is true?"

"I'm afraid it is."

Luisa stood back with her hands to her cheeks. "Oh, Julie!"

"It's okay. I'm okay. We're getting divorced, and I'm living in Osprey Tower for now."

"Ohh." Luisa's eyes went round.

"How are you and Ferdy?"

"Fine. Fine." She hooked her arm through Julie's. "Come. Come back to the kitchen and have supper with us."

The foyer was in darkness and so empty and still that their footsteps echoed through the cavernous space. But the second Luisa pushed through the swinging door to the kitchen, they were swept up in a swirl of bright lights and loud music and steaming pots and wonderful aromas. Ferdy was there, and he nodded and smiled at Julie and jumped up to turn off the radio while Luisa hurried to pull a pot off the burner. "You'll have some pozole, yes?" she asked Julie.

"Thanks, but first I have to ask you something. Could we sit down for a minute?"

Luisa turned from the stove with a sudden wariness. She cut her eyes to Ferdy. His shoulders hunched in a helpless shrug. "Yes, all right," she said.

Julie sat down at the kitchen table. Ferdy pulled up a chair across from her, and Luisa stepped around the empty chair beside Julie to sit beside him. Julie felt awkward in this arrangement, like she was interrogating them. They already seemed so on edge. She wished she could put them at ease, make some small talk, but she couldn't. She couldn't put this off any longer.

"Luisa." Julie looked directly at the woman who'd been a second mother to her all those years. "That morning—when I found my mother and I fainted—" She got no further than that before dread crept into Luisa's eyes. She groped for Ferdy's hand.

"I'm sorry to bring this up," Julie went on. "But I've realized some things about my mother and the, um, condition she was in those last weeks? And I need to know—when you found me on the floor beside her bed, did you find anything else?"

Luisa made a choking sound and pressed her free hand over her eyes. Julie looked to Ferdy. He didn't look at her. He was staring at the tabletop. Slowly, he nodded.

"Please understand," Luisa cried. "I did not want you to go through that again!"

Confusion spread over Julie's face. "Go through what?"

"You found your father killed himself, and now to find your mother, too—I did not know if you could bear it again. I thought, I thought—*Nobody needs to know. They will think it was a stroke, and you will never have to know.*"

"Luisa," Julie said slowly. "What did you find?"

Luisa took her hand from her eyes to look at Ferdy. At his nod, she laboriously pulled herself to her feet, seeming decades older than she was. She went to the refrigerator and pulled a plastic bag out of the produce drawer and laid it on the table in front of Julie.

It looked empty. It was a clear plastic bag, sandwich-size, with a zip closure. It wasn't until Julie picked it up that she saw there was something inside. Something colorless and folded in such a way that its original shape was obscured. But when she held it to the light, two shapes emerged: the shape of a finger and the shape of a thumb.

"Latex gloves," she breathed.

"I took them and hid them in the cabana until the police were gone."

"And then you put them in the refrigerator?"

"I thought, in case—I do not know what. I thought they would say she had a stroke, and nobody would have to know the truth. But then they said Mr. Mull did this. I thought, *No, he could not, and I should tell the police I hid the gloves.* Then you told me yes, he did do it, and I thought she must have put the gloves in there some other time." Luisa collapsed back in her chair. "So I did nothing."

"Luisa." Julie kept her voice soft, but she couldn't keep the sadness out of it. "I was wrong about that. Charlie didn't do it. Mom—she wasn't right at the end. She had a blood vessel burst in her brain. It made her imagine things. Crazy things. Horrible things about Charlie. It made her want to die, and it made her want Charlie to be blamed for it." Julie reached across the table and took her hand. "We can't let him be blamed anymore."

The look Luisa threw at Ferdy was terrified, and he was giving her the same look. "If I tell about the gloves," she cried, "they will deport us!"

Julie couldn't help a short laugh. "You're both American citizens. They can't deport you."

Ferdy snorted as if to say he knew better, and maybe he did.

"Okay, listen," Julie said. "Did the police ever ask you if you found a pair of gloves?"

"No—"

"Did they ever ask you if you removed anything from the room?"

"No."

"Okay." Julie reflected. Long and Russo might be planning a trip out here in the morning to question Luisa further, but they hadn't made it yet. "Then they can't accuse of you of lying about it. And as far tampering with evidence goes? You didn't have the requisite intent."

Ferdy looked to his wife for a translation of that phrase, but Luisa didn't know it, either. She sent a helpless look to Julie.

"You didn't think it was evidence of anything. You were just tidying up the room like you always did."

"But—but I saved it. In the refrigerator!"

Julie had to think about that for a moment before she came up with an explanation. "You saved it because you thought it might become important later. So you preserved it. But you forgot about it until I came over here tonight and asked you."

Luisa looked at Ferdy again. Slowly, she shook her head. "That would be a lie."

Julie felt a little sting of shame. Of course it was a lie. Dressing it up as a counternarrative wouldn't change that. She had no right to ask Luisa to lie, just as she had no right to ask her to tell the truth and open herself up to prosecution for evidence tampering. Especially when she'd taken the gloves only to protect Julie. Ferdy could be implicated, too, since he knew about the gloves. They'd both be taking a big risk if they came forward now.

"You're right," Julie said. "You have to decide for yourself what to tell the police. Or whether to tell them anything at all. It's all up to you."

Luisa and Ferdy looked at each other for a long time. A lifetime of their shared toils and struggles seemed to pass unspoken between them. Just when they were on the verge of a carefree retirement in Key West, they could be losing everything. They could be facing prison. "But Mr. Mull," Luisa said finally.

Ferdy's face sagged. "*Sí,*" he told her.

"Yes," Luisa said, as if translating for Julie. "We must do this for Mr. Mull." Julie reached both hands across the table to grip theirs.

CHAPTER 44

Julie," Tad answered when she called him. It sounded like he was at a party. She could hear excited voices in the background, the sound of water splashing, and motors. Maybe a Jet Ski. Sarasota kids liked to party on the sandbar in the Big Pass inlet, and she could easily imagine Tad among them, swigging a can of organic beer.

"Julie, I'm sorry I didn't call," he said. "I—I didn't know what to say."

For a second she didn't know what he was talking about, until she remembered Eric's arrest. Everybody knew by now, everybody was talking about it, and it was the last thing on her mind.

"No, I'm calling about Charlie," she said. "He's innocent. And I have the proof."

"What?"

"Can you come out to my mother's house?"

JULIE WAS WAITING at the gates of the courtyard when he drove up in his beat-up truck. It wheezed and rattled as he shut off the engine, and Julie couldn't imagine that a more disreputable-looking vehicle had ever crossed these pavers. Tad jumped out looking not much better than his truck, in denim shorts and a muscle shirt with three-day stubble on his face.

"Sorry to pull you from your party," she said.

"That's okay. We untangled the net and kept her cool. They think she'll be okay."

It had been a long day, she was tired, and she had no idea what he was talking about. "Who?"

"The marine responders."

"No." He had no idea how exasperating he was. "I meant who did you keep cool?"

"The dolphin," he said, as if it were abundantly obvious.

"Ah." Now she understood. "You were rescuing a beached dolphin. Of course you were."

He cocked his head. "What's with the sarcasm?"

"Don't you ever get tired of being such a do-gooder?"

He grunted a laugh. "Look who's talking."

"Me!"

"Not many people would look for evidence to clear the man accused of their mother's murder. Assuming you've actually found any?"

"Come inside," she said.

She brought him through the darkened house and into the kitchen where Luisa and Ferdy stood waiting. They'd met before, sort of, at the lawyer's office, and they acknowledged their brief acquaintance now with head bobs all around.

"Okay," Tad said and turned expectantly to Julie. "You said you had proof of Charlie's innocence?"

"My mother killed herself," Julie said. It hurt to say the words, to hear them spoken out loud. She took a breath and pressed on. "And she deliberately made it look like Charlie did it. I have testimonial proof, and Luisa has physical proof."

Tad was no poker player. All of his emotions played out across his face. Shock. Hope. Skepticism. And mostly impatience. "If that's true—" he began.

"Shall we sit?"

They all pulled up chairs around the kitchen table. Julie started with the ME's discovery of a ruptured aneurysm, then ticked off all the symptoms she'd observed and discounted during the week after the wedding. The unsteady gait, trembling hands, hearing loss, confusion, forgetfulness. Luisa nodded as Julie listed them. She'd observed all of that and more.

"Later on, facial paralysis," Julie said. "One side of her face drooped."

"Charlie mentioned something about that," Tad said. "But he said she had a touch of Bell's palsy."

Luisa gave a vigorous nod. "This is what she told us."

"She probably believed it herself," Julie said. "That's one more symptom of this kind of brain bleed. Hallucinations. The damage to her brain was getting worse and worse the whole time. I think to some extent she realized that. Her heart was broken, and she was afraid she was losing her mind, and that's when she decided to kill herself."

"You saw signs that she was suicidal?"

"I should have," Julie said, and she squeezed her eyes shut for a second, remembering all the clues she'd missed. "During the hurricane, she went walking on the beach. Right into the storm. She was drenched, but she wouldn't get in the car, and I said, *Do you have some kind of death wish?* And she said, *Wishing never gets you anywhere.*"

Tad's face scrunched up. He didn't think that was enough, and Julie held up a hand as if to say, *Wait, there's more.*

"The prenup gives Charlie this house in the event of her death. But she told me there was a way around that. A way for him to get nothing at all. And when I asked her what that could be, she said the Slayer's Act."

"Whoa." Tad rocked back in his chair, his eyes wide. Ferdy looked to Luisa. She shook her head, and Tad did the translation this time. "That's the law that says you can't inherit from somebody if you kill them."

Julie continued, "So I said, *Mom, Charlie hasn't killed you,* and she said, *Hasn't he?*"

"Huh." Tad's eyes were moving rapidly. He was processing.

"She wanted to die," she said. "She wanted to die, and she didn't want Charlie to get any of her money."

"Okay." He accepted that much with a nod. "So that's your testimonial proof. Where's the physical proof?"

Julie looked at Luisa, who took a deep breath and told her story. "That morning I heard Julie scream upstairs. I ran up and found her on the floor and Mrs. Sawyer in the bed. I checked. Julie was alive, but Mrs. Sawyer—" She shook her head. "I thought it was a stroke? I hoped it, anyway. But I was afraid she did it herself. And I thought, *Julie cannot go through this again.*"

"Again?" Tad interrupted.

Luisa gave Julie a sad apologetic smile, as if she hadn't meant to spill her secrets. But it was part of the story, an important part, and Julie nodded at her to continue.

"Julie's father killed himself when she was only thirteen years old. She was the one who found him, and it was awful for her."

Ferdy's eyes filled with sadness, too. They'd both endured the aftermath of Julie's trauma; they'd both awakened to her screams during the night.

"I'm sorry," Tad said. "I didn't realize."

Luisa went on, "I could not let that happen to her again. I thought, *If there is a note, I must find it and burn it. Julie must think this was a stroke.* So after I called 911, I went searching for a note. Under her pillow, on the nightstand. There was nothing there. The needle was on her vanity table. *She did it there,* I thought, so I searched through all her makeup and lotions. I needed more light to see, so I pushed the switch on her makeup mirror. This one." Luisa outlined the shape of a twelve-inch square in the air in front of her. "The lights did not come on. So I opened the battery compartment in the back. There were no batteries inside. Instead, there was this." She got up and went to the refrigerator and put the plastic bag on the table in front of Tad.

He leaned forward to eye it and exhaled a long, slow breath. "Latex gloves," he said. He sat back again as he put it together. "Charlie had already injected her with the peptide cocktail. She had his prints on the syringe. So she put on latex gloves and did the alcohol injection herself. Then hid the gloves in the battery compartment." He looked at Julie. "Ingenious."

Julie nodded. "She might have been losing her mind, but she was still brilliant."

He turned back to Luisa. "There was a bottle of Everclear. Pure grain alcohol—"

"Yes, it was always here. In the pantry." Luisa pointed to the door on the far side of the kitchen. "I do not know why it was in Mr. Mull's closet."

"She might have moved it there," Tad said. "But the thing is—he's the one who bought it."

"For me!" Luisa said. "I used it to clean windows sometimes. I had a bottle from a long time ago, but it was gone, and it is against the law to buy it here. I mentioned this to Mrs. Sawyer, and she told Mr. Mull to buy it when he went up north."

Tad asked Luisa to go through it all again, and she squared her shoulders and told the whole story from start to finish. Julie thought it was the bravest thing she'd ever seen.

So did Tad. "Mrs. Barrera," he said, "you've just saved a man's life."

IT WAS AFTER ten by then, and nobody had eaten. Luisa reheated the pozole and ladled out servings for each of them. While they ate, Tad and Julie debated their next steps. He thought they might need a forensic neurologist to review Kate's medical history and give expert testimony about her state of mind, and Julie agreed to pay the fees if an expert witness was needed. But then she told him about the detectives' line of questioning that afternoon, which made Tad wonder if the government was already halfway there. The gloves would have to go to forensics, but assuming they tested positive for Kate's DNA, that much combined with Julie's and Luisa's statements might be enough to convince the government to drop the charges.

They decided Julie would call the detectives in the morning and tell them that after reflecting on their questions yesterday, she'd remembered some additional details and wanted to amend her statement. Luisa could do the same, but Tad thought she should be represented by counsel when she gave her statement, just in case. "Let's have your attorney make the call and say you want to come forward with some important evidence."

Luisa and Ferdy exchanged a panicky look. "I do not have an attorney," she said.

Tad put up a hand. "Will I do?"

"You have a conflict," Julie said.

"Not if Charlie and Mrs. Berrera both waive it. I think I can skate through the interview, and hopefully, it won't go any further than that."

Luisa put up her own hand. "I waive it," she said.

IT WAS AFTER midnight when Tad finished Luisa's witness prep. She and Ferdy retired to their apartment, and Julie got up and stretched out her spine and rolled the kinks out of her neck. She was wondering whether to drive back to her new apartment or sleep in the guest room when Tad said, "Now we need to prepare your testimony." She made a face. He clarified, "You have to be able to explain why you didn't tell the police about your mother's condition before."

That meant unpacking thirty-three years of their mother-daughter relationship.

Julie went to the wine refrigerator and came back with a bottle of California chardonnay. "I'll need a drink to get through this," she said. She put the bottle on the table and was wrestling with the cork-screw when she noticed him studying the label. "No, I don't know if the grapes were ethically grown or whatever," she griped.

"Pour me a glass, too," he said.

IT PLAYED LIKE a confession. Over the next thirty minutes and two glasses of wine, she told him about her fraught relationship with her mother. How Kate sucked all the oxygen out of every room she ever entered, but how she also brightened every room. She was like the sun, so brilliant, so dazzling, that she eclipsed everyone around her. Including Julie. Especially Julie. She grew up in that shadow and felt starved sometimes for a little bit of light to call her own. She told Tad how much she loved her mother and how much she resented her at the same time.

"She always seemed larger than life to me," Julie said. "I think that's why I missed all those symptoms and dismissed all those con-versations. It was impossible for me to imagine such a larger-than-life person could ever want to end that life."

"You know," Tad mused after a moment. "If the state attorney agrees to drop the charges against Charlie, he'll need to explain why. That'll probably mean a public announcement that your mother killed herself. From what you tell me about her? I'm guessing she wouldn't want that out there."

Julie thought about that. "You're right. But you know what? She doesn't get to control everything anymore. Not when Charlie's life is at stake."

The realization seemed to strike both of them then. This was really happening. Charlie was going to be exonerated. They should be celebrating.

They polished off the first bottle and opened a second and went outside to drink it in the cooling night air. They pulled two chaises together on the pool deck, then they stretched out side by side and watched the city lights twinkling across the bay.

"Julie?"

"Hmm?"

"What you did tonight? Getting to the bottom of this and convincing Mrs. Berrera to tell the truth? Facing the truth yourself? It took some guts. Some smarts, too. And I just want to say I really admire you for it."

"You might be drunk."

He ignored that. "I didn't know your mother, but I have a feeling she'd be full of admiration, too."

"Now I know you're drunk," she said, laughing. But in a softer voice, she added, "Thank you, Tad."

They fell into silence. The night was so quiet at this hour. They could hear the water lapping against the dock, but there was no boat traffic on the bay, and no car traffic on the bridge or the island, only a distant drone of motors on the mainland. Julie was relishing the utter peacefulness of it until Tad ruined the moment by bringing up what he called an exciting new research project: passive acoustic recorders were stationed in the bay to measure the decimation of the fish population as a result of red tide.

She heaved a loud sigh. "Here's the fallacy in that research. You assume there's no noise because the fish are dead. But what if they just want a quiet night once in a while?"

He laughed, but of course, he had the facts and figures to back up the premise of the research. He refilled their glasses, and they launched into a debate over climate change: environmental steward-ship versus economic growth; clean energy versus the plight of the coal miners. Julie scored a few points, but she was only playing men-tal gymnastics. Tad was passionate about all of it. He talked about the microenvironment and how much he loved the Gulf Coast and all the things he'd seen that made him fear for it. He talked about the macroenvironment and his fear for the future of Planet Earth and what his someday children would inherit.

"Some people decide not to have children," she said. "For exactly that reason."

"No, no," he protested. "We have to hope for the future. For hu-man beings in the future. Or what's the point of any of this? We can't just throw up our hands. We can't just abandon the planet and let the jungle overtake it. We need to fix the mess we've made. We need to build. But we need to build smart."

When the wine was gone, they lay back on their chaises and watched the stars glitter overhead. Julie's head was spinning with a hundred ideas, and finally she spoke one. "I have a proposition for you," she said.

He rolled his head her way and cracked an eye open with a sleepy grin. "I accept."

"Shut up and listen."

Both eyes opened wide as she laid out her plan. He sat up straight on the chaise and stared at her, unblinking, for a long moment. He got up and paced circles on the pool deck. He raked his fingers through his hair. He stopped and stared at her again. Then he turned around and jumped fully clothed into the pool.

She laughed. Her mother wanted her to take risks, to be bold, and she couldn't think of anything riskier or bolder than this. People might think she was crazy. But if she made it work? She lay back, basking in the possibilities.

Abruptly, she sat up. Tad had been underwater too long. She bolted to the edge of the pool and saw him six feet down, submerged in the murky water. She crouched, ready to dive in, and at that exact moment he geysered to the surface, sputtering and panting for breath. "Ask me that again when you're sober?" he said.

She thought about it. She needed to do a lot more research, talk to some lawyers, hire some consultants. But after that? "I just might," she said, and she reached down and grabbed him by the hand and reeled him in.

CHAPTER 45

The wheels of justice turned, but as always, they turned slowly. It was a sweltering day in July before Charlie was finally released. Julie waited in her car two blocks from the jail with the AC blasting. When she got the text from Tad, she drove up to the main entrance and parked in the fire lane with her flashers on.

The plan was for Tad to hustle him out and run to the car before anyone noticed and snapped a photo. But when they came through the door, it was obvious that Charlie couldn't run. He leaned heavily on Tad and hobbled slowly across the pavement toward the car. His once-ramrod-straight back was bent, and his once-long stride was now a halting shuffle.

He didn't lift his head as Tad opened the car door and helped ease him in. He collapsed with a groan on the backseat, and it was another minute before he looked up and saw Julie watching anxiously from the driver's seat. "Oh, hi, honey," he said mildly.

"Oh, Charlie," she choked, on the verge of tears.

"Not now," Tad whispered as he slid into the seat beside her. He pointed at a man on the sidewalk who was squinting at his phone to line up the picture. Julie nodded and stomped on the gas. It was another block before she remembered to turn off the flashers.

No one spoke, and when she glanced in the mirror, she saw that Charlie was slumped against the door with his eyes closed. His chin was on his chest like his neck couldn't hold up his head anymore. His jowls sagged into the gaping collar of his shirt.

"What did they do to him in there?" she whispered.

"What d'you mean?"

"He's aged twenty years!"

Tad shook his head. "This is what he looked like the day after his arrest. It wasn't jail that broke him."

Tears filled her eyes, and she had to blink hard to see the road.

Her therapist was working with her to let go of the guilt, and she thought she mostly had, but seeing Charlie like this brought it all rushing back. Yes, she was back in therapy, though not for PTSD. The nightmare reel hadn't played since the day her mother died. And not even because she'd lost her mother, husband, and best friend all in the space of two weeks. No, it was guilt that left her feeling hollowed out. It was crippling sometimes.

While Charlie slept, Tad worked on his laptop, and Julie drove the old familiar route, south through the city, west across the bridge, north to La Coquina. She slowed down when she reached the beach road, and Charlie blinked awake and hauled himself up a little straighter. "There it is," he said softly. She glanced in the mirror. It wasn't the house he was looking at. His head was turned the other way. He was gazing out at the sparkling waters of the Gulf.

Becky came barreling out of the front door when they arrived. She and her husband had been living here the past week, enjoying the beach and selecting the furniture that would go to the new, smaller house in Tampa where they'd be moving after the sale closed on La Coquina. Charlie had sold it within days of receiving ownership of it. He couldn't afford the upkeep, he'd said, but Julie knew that any bank in town would have been happy to do a reverse mortgage on the place. That wasn't the reason he wanted to move.

Julie and Tad hung back as Becky pulled her father out of the car and wrapped him in a big joyous hug. Charlie eased himself free to shake hands with his son-in-law while Becky swallowed Tad in her next bear hug.

Julie couldn't hold back the tears any longer. How could she ever have believed that this dear, sweet man was capable of murder?

"What's this now?" Charlie said softly as he shuffled toward her. "This is supposed to be a happy day."

Tears streamed down her face as she hugged him. "I'm so sorry, Charlie. I'm so sorry!"

"Hey, now." He patted her on the back. "None of this was your fault. Not one bit of it."

"It was. If I'd seen the signs. If I'd paid attention—"

"No." He held her back and looked at her with a sad smile. "Like anyone could ever get the jump on your mother."

TAD AND JULIE left Charlie with his family and drove back to the mainland and into the driveway where Tad had left his bicycle that morning. He buckled on his helmet and threw a leg over the bike. "See you at the office tomorrow."

"Eight o'clock sharp," she said.

She waved him off and went up on the porch and through the front door of the little yellow cottage. Her new home. It turned out that you really could knock on somebody's door and make them an offer.

She was in the process of selling everything she'd inherited from her mother. The cash to buy this house was all she'd kept for herself—along with KS Development, of course. As for the rest of the sale proceeds, she'd made a generous gift to the Harvard Radcliffe Institute, earmarked for research on climate change. This, she felt, would honor her mother's original intention, if not exactly her wishes.

Everything else was being plowed into the company. They were going to need a substantial cash cushion to get them through the next few years. Take risks, Kate had said, be bold, but she never could have envisioned the risks Julie was taking with KS. She'd given away forty-nine percent of her ownership to Save Our Shores. She'd committed to sustainable development, and she'd partnered with a notorious climate activist. Julie was now CEO and Tad president, and green growth was the new company mission. Tad was in charge of green, and Julie was in charge of growth, and she expected they'd butt heads regularly.

CHAPTER 46

The memorial service was almost a reprise of the wedding. Charlie made all the arrangements, and he followed Kate's blueprint nearly to a T. A sunset service on the beach followed by dinner in the courtyard. The same caterer, the same string quartet, even the same guest list, albeit with a few additions and deletions. Tad was in; Eric and Greta and Alex were out. Charlie hired the same party boat to bring the guests from the mainland to La Coquina, though they weren't calling it a party boat this time. It was just a ferry.

It was an evening service, which was unusual for a funeral but much appreciated by the guests, since the full weight of summer heat was upon them by then. It was also a black-tie affair, which was unheard of for a funeral, but Charlie thought it was fitting for a woman as elegant as Kate and a touch that she would have appreciated.

The actual service was very brief. The strings played Elgar's "Nimrod" and Barber's "Adagio." Becky read "Do Not Stand at My Grave and Weep" because she'd heard it once and loved it, and Charlie couldn't say no to his daughter.

There was no danger of anyone standing at the grave, because Kate didn't have one. She'd been cremated, and her ashes were delivered into an urn made of handblown glass in swirling colors of the sea. The urn was inside the house tonight, standing on the center table in the foyer, the same table where Charlie's wilted daisy bouquets once stood. The memorial service did not include a casting ceremony; Charlie wanted to scatter the ashes later in private.

After the music, after the poem, there was a long silence while everyone watched the sun slowly sink into the sea. When it was gone, when there was nothing left of the light but long streaks of rose and peach painted across the sky, a single gong sounded, deep and sonorous and sorrowful. Everyone remained seated until its last echoes faded into nothing.

Dinner followed in the courtyard, at a dozen round tables seating ten people each. There was no head table and certainly no sweetheart table. Instead, a lectern stood by the courtyard gates, and the dinner speakers made their way there to deliver their tributes and remembrances.

First up was Senator Richards, who couldn't stay to eat; sorry, but he had to catch a flight back to Washington. He spoke of all Kate had done to foster the booming economy of the great state of Florida and how she was proof that anyone could make something of themselves no matter what the supposed barriers were and do it all without affirmative action or quota assistance or any other help from the government. Tad rolled his eyes across the table at Julie, but most of the guests were the senator's target audience, and they applauded appreciatively.

Next was Dory Kaplan, the founder of the nonprofit Julie once clerked for. Dory had always been Kate's principal rival for coverage in the society pages, but tonight she spoke fondly of Kate and her commitment to philanthropy. If Dory felt betrayed that Kate's last will left nothing to charity, she didn't let on.

Jack Trotter got up to speak about Kate's vision and her brilliance and what a privilege it had been to work with her. Then Vincent De-Marco, president of DeMarco Construction, joked about her tenacity in contract negotiations. "I always had to check my pockets when I left her office, to see if she'd robbed me of my wallet, too!" The crowd howled at that. Everyone remembered being on the short end of some kind of exchange with Kate.

There was no after-dinner dancing, but when the dessert plates were cleared, most of the guests got up and circulated or made their way to the bar for a nightcap. Charlie sat alone at his table, and when well-wishers stopped by to pay their respects, he nodded his thanks but barely made eye contact. His rheumy gaze always returned to the darkness beyond the courtyard, out to sea.

Julie made the rounds for him, thanking everyone for coming, acknowledging their condolences, reminding them of the ferry's departure time.

Tad appeared at her elbow. He wore a tuxedo but shoes without socks—his own micro-rebellion. He held two glasses and handed her one.

"Thanks." Her eyes kept returning to Charlie. He must have asked someone to bring him the urn. He held it in his arms, clasped to his chest. She thought of his speech at the wedding, all the charm and humor, all that vigor. It was impossible to believe this frail shell was the same man. He looked like he barely had strength to hold his head up. "I'm worried about him," she said.

Tad gave a grim nod. "I don't think he'll ever recover."

Vincent DeMarco bore down on the pair of them with a whiskey in his hand. He wanted their assurance that nothing in their business relationship was going to change. "Sorry, Vinnie," Tad said with a cheeky grin. "Everything is."

Julie left them to argue about it and made her way to the table in the corner of the courtyard. Charlie had included Luisa and Ferdy in the event as guests, not servants, and he'd seated them with Becky and her husband, where he thought all four of them might be more comfortable. Julie bent to whisper to Becky. "Have a minute?"

Becky pushed back from the table, and they stepped into one of the archways, away from everyone else. "I'm so worried about your dad," Julie said.

"I know." Becky heaved a sigh. "This darkness that's come over him—it's even worse this time than it was before."

Julie gave her a puzzled look. "Before?"

"When Nadia died. And my baby brother. I mean, it was really sad. The big coffin and the little tiny coffin. Dad was already in bad shape from the war and all, but this just put him over the edge. My grandma said she didn't even know him anymore. Her own son. He was just broken."

Broken, Julie thought, gazing across the courtyard at Charlie. That was the same word Tad had used. She caught herself and spun back to Becky. "Wait, you were at Nadia's funeral?"

Becky nodded. "My grandma took me. It was my first time on a train."

Julie wasn't following. "A train to Lebanon?"

Becky laughed. "No, silly. She was living here when she died. The funeral was here. Or not here, exactly. In Chicago."

Julie stared at Becky as her husband called her back to the table with a question about furniture. By the time Julie looked back over to Charlie's table, he was gone. "Excuse me," she mumbled.

She threaded her way across the courtyard, through the tables, searching for him in the crowd, asking people if they'd seen him. Somebody thought he might have gone inside; somebody else speculated he was on a bathroom break. It was finally Jack Trotter who said he'd seen him heading out to the driveway. Seeing somebody off, he imagined.

Julie hurried out of the courtyard, and the din of party voices faded to a murmur behind her. Only a few cars were parked in the circle drive, and Charlie was nowhere among them. She went out to the road. There was a half-moon tonight, and it lit the beach with a pale glow. She could see a figure hobbling over the dunes, black suit over white sand.

She kicked off her shoes and ran after him. "Charlie!" she called, then shouted it again, over the roar of the surf.

He turned. He was cradling the urn in his arms.

"Charlie." Julie stopped dead six feet away. "Your wife Nadia. She was living in Chicago. She died in Chicago."

"Yes?" he said uncertainly, waiting.

"You got leave from the military hospital to go to her funeral. In September 1982, you were in Chicago."

"Oh." He blinked hard, once, twice. "Yes."

She lurched back, so violently she nearly lost her balance. "My God!" she gasped. "Who are you? I don't even know who you are!"

He looked away, out over the black waters of the Gulf. The moonlight made the tears shine in his eyes. "I'm the man who loved your mother," he said. "All my life. With all my heart and all my soul." The tears spilled from his eyes and streamed through the runnels of his face. "I thought she loved me the same. I thought we could share our secrets. Our worst secrets."

"Those people," Julie whispered. "All those people."

"I know." He looked down at the urn and clasped it even tighter to his chest. "I guess I broke her heart. Then she decided to break mine."

He turned away, stumbling to the edge of the sea. The surf lapped at the toes of his shoes, then his ankles. He stared out over the Gulf with the urn hugged tight to his chest. Then he squared his shoulders and marched ahead, plowing through the water to his knees, then his chest.

Julie's arms reached out for him, for the urn, in pure reflex. But slowly she pulled them back, and she stood and watched until he disappeared into the darkness.

A long horn blast sounded from La Coquina's dock. It was a plaintive sound, as deep and sorrowful as the gong that marked the end of Kate's memorial.

Julie turned and picked up her shoes. It was time for the ferry to leave the island, and it was time for her to leave it, too.

AUTHOR'S NOTE

An in-depth investigation of the actual events and circumstances surrounding the horrific crimes known as the Tylenol murders was conducted by *Chicago Tribune* investigative reporters Christy Gutowski and Stacy St. Clair. Their work is reported in the October 27, 2022, issue of the *Tribune*. I also recommend the podcast they produced entitled *Unsealed: The Tylenol Murders*.

James Lewis was the sole suspect who investigators believed was responsible for the Tylenol murders. He died in July 2023. He was never charged, and the crimes remain officially unsolved.

ACKNOWLEDGMENTS

I might be a bit notorious for writing in isolation (i.e., no critique group, no beta readers, no developmental editor) but it's impossible to publish in isolation. It takes a village to deliver a novel to its readers, and I'm so grateful to all the talented and hard-working inhabitants of my village.

First and foremost, my agent, Jennifer Weltz, without whom I never would have emerged from isolation. Thank you, Jennifer, for everything you do for me. Thanks also to the rest of her team at the Jean V. Naggar Literary Agency, including especially Ariana Philips and Cole Hildebrand.

My editor, Sara Nelson. *Shell Games* is our third book together, and I grow more grateful each time for her keen eye and wise counsel. Thanks also to the whole team at HarperCollins, including especially Edie Astley, Heather Drucker, Lisa Erickson, Megan Looney, Suzette Lam, and Natalie Miller. And like every author, I owe a big debt to my copy editor. Thank you, Beth Thomas.

Finally, I'm grateful to Alison and Jordan, my steadfast supporters and sounding boards. They're the smartest people I know, and the wonder of it all is that I made them! With a little help from—

Bob, always.

ABOUT THE AUTHOR

BONNIE KISTLER is the author of *Her, Too*, *The Cage*, and *House on Fire*. A former Philadelphia trial lawyer, she now lives in Sarasota, Florida, and the mountains of western North Carolina. Her website is bonniekistler.com.

READ MORE BY
BONNIE KISTLER

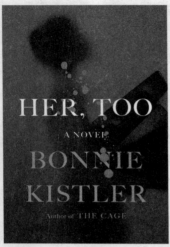

HER, TOO

"A timely, fast-paced, and unputdownable thriller with everything a reader craves. Kistler nails the villain and has you cheering for all the heroic women through every surprising twist and sadistic turn along the way." —JAIME LYNN HENDRICKS, bestselling author of *Finding Tessa*

THE CAGE

"From its audacious opening scene to its wallop of an ending, *The Cage* is a delicious thrill-ride of breakneck twists and turns, underpinned by complex characters ensnared in risky relationships . . . deftly weaving together the worlds of fashion, high finance and white-shoe law to reveal their seamiest secrets and shared underbellies, all via characters who live, breathe, and scare the hell out of us on every page." —CASSIDY LUCAS, author of *Santa Monica*